CASS TELL

NAKED

ISLAND

destinēe

BOOKS BY CASS TELL

Novels
Naked Island
The Coffee Lover
Dance With Poetic Sea
The Savant
The Cookbook
Pale Tides
A Smile Forever, A novella and short stories
Virtual Eyes
Social Code
Blue Fate 5: Pursuit
Blue Fate 4: Squeeze
Blue Fate 3: Dropout
Blue Fate 2: Buyout
Blue Fate 1: Startup

Wings Series
Wings Series Box Set 1
The Hollywood Burn – Wings Series 6
The Brussels Atonement – Wings Series 5
The London Inferno – Wings Series 4
The Paris Crossing – Wings Series 3
The Prague Transit – Wings Series 2
The Munich Shift – Wings Series 1, The Beginning

Children's Stories
The Wise Girl and Baba Yaga's Son

The Adventures of Amy and Jack - Series
The Insidious Hope
The Impossible Storm
The Amazing Rescuers
The Impossible Prize

COPYRIGHT PAGE

Naked Island
By CASS TELL

Published by Destinée Media www.destineemedia.com
Written by Cass Tell www.casstell.com
Cover concept by Per-Ole Lind www.perolelind.com
Cover image: by zizwix on Pixabay
Palm Tree Illustration by gstudioimagenl on Freepik

ISBN: 978-1-938367-73-1

TABLE OF CONTENTS

DAY 1

It's bizarre to stand buck naked in front of two unknown women who wear nothing but their birthday suits. A hasty decision got me here.

We are in a small clearing in a jungle on a tropical island, and I have this impression of meeting two perfectly created Eves in the Garden of Eden. One has red hair, the other is brownish-blond, and they are both tall. It's a noticeably different planet from where I was twenty-four hours ago.

Compounding the strangeness is to have two other people here, a guy with a fancy video camera and a woman standing next to him holding a clipboard. Their names are Frank and June, and I've seen them at the film studio in Hollywood but have never spoken with them. They are experienced production staff for the Naked Fear TV shows. The rules are that we are not to converse with them except for emergencies.

Frank and June have the luxury of wearing jungle fatigues and ankle-high boots. In his mid-forties, Frank is skinny, about five feet ten, and has a slightly hunched posture, perhaps caused by lugging a camera for many years. He has a gaunt face and dark, expressionless sunken eyes, reminding me of a vulture staring at roadkill. He would not be considered photogenic, except perhaps for a horror movie. Therefore, he should stay on the other side of the camera.

June is slightly shorter than Frank, perhaps in her mid-thirties. She wears her brunette shoulder-length hair in a ponytail, has smooth olive skin, and seems athletic. Unlike Frank, June belongs in front of a camera, and I could see her in an action movie. I suspect she was at one time an aspiring actress. But, like many who come to Hollywood, she probably didn't get the right parts and eventually ended up working in film production. Her job is to direct the show's filming and keep the

1

storyline on track or adapt it as we go along.

Frank and June's current goal is to capture that first awkward moment when the naked folks meet up. Then they will film the ensuing successes, conflicts, and failures. A few small triumphs are scripted into the plot, but most important are the disputes, breakdowns, and misery. That's what makes good television drama. The entire scenario seems perverse when you think about it, but people enjoy watching this stuff on TV. I suppose it's a reflection of the values of our culture.

That's enough philosophizing because my primary goal here is to survive.

It's strange to have two stunning nude women in front of me, combined with a cameraman intently pointing his camera at them. Still, it gets weirder when he swings the camera around and faces me. With my hands, I cover my private parts. This will take some getting used to. Most annoying is this thorn sticking into the side of my shoeless foot. I bend down and pluck it out while thinking, *what am I doing here?*

The two women approach me with sparkling white smiles. They have been through this before and know the protocols. It's like on a Hollywood set when someone calls out "action," and the actors play their parts. I am a rookie. To have such perfect bare-skinned females entering my comfort zone only increases my uneasiness.

"Hi," the redhead says. "Are you lost?" She laughs.

"Uh, uh . . . uh," I stammer, and my mind goes blank, not knowing what to say.

She waits expectantly and then seems startled, perhaps anticipating something more from me, a cute and quirky comeback, such as "story of my life" or something like that. Unfortunately, I had zero coaching for this experience.

The redhead gets back to smiley mode. "My name's Pandora."

"And I'm Ada," says the blond.

"I know that. I've seen your Naked Fear episodes on TV." They are both experienced survivalists, each making it through twenty-one-day challenges and finishing solo. In Pandora's case, her male partner tapped out after being driven crazy by her constant bickering. Regarding Ada, her partner got an infection in his leg and was extracted. Ada is calm and calculated, looking for solutions, at least from what I saw in her Naked Fear episode.

Other than seeing their episodes, I know that Pandora lives near

Seattle and runs a small construction company specializing in drainpipes or something like that. She also teaches survival courses between construction jobs. Pandora is in her early-thirties and strikingly attractive.

I know less about Ada, except she does something on social media. She is perhaps twenty-six or twenty-seven years old, a bit younger than me. She is also beautiful and belongs in a high-end fashion show rather than on a grimy jungle reality show. So why did the producers pick such stunningly gorgeous specimens of humanity? Even more perplexing is why was I thrown into this mix?

"And, what's your name?" Ada asks.

"Oh yeah, my name is Bartholomew."

"Bartholomew? What kind of a weird name is that?" Pandora asks.

There she starts, picking away. "A Scottish ancestor," I reply. It would be easy to belittle her unusual name, and I want to avoid getting into a verbal battle during the show's first few minutes.

"Okay, Bartholomew," Ada replies. "Nice to meet you."

As a greeting, Ada comes to me and gives me a discrete sideways hug so that her lovely curves don't touch my chest. Her blond hair smells of shampoo. I try to keep eye contact but am tempted to survey what's below the neck level. I believe women must be respected and not treated as objects, but I can't deny my natural instincts. This unexpected physical encounter magnifies the absurdity of being here and only deepens my uneasiness. I'm a deer caught in the headlights.

Pandora follows Ada with a frontal hug, and I feel strength in her arms and shoulders. It appears more than a friendly "nice to know you" but a supremacy demonstration, an aggression. I'm taller than her, but it's like she is the primal Amazonian woman and wants me to know it. Her skin-to-skin approach further unnerves me, and it seems her goal is to put me in my place way down the pecking order.

They both wear makeup and colorfully painted fingernails, and their hair is combed and silky. That will all disappear during the first few days when insects, dirty living conditions, and starvation become real.

"I haven't seen you on any previous challenges," Pandora declares.

"First time," I reply with a grin while attempting to gather my emotions.

"That can't be," she declares. "This is an XL challenge, and they

3

only take experienced survivalists."

"It was a quick decision."

"Are you a survivalist?" Pandora asks.

"No. I work as a bookkeeper for the film production company that creates this show."

In reality, the producers were desperate when one of the Naked Fear participants got sick at the last minute, and they urgently needed a replacement. Then they had this insane idea to send any available, expendable person. Looking far across the room, they spotted me at my desk in my isolated corner cubicle. And, what better script than to insert a neophyte into a group of proven survivalists?

"Oh my," Pandora exclaims. "Have they lost their minds? You'll never make it."

With a big smile, I proclaim, "Who could refuse a holiday on a beautiful tropical island?"

Ada says, "Believe us. This will be anything but a holiday."

Pandora looks at Ada and raises her eyebrows. Then, she turns to me and says, "Okay, bookkeeper, we have our doubts. From now on, we call you Bookie."

It might be best not to tell them my bosses said I could tap out after five days but hoped I might last longer. One laughingly said they needed to film at least five days of my misery. He told me to fake the pain to enhance the drama.

"Well, let's get oriented," Pandora says. She points at three brown burlap bags hanging on a green bush at the edge of the clearing.

We walk to the bags, take them, and go through the routine of examining what each person chose for the trial. This XL challenge is exceptionally long, for twenty-eight days, and therefore, each participant is allowed two survival items.

Pandora reaches into her bag and takes out a long machete and a fire starter.

"Perfect," Ada says, and from her bag, she takes out a hatchet and a mosquito net. Then, holding up the net, she says, "I hate bugs."

Pandora laughs.

I reach for the remaining bag, which has five arrows in it. Then, behind the bag, I notice a long archery bow.

As I take the bow, Pandora says, "That's a useful piece of equipment, although it seems odd that a bookkeeper would choose it."

4

"I didn't choose a thing. It's the first time I've seen it. The producers picked out my survival tools."

"They are nuts," Pandora comments.

My bag also has a seven-inch saw-back hunting knife with a rubber handle.

Our bags also contain small handheld cameras called 'diary-cams.' When the camera crew is not around, we are supposed to use them to record our thoughts and dramatic events.

Each of us also has a leather necklace with one wooden-looking bead on it. It's there for a purpose. The bead is a microphone. TV viewers don't know that something else is in the bags, small transmitters that capture and send the signals from the microphone necklace. For being in such a primitive situation, there certainly is a lot of high-tech equipment around us.

Hanging on the bush is a metal pot, which means we now have tools for chopping, hunting, cooking, and purifying water.

Pandora takes a map from her bag, and we look at it. It shows the island, which seems approximately eight miles long and three miles wide, stretching south to north. The map is simple, without much detail. Dark green patches depict a thick jungle, with some rocky hills in the north and another rocky area toward the south. An airplane landing strip is in the middle. We are now in a small clearing near a beach on the island's east side.

Our goal is to hike to an area in the southwest, where there is a lagoon, and then join three more survivalists. Somewhere past the lagoon, a production crew set up a camp with tents, cots, and an abundance of equipment and food. Unfortunately, the show's participants are not so lucky.

Another camera crew is filming the other three survivalists. After meeting up, our adventures will be videoed, along with the tensions between a group of naked, stressed, starving people.

Aren't the deviant imaginations of Hollywood a wonderful thing?

It's already afternoon, as the start of filming was delayed because of my late arrival. We won't make it to the island's south side before nightfall, so somewhere we need to make a temporary camp to spend the night.

I flip the strap of the burlap bag over my shoulder and hang the bag in front to hide my private parts. This nakedness in front of strangers still feels unnatural. After all, even Adam and Eve realized they needed to be covered. I carry the bow in my left hand.

"Lead the way," I say, knowing that Pandora is happy to take the commanding position. She removes the pot from the bush as though taking personal possession of it, and as suspected, she is first to head toward a trail. Frank, with his camera, and June, with her clipboard, follow us, and we wind our way into the jungle.

Pandora and Ada move ahead while I stop to pick up a dried bird's nest that has fallen on a bush. Jungles are damp and collecting a fire starter is good.

I see Pandora turn to Ada and whisper. "This guy knows nothing of survival and won't make it and will become a burden to us. The sooner he taps out, the better. I'm certainly not going to baby him."

Ada remains expressionless.

Ignoring Pandora, I notice various animal tracks of peccaries, rodents, and small deer on the trail. Peccaries, also known as javelinas, are a type of pig smaller than the razorbacks in the United States.

The others move on, and I pause to observe the surroundings. The trees and plants are familiar. Besides the weird situation of having two undressed women in front and a camera crew behind, I feel at home.

* * *

We are on the Isla San José, the second largest island in the Pearl Islands chain in the Pacific Ocean, about thirty miles off Panama's west side and one hundred miles north of Colombia. The island is privately owned and virtually uninhabited, except for a guest house on the east side, which is run by a few staff. Wealthy tourists visit the guesthouse, a few at a time.

Searching for out-of-the-way places, The Naked Fear TV production team found this location many months ago. Back at our studio, I learned that the island's owner was happy to allow filming as it might increase tourism to the guesthouse. But now, it seems the island was recently bought by a new person, a billionaire, and he didn't want the filming to take place. Eventually, he reluctantly agreed we could be here if we stayed on the island's south side.

The island has many deer and wild javelinas, potential food sources. Culling these animals is welcomed if the survivalists are lucky enough to trap one. During the past weeks at our Hollywood offices, I overheard some planning discussions for this show's episode but not everything. At that time, it wasn't of much interest. Now, I regret not listening more.

The jungle is dense, and Pandora does an okay job of finding trails heading toward the southwest. She charges ahead as though on a single-minded mission. I lag, and eventually, Frank and June pass me.

I'm suffering some form of jetlag, and the intense afternoon heat is getting to me. The body and mind need time to acclimate to a new environment. Pandora, Ada, Frank, and June probably had several weeks to prepare for this experience, and they arrived in Panama a couple of days ago.

My preparation time consisted of a quick drive from the office to the airport in Los Angeles and then a sleepless night on a commercial flight to Panama City. After a long wait at Panama City Airport, there was a twenty-minute flight to this island in a private aircraft. That was followed by a bumpy boat ride to the beach and a short hike to the clearing. That takes a toll.

My goal now is to endure the five days, perhaps a bit longer, and try and get along with my fellow survivalists. Pandora and Ada know that other survivalists are on this challenge, but not how many and who they are. It is scripted that we are supposed to find them and then go through that exciting moment of discovery caught on camera where everyone becomes instant friends. After that comes hardship and conflict.

Back at the office, for the past weeks, I was busy trying to keep up with an ever-growing mountain of expense reports. Therefore, I ignored the selection of candidates, but know they all completed their twenty-one-day challenges. The producers mentioned that "the dynamics will be outstanding, perhaps the best show ever."

I never caught the reason why.

As we walk, I notice various types of plants and trees. Some can be used for medicinal purposes, and others are edible. For example, there are *cordoncillo negro* shrubs, known as *mantico*. The leaves can be chewed to treat digestion problems like vomiting and dysentery or rubbed over cuts as an antiseptic. I take some leaves and put them in my burlap bag. There is also a coco plant from which cocaine is produced and *suma* plants that makes a calming tea. It is also known as an aphrodisiac.

I see a *manchineel* tree and stay clear of it. The Caribs of the Caribbean make poison from the tree's sap for the tips of their arrows. It has a fruit that looks like an apple, and in Central America, it is known as the *manzanilla de la muerte*. Or little apple of death. It is one of the most toxic plants in the world.

There are eucalyptus trees, and I break off green leaves and put them in my bag. And as we pass through a large clearing high on a hill, I take leaves from a *sabia* plant, a type of sage that grows in sunny, dry places. Eucalyptus and sabia make excellent insect repellents.

I make a mental note of edible plants, particularly jungle palms, from which one can eat the core. They are a good source of carbohydrates.

The tracks of deer and wild pigs are everywhere, meaning an abundance of wild game. The island's previous owner brought in predators to keep the animal population balanced, like a puma for the larger game and *oncillas*, a smaller spotted cat, to keep rodents in check. Where I come from, we call them *tigrillos*. There was a question of whether these predators would pose a problem to the survivalists. The producers laughed because they had put people in more dangerous situations.

I wonder what kind of snakes are on this island and whether Pandora thinks of this as she charges ahead.

Far across the clearing, I hear Pandora call out, "What are you waiting for?"

I look up and ask, "Who me?"

"Yes, you, Bookie. You slow us down. We'll never get to our meeting point."

"Just a minute," I say, stopping to pick up some salvia leaves.

Pandora turns to Ada and, with a low voice, says, "He will only become a burden and shouldn't be on this challenge."

Ada doesn't respond but points to the south and says, "That's a thick jungle down there, and it won't be good to be there in the dark. Let's camp here."

Their voices carry across the large clearing, and I hear their conversation. Ada made a wise choice. Who knows where that puma might be lurking?

Pandora peers down at the forest and says, "Okay, let's make a quick shelter, but we need to dump this guy as quickly as possible."

Frank films their conversation. He films them a lot more than me.

Before I get to their side of the clearing, they have already placed poles against a low branch on a tree, covering them with large palm leaves.

Pandora glares at me and declares, "You make the women do all the work."

I smile. "It looks that way." I could have jokingly said, that's why women were created, but who knows how a hardcore feminist like Pandora would react? After all, she carries a machete.

"Bookie, what were you doing back there? This is not a leisurely walk in a garden. This is survival. Our objective is to join up with the others. Now because of you we are a day late."

"Why are we stopping?" I ask, already knowing the answer.

Like a harsh schoolteacher, Pandora says, "Night comes more quickly when you get closer to the equator, but I regret that we did not meet up with the others."

Knowing Pandora, I suspect she wanted to get there early to gain control of the group. What more would you expect from the supreme Amazonian woman?

Ada stays quiet and places a final palm leaf on the others. Then she takes out her mosquito netting and rigs it inside the shelter.

Frank and June find a place two hundred feet away, where they remove tarps and lightweight sleeping bags from their backpacks and use matches to start a fire. Then, they drink water from plastic bottles and eat something from tin cans.

Pandora, Ada, and I have nothing to drink or eat, so we sit on the ground and watch a magnificent orange and yellow sunset over the Pacific Ocean to the west. Pandora describes her previous Naked Fear challenge and how "they hooked me up with a loser who couldn't last three days in a tent in his backyard." When she says this, she glances at me, and instead of meeting her eyes, I gaze at the sunset. Quickly it turns dark, and Pandora and Ada head for the shelter.

I get up and walk away from their shelter, and Pandora calls out, "Where are you going?"

"I'll sleep over there," I say, pointing to another place in the large clearing."

"Why are you doing that?"

9

"There is a spot I like."

"You will be eaten alive by mosquitos and a zillion other kinds bugs. If you want to be that stupid, then go ahead."

Pointing across the clearing, I say, "The stars are magnificent. I want to look at them." That should throw her off.

"You are crazy." She turns, crouches down, and disappears into their shelter.

I head across the clearing, for I had identified a spot with a natural covering, which requires little effort to set up. It is March, and there is not much rain in Panama. However, in October, it will be a deluge.

I whack off the leaves of small jungle palms with my knife to make a ground cover and a simple blanket. However, there is a more fundamental reason for not staying with them. I am uncomfortable sleeping beside two beautiful nude women. I'm tired from the trip, need to rest, and can't spend the night struggling with man thoughts.

It takes a few minutes to set up my sleeping arrangement. Then, I peel the skin off the stalk of a palm branch and savor the delicious heart-of-palm. It provides nourishment and much-needed liquid. I don't eat much, for my body needs time to adjust to jungle food.

Taking the salvia and eucalyptus leaves from my bag, I rub them over my body and sprinkle the crushed leaves around my bed. I have slept like this before.

In a few minutes, I am fast asleep.

DAY 2

Morning light hits my eyes, and there is a movement across the clearing. Ada stands next to their shelter, holding her mosquito net. Pandora slings her brown bag over her shoulder. It is disconcerting to see their goddess-like bodies at sunrise. Some Naked Fear participants say that nudity is not an issue when survival is the goal. That's certainly not what I'm sensing, for these women are attractive, and my thoughts are on anything but survival.

I'm wondering what Frank is thinking. He is fifteen feet away from them with his camera focused on them and nothing else.

With a low voice, Pandora says, "We've got to ditch Bookie, who is totally lost out here. He's sleeping, so let's go."

"We can't leave him," Ada exclaims as she rolls up her mosquito net and stuffs it in her burlap bag.

"For sure we can. After a night on the ground, he has certainly been devoured by insects, and his day will be miserable. Missing the comforts of home, he's bound to tap out. It's the best thing for him and for us."

She doesn't know that I slept well and surprisingly don't have insect bites.

"I don't feel good about it," Ada whispers.

"Think about it. Bookie will pull down the entire team, and it's a mistake he's here. Did you see how he wandered around yesterday, like living in a dream world? We can't let emotions get to us and must make good decisions. This boy will drain our energy."

"Okay. Let's see if he joins us, but this doesn't seem right."

They leave the clearing and head southwest down the hill on a jungle path, quickly disappearing into the jungle.

Frank stops filming and rushes over to me. With a loud voice, he says, "Wake up. They are leaving. You need to catch up with them."

"I heard them," I say. "Let them go." I remove my palm leaf blanket, stand up, and cover my essentials with my burlap bag. I know that the body's private areas are blurred when the show goes on television. Still, this nude business in front of a camera bothers me. And I've been in the studio and heard the technical team's wisecracks as they go through the raw footage and how they jest about body geometries and camera angles.

June joins us, carrying her backpack and clipboard, and asks, "If you don't go with them, what's your plan?"

Waving a hand through the air with a dramatic theatrical gesture, I gaze beyond the trees and proclaim, "I'd want to explore the island's biodiversity and experience nature's expression. And eventually, in two or three days, I'll introduce myself to the group once fully functional." Maybe I should have taken acting lessons? There's also the reality that groups on Naked Fear never fully function.

Frank and June look at each other with bewildered looks.

"Do you know where we will be?" June asks.

"I think it was on the map, somewhere that way, on the other side of a blue lagoon." I point south. I had observed precisely where it was on the map.

"Yes, that's where the film crew has set up camp. You will probably see our boat in a harbor.

Frank looks toward the path where Pandora and Ada disappeared, and he seems anxious to catch up with them. He turns to me and asks, "Are you sure you will be okay for three days. You've never been on one of these challenges."

With eyes drawn like a lost puppy, I mutter, "When I get hungry, I'll come into the camp. Although, Pandora, the boss-lady, decided I was not welcome. And aren't you breaking the rules? That unsettles me and makes me feel guilty."

June frowns and asks, "What do you mean?"

"You are not supposed to be talking to me." I hold back a smile.

June glances again at Frank, hesitates, and with a low voice, says, "The rules are flexible. This is exceptional, but okay, we agree on three days. We will have plenty of work with the others during that time, so just be careful. And use your diary cam."

Frank is already moving in the direction of the path. He has fascinating scenery to capture with his camera and doesn't want to miss a second.

"Be careful," June says as she glances at Frank. She seems unsettled when she says this, as though unsure she made the right decision, or does she think I might be in some kind of danger. Or is there something more?

June catches up with Frank, they vanish into the jungle, and I take my knife, cut out a palm heart, and eat it. It will give me some energy for the morning.

There's a reason I don't want to go with Pandora and Ada. I've watched many of the Naked Fear episodes and understand the dynamics when survivors get together, whether two people or more. It starts with negotiations on where and how we will build our shelter, collection of firewood, water, and food, and who will do the work. But, most often, having different points of view, personalities come into conflict. As a result, physical and mental energy is wasted when attempting to establish a working relationship. Typically, there is a conflict when one person absolutely knows they are right and attempts to impose their will on others. And then, everything breaks down and becomes dysfunctional, with basic survival tasks not performed.

I don't want to be part of that. Instead, one must explore the territory to determine the survival resources available. That's why I need two or three days to survey a broader terrain which I expect Pandora and the others will not do.

Except for birds chirping and a slight breeze rattling leaves in the trees, there are no other sounds, and in some way, it feels good to be alone. And I've been thinking. What happens when Pandora gets to the camp? The last thing I want to do is join a team of macho survivalists who may be jockeying for leadership positions. I'm not here to win friends and influence people but survive at least five days as my bosses requested.

I trace what I remember of the map on the ground with a stick. Pandora and Ada are now on their way to join the others on the south side of the lagoon, which means they must cross a stream or river. There was a hill or rocky bluff just on the north side of the lagoon. That places the group on the southern tip of the island. There will be five of them, and they will tromp around the forest down there, seeking food over the coming days. Unfortunately for them, the wild animals won't like it.

The animals will become wary and move out, so finding adequate food for five people will become increasingly difficult during the twenty-eight days.

The river, lagoon, and rocky bluff form a natural barrier, which will make the team reluctant to go north. People are creatures of habit, stuck in routines, and unwilling to change even if their patterns are subliminal. I'd bet a million bucks that the producers of Naked Fear have this figured out, as they will do anything to create despair and conflict. It sells.

So, my territory is north of the bluff, which gives me much of the island.

Carrying my brown burlap bag and archery bow, I circle the clearing. Instead of following the others to the south, I take a smaller trail heading west toward the sea. My pace is different than yesterday when we charged up to the clearing. Now, each step is slow and deliberate, careful not to make any sounds, and I frequently stop to survey the area. The last thing I want is to disturb animals.

Jungles are alive with life, but many people who enter them never see anything. To appreciate what's there, you need to blend with the environment. Stopping at a stream, I spread mud on my shoulders, as it will be a long day in the sun, and I want to avoid sunburn. I have a tan from going to California beaches on Saturday mornings, but the tropical sun is intense. The jungle is thick and wild, and I love the pungent smells.

Halfway down the hill, I see movement and count five wild javelinas digging with their snouts in the dirt. They are on the other side of the stream, and while I would like to stalk them, I need to construct some infrastructure before hunting. It is warm here, and meat spoils rapidly, so having a ready fire is essential.

I quietly move on, and the pigs continue digging into the ground as though they never saw me. Was it a mistake not to take one?

Angling south, I climb up to the top of a rocky hill, which is more like a bluff, steep on both sides. It must be what I saw on the map. It runs east to west. The blue lagoon to the south and the survivalists' camp must be beyond it. I walk along the top of the bluff and then find a narrow path descending west toward the sea. At the bottom, I discover water trickling down the rocks through a long moss covering. This seems like a good water source, and I put my head at the bottom of the moss and let the water drip into my mouth. Moss is a natural purifier, and I hope it has done its job. Boiling water is preferable. I'm generally cautious about the water I consume, having learned from experience.

The water is refreshing, and I wish I had a means of collecting it.

I follow a small animal trail not far from the sea and quickly pass through a thick wall of jungle vegetation. Then, an open area of sandy dirt spreads up to an indent in the bluff as though a backhoe carved the hill and smoothed out a circular area. This is an excellent location to set up camp, as it is near the beach and will benefit from sea breezes, but not too close. On beaches, sand flies often come out during sunset, biting you to death. I first need to determine if that is the case here before building a camp on the beach.

Next to the rocky bluff, this location provides protection and invisibility to anyone walking along the beach. Most survivalists say the most important considerations are shelter, fire, water, and food, and they set their priorities accordingly. However, I was taught something different. The first consideration is safety and protection from enemies.

Before expending energy on building a shelter, I need to better orient my surroundings to determine available resources and dangers.

I walk out to the beach and head north and a few hundred feet away is another lagoon, much smaller than the one in the south. On one side is a large bamboo thicket, which gives me a good feeling. Bamboo is a highly versatile plant with edible roots, and the stalks are ideal for building shelters. In addition, bamboo leaves can be used to make tea or woven into baskets and hats.

Walking further along the beach, I see something that angers me. Rubbish has washed up on the sand. It is a horror how much ugly stuff mankind dumps into the waters of this world, but I will try to put some of it to good use.

Scattered across the sand, I find a few empty water bottles, a tangled roll of thick nylon fishing line, and various lengths of rope, both nylon and cotton. Buried in the sand is a ripped fishing net about eight feet long. The net can be repaired. After carrying those items back to the campsite, I head back to the beach, where I find a tattered long-sleeved shirt in pitiful condition. The previous owner was big, but my chest is larger. Wearing it unbuttoned will help in the cool evenings. However, it's not exactly what one might wear to a weekend dance.

At the end of the beach is a massive pile of driftwood that will come in handy, and then there is a rocky jetty going out into the sea as though nature purposely put up a sea wall. This would be a great place to go fishing if I only had a hook for my newly found tangled fishing line.

In the pile of driftwood, I pick out pieces of wood to form a bow drill fire starter, a straight round piece of hardwood for the spindle, a piece of flat dry wood as the base fireboard, a handle for the spindle's top, and a curved piece of wood for the bow. All that is placed in my brown bag.

Lugging several large pieces of driftwood, I go back to my campsite. As the weather is expected to be dry, making an elaborate shelter is not urgent. The first priorities are water, fire, and food.

Taking one of the pieces of rope collected from the beach, I construct my bow-drill fire starter. I use the dry bird's nest found yesterday and quickly make a fire. It burns well against the stone wall of the small cliff, making little smoke. Then, I put the larger driftwood logs on top of the fire, knowing it should burn for many hours.

It is mid-day, and my stomach rumbles, setting my next priority.

On many Naked Fear shows, the participants exist for twenty-one days on very little, perhaps only eating a lizard or snake. They end up starved and emaciated, looking like scarecrows. I have no intention of doing that for the five days I will be here.

* * *

Taking my archer's bow, I quietly circle the far side of the lagoon, looking for trails and places where animals come down to drink. Further around the lagoon, I find a broader, straight path leading to the north. It feels like humans used it in the past.

Walking up a hill, I come out at another clearing, and at the far side are the ruins of a house. The four walls of mud and rocks still stand, but the roof has caved in. While heading to explore it, I sense something moving in the grass, so I take one of the arrows from my bag and place it in my bow. I slowly stretch the string back and hold my breath, not making a sound.

A moment later, something gray moves through the tall grass, and in a split second, I know what it is and let the arrow fly. Then, with a thud, the arrow strikes the animal. It's a *tapeti,* a forest cottontail whose range extends from Mexico to northern Argentina. I won't go hungry tonight.

Instead of exploring the ruins, I immediately head back to my camp with a feeling of satisfaction. The tapeti needs to be skinned, and I am hungry.

After putting more wood on the fire at camp, I prepare the rabbit and cook it on a stick above the fire. Then, to minimize the number of flies, I take the rabbit's guts away from the camp and put them in the water at the lagoon's edge. I'm curious if anything will eat it, either fish or, of more interest, a Cayman. It's uncertain if they are on this island, so one must be cautious.

As the tapeti continues to cook, I cut some bamboo stalks and quickly make a ground-level bed. Tomorrow I can build something more sturdy and higher off the ground. Then, I go to the sea, swim, and wash off the mud on my shoulders.

The sun lowers over the western horizon, and the colors are beautiful. I put on my tattered long-sleeved shirt leaving the front buttons undone. Then I take the cooked tapeti and a plastic bottle of water collected from the spring in the rocks, go to the beach, and watch the sunset.

I wonder what Pandora, Ada, the film crew, and the other survivors are doing? It's the first time I have thought about them, as my day was too busy and enjoyable.

How are the survivalists getting on? Did they decide on a campsite and find water and food? Are they getting on with each other? That's the big question, and I suspect that after initial greetings and niceties, they quickly disintegrated into the process of establishing a pecking order. Pandora is a handful with a domineering personality. Who else was brought on this challenge? Some survivalists have big egos, and when the stresses come, it creates conflict. And there you go again. Conflict makes good drama, which means more TV viewers, creating more revenue.

It's all about the money.

I wonder when to join the team, as I promised June to show up at their camp in a couple of days. But honestly, after seeing the beach and experiencing tranquility on my side of the bluff, I'd prefer to stick to myself as much as possible before tapping out in four days.

17

The production team said I should film myself if the camera crew was not around, but my diary cam sits at the bottom of my bag. I haven't taken it out once. Filming my experience for the sake of unknown television viewers seems to be an invasion of my privacy. So, for now, the camera will stay where it is.

This beach reminds me of my upbringing when tribal elders took us on sailing and fishing trips to the sea. I grew up in a small town called Mabaruma on the west side of Guyana. Guyana is a low-populated country sandwiched between Venezuela and Surinam and touching the north of Brazil. That's where my parents are doctors, medical missionaries, and working in a small hospital. They originate from Kansas, where I was born. Somehow two young mid-western doctors got the call, and they spent a lifetime serving people needing medical and spiritual attention. I have a younger sister who was born in Guyana and is studying to be a doctor who will someday join my parents.

Most people living in Mabaruma are Amerindians, including Arawaks, Caribs, and Warao. Growing up, they were my friends, and the tribal men taught us to hunt and fish. They taught us about the trees and plants, what you can eat, and what is poisonous. Besides going to school in the village, my education was in the jungle and the Caribbean Sea. That probably accounts for my "missionary kid" strangeness. It's curious how I went from that to being a bookkeeper, which I consider a temporary job. It is a stepping stone to something else, but I'm uncertain about the next step, and it feels like I am stuck in a holding pattern.

As I take a bite of the cooked meat, I hear a noise behind me and then the whine of an animal. Startled, I turn around, and not far away, standing by a tall coconut palm, is a medium-sized male dog. He is a short-haired, pure white crossbreed. The dog is exceptionally skinny, with ribs clearly visible. He whines and shakes, but the giveaway is his wagging tail.

I hold out a piece of bone and meat, and the dog slowly approaches, his tail wagging faster.

"Want some food?" I ask.

I put the bone and meat on a rock next to me, and the dog quickly comes forward, devours it, and then sits and looks at me with expectant eyes. There is a guest for dinner, which means sharing a meal or most of it.

DAY 3

The dog is still there in the morning, curled up on the sandy ground about three feet away from me. It stirs when I get up, flops its tail a few times, then shuts its eyes and sleeps. I don't know what to make of the skinny mutt.

He is obviously accustomed to human company, and while skittish at first, he quickly warmed up to me. His presence raises questions. How did he get here? Was he abandoned? What happened to his owner? Did he wander off and get lost from the guest house on the other side of the island?

The dog isn't in the best shape, as it seems he existed on meager food for many days. It might be good to have a watchdog around, as the puma would be wary of the dog, even a mangy mutt like this.

It doesn't seem right to keep calling it 'dog,' so it needs a name. The names 'spike' or 'fido' don't seem to fit, at least for this pathetic-looking thing, but I recollect the first time I saw it under a coconut tree. So, his name is 'Coco,' which is more respectful than calling him 'nut.'

This means I have another mouth to feed. It is early morning and an excellent time to go hunting, so I take a frayed nylon rope found on the beach, make a collar and leash for Coco, and tie him to a tree. It would be foolish to take him on a hunting trip. I remove the tattered shirt, which was helpful for sleeping during the night, and then take my bow and head over to the lagoon.

It's refreshing to feel the coolness of the morning, and I pause to survey for animals and take in the morning's beauty. Birds hop between reeds in the lagoon, chirping and whistling their different sounds.

The rabbit entrails I left in the water are mostly gone, and small fish nibble away at the remains. Small fish typically means bigger fish are around, so I need to repair the fishing net found yesterday. There is no sign of any Cayman, meaning one less danger, although barbecued, their meat makes a good meal.

I move slowly along a trail near the water's edge and come upon a Capybara. This large rodent is found throughout Central and South America.

Arming my bow, I take a shot and hit it in the chest, just behind its front leg. It takes two steps and falls to the ground. My Amerindian elders would approve of this, a respectful shot of the animal. Carrying it to the water's edge, I skin and clean the Capybara, a small one, maybe ten pounds. There are different kinds of Capybaras. In Central America, they are smaller than the giant ones we have in Guyana. They tend to live near rivers and swamps. In Guyana, they are considered a delicacy and are used in a traditional dish called *pepperpot*.

Back at camp, I turn Coco loose, restart the fire, and then hang pieces of the Capybara directly above the flames. The rest is hung higher, which will do for now, knowing a proper smoker is needed. It quickly starts to cook, and Coco takes an interest, and twenty minutes later, Coco and I have a filling meal. Capybara tastes something like a blend of chicken and pork. Coco and I both eat plentifully, and he devours the bones, and we now have enough meat to last a day or two.

While a meat diet is more than welcome, I eventually need to complement it with coconut, bamboo roots, the heart of palm, and other edible vegetation taken from the forest. In addition, there is salt available in the rocks by the sea, formed from evaporated seawater.

Near the fire pit, with bamboo stalks, I spend the rest of the morning building a hut frame and constructing a bed that gets me higher off the ground. And by stacking rocks out from the rock cliff, I make a four-foot wall to create a three-side fireplace enclosure, with a plan to close off the chimney with bamboo stalks to create a smoker.

The dog sleeps through the morning and occasionally opens his eyes as though supervising my work. At noon he is wide awake, especially when I take strips of meat from the fireplace for a meal. Then, giving a piece to Coco, he quickly gulps it down as though making up for lost time.

I wish he could describe the adventure of how he got here.

After lunch, I rest for an hour, at least according to a primitive sundial I made. I stuck a straight stick upright in the ground and placed pebbles in an arch to track the movement of the stick's shadow.

It is a pleasantly warm day, and I feel contented. The tranquility here sure beats the hectic office life back in Hollywood, where I am typically stuck at a desk going through expenses. When films are made, whether a short half-hour sitcom or a mega feature movie, it means budgets and costs. That endless list of credits scrolling down at the movie's end means expenses. Everyone from actors to electricians, hairstylists, and stuntmen need to be paid. My job is simple. Log every expense and tell the finance manager when there is an overrun.

My journey to that job was untypical. After completing high school in Guyana, I joined the United States Marines for two years. My parents thought it would be good for me to socialize with western people, and it was an excellent experience. Some abilities learned in the jungle were applied to the Marines. For example, my marksmanship skills were among the best. More than that, I had an innate awareness of hostile environments, as growing up in the jungle developed a sensitivity to every movement and danger. I saw horrible things in the Marines, which I try to forget.

Some of the guys in my unit came back with PTSD and had difficulty reintegrating. I was never integrated, even before the Marines. Some of my fellow soldiers couldn't find jobs and ended up homeless. I moved on, but I can't say the combat experience didn't impact me somehow. Maybe that's why I can't find an occupation that feels right, one that motivates me to get out of bed in the morning. But I suspect there is more to it than that.

My parents have very little, so one reason for joining the military was to get government funding for university studies. It worked. After the Marines, I went to university in Los Angeles and earned a degree in Business. Then, I made some money, saved it, traveled, and drifted through a few jobs. Nothing fits. Someone advised me that it's just a process of finding oneself. At twenty-nine years old, I'm still searching.

Regarding religion, I believe in God, which isn't always popular today. That's another reason I'm out of sync with many around me, especially with my Naked Fear Production Company colleagues. My Amerindian friends in Guyana have a greater sensitivity to a supernatural reality, sometimes on the spooky side. Yet, I am more comfortable around them than with many people in California who can't see beyond the material world. The people I work with seem to position their lives on their dress and what they own. And sometimes, it feels like each person makes up their own unique morality. The world rotates around whatever gives them pleasure. That's not me.

My main question is, what to do with the rest of my life? That's probably a question for everyone, yet I've seen that most people are caught up in routines, often hindering them from reaching their full potential. That's how I feel now, treading water in a job that doesn't fit. It's strange how finding a trail in a jungle is no problem but finding the right life path is something else. Maybe I should trust more in the God I believe in. Perhaps my time on this island will give me time to rethink my life trajectory. Maybe I'm being too introspective.

The primitive sundial on the ground tells me an hour has passed, so I decide to get more wood from the driftwood pile at the end of the beach. I walk down to the water's edge, where the sand is damp and firm. Coco runs ahead of me, and when we approach the driftwood pile, he runs to the rocky jetty. He stops and barks, excited, like wanting me to join him.

I climb across the rocks and around the bend and then see a small sailboat washed up on the sand. Coco charges across the beach and circles the boat, his tail wagging furiously.

22

I jog across the sand to join him.

The boat is tilted on its side, its wooden hull painted white, with chipped and faded yellow trim and a yellow mast. A small outboard motor is attached to the rear.

Then, I notice a string of bullet holes spread horizontally above the waterline. The gun was a powerful automatic, perhaps an AK47, for the bullets sunk deeply into the thick wood but did not make complete see-through holes.

Inside the boat, near the mast, are unusual dark stains. Coco jumps in the boat, goes to the stains, sniffs them, and whines. I suspect the dark coloration came from blood. A bullet hole is in the mast at chest height. Is it possible someone was shot? Perhaps the wounded person fell overboard and never made it to shore, for I don't see any signs of footprints in the sand, but there is no telling how long the boat has been here.

The boat contains a small box with a few hooks, sinkers, and a roll of nylon fishing line. At the bottom of the box, I'm surprised to find a box of bullets. Then my foot hits something which clinks on the floor of the boat. I didn't notice it before, but it is a .38 pistol. Fishermen sometimes carry guns to shoot sharks close to their lines, but this boat contains little fishing gear.

I pick up the pistol and examine it. The cylinder has six fired shells, which tells me that the boat's owner did some serious shooting. From what I've seen here, I assume it was to defend himself, but from what? Did he put up enough of a fight to escape his attackers?

I eject the empty shells from the gun, put in new bullets, and then set the gun to the side.

A red ten-liter jerrycan full of gas is in the back. The boat is old and worn but solid. It would take some work to get it back in the water, but it might be possible with some digging and a favorable high tide. I pull the rope to start the motor, and it immediately comes to life, but I quickly turn it off to avoid burning it out. It needs to be in the water to cool the motor.

Looking around, it's evident this fisherman was equipped with cooking supplies. In the middle of the boat is a pot for cooking, and a box of matches, a metal tea kettle, a small single-flame gas cooker, some plastic plates, and two ceramic mugs.

A plastic box contains four cans of sardines, crackers, and dog food. In addition, packages of tea, a large bag of Colombian coffee, a plastic bottle of mosquito repellent, and a bar of soap are of particular interest. In addition, there is a roll of plastic sealable baggies, which could be handy for storing food.

This is a fantastic find, as everything can be helpful. I am one lucky dude, and I'm sure Coco will like the dog food. Who said you had to suffer on Naked Fear? But is this stealing from someone? The owner of the boat might still be around.

A thought comes to my mind. What would the producers say if they knew I stumbled onto these things? And what about the viewers of the show? Some will go crazy on social media with "this guy is a cheat" and other cynical comments. The scoffers will have a great time with this, and there are many on the internet with nothing better to do than say vicious things and hide behind anonymous names. To be honest, I could care less about them. I got lucky, and I'm not here to suffer. Anyway, I will keep all this stuff hidden. No one needs to know about it.

Lifting the cover of a long wooden box, I find a folded sail, a pair of binoculars, and a map. It's a nautical map of the Pacific Ocean on the west side of Colombia and Panama. An X is penciled over a town named San Miguel on the Isla del Rey, the largest island in the Pearl Islands. It is not far from our island of Isla San José, and I remember seeing Isla del Rey when flying here.

The box contains various clothing items, including cotton pants, two t-shirts, and shorts. There is also a canvas army jacket and an oversized rain jacket with a hood. The clothing is XL, so it will fit me. There are a pair of flip-flops, one size smaller than my feet. They may be of use.

In the box is a newspaper from Colombia dated three weeks ago. It could mean the dog has been on his own for some time.

Under the sail is a plastic bag containing money, a stack of Colombian Pesos, not worth much, and two thousand nine hundred U.S. Dollars. That's quite a bit of cash for a Colombian fisherman and seems hugely unusual.

This is amazing. The dog found me, and then he led me to this. How unique, and I smile. What other Naked Fear participant has a dog?

Another sizeable wooden space is built into the boat's bow, which appears to have a false floor, which has been removed. Then I notice white powder and suspect it isn't flour. If this boat had come from Colombia, it might have been used for drug smuggling.

My smile goes away.

There are several scenarios, but only one seems plausible. This sailor was not a fisherman but a drug runner who encountered the police or a rival gang of smugglers, and he came out on the short end.

I look at the dog and say, "Coco, it seems you were hanging around with the wrong people, but I'm sorry about the fate of your owner."

His ears perk up, and he tilts his head as though he understands.

For the rest of the afternoon, I make several trips carrying everything but the boat's motor to my campsite. I'm thinking about what I found during those trips, and I have a serious concern. There are different possibilities about what happened to this fisherman. Still, there is enough evidence to show he was shot, and the likely reason was the cargo he carried. If drug runners are here, we have a greater danger than snakes and pumas. Drug cartels are heartless, and destroying lives means nothing to them.

As much as the Naked Fear producers like suspense and drama, I'm sure they never imagined this one.

From what I saw, I'm troubled. The sight of dried blood in the boat was anything but pleasant, and it wasn't from fish. I'm sure it came from Coco's owner, and the cans of dog food are a giveaway that the dog was on that boat. It is uneasy to think that drug traffickers are cruising past this island. Maybe I'm overreacting. I'm a cautious person, a trait gained from spending so much time in the jungle. One learned to look out for jaguars, venomous snakes, poisonous frogs, fire ants, and other nasty creatures that could kill you.

After a good Carabaya meat meal, I try my new bed when night comes. While tired from the work of the day, my sleep is restless. The bed will take some acclimation, but something else is concerning. It's the thought of that sailboat. Although, I don't plan to stay here all that long, so why worry?

DAY 4

This morning I'm faced with making a choice. On Day One, I told Frank and June that I would show up at their camp in three days, which is today. So should I go or just hang out here and enjoy one more day by the sea?

If I stay another day, it will meet the five-day limit requested by my bosses, although they hoped I might hold out a bit longer. They have little of me on film, except for the first day's tromp through the jungle and the conflict with Pandora, which isn't much. They told me to fake some pain in front of the camera before tapping out.

So, I made a promise and need to be a man of my word. First, I'll visit the survivors' camp and do what's expected. Although it sounds phony to "fake pain," whatever that means. I'm not much of an actor, but I'll try it, and this might turn out to be the funniest, most ridiculous scene ever on Naked Fear. After that, I'll tap out and return to California's comfort. I'll take the money found on the sailboat and leave all the other stuff behind or give it to the survivalists to make their life easier.

But then, I look at Coco, and he stares back at me with sad brown eyes. He would starve if I left him on this island alone, so what should I do with him? It would be wrong to leave the dog.

Coco and I eat the last of the Carabaya meat. Then, I boil water, put a teaspoon of Colombian coffee in a ceramic cup, and pour hot water over it. It's in the category of Turkish coffee, not filtered. After letting the grounds settle, I drink the coffee, which lifts my spirits.

Then, I hide the archery bow, the handgun, and a box of bullets in a crack in the rocks. I've seen Naked Fear shows, and participants covet archery bows. I know how Pandora can be, and if there are others like her, it's best to remove temptation from them.

Calling Coco, he follows me up the narrow trail that heads to the top of the bluff. From here, I see the large lagoon to the south and get an orientation of where we are going. Then, I discover a tricky path where we traverse down the other side. This seems the only possibility to go to their camp unless we take the long way around where Pandora, Ada, Frank, and June walked the other day. Unfortunately, it is impossible to walk along the sea, as the bluff forms a cliff out into the water, and to go that way, one would have to swim.

Coco and I find a trail around the lagoon until we come to the beach and then walk through a shallow stream where the lagoon's water slowly flows out into the sea. The beach is long, and another rocky outcrop circles into the ocean at the far end. Again, remembering the map, the natural harbor is where the production team keeps a boat.

I hear voices halfway down the beach, so I position the brown bag over my private areas. This nudity business in front of others still feels bizarre.

I step into the forest and carefully make my way to the voices. It's Pandora, and she is arguing with someone. They stand in front of a group of shelters of various constructions. One is a lean-to, and another is a poorly constructed hut. A third resembles an indigenous tribe's teepee or wickiup, where all poles meet upward at a central point. I can imagine the discussions and arguments when building these shacky structures, having little agreement on the best way. The producers of Naked Fear love this sort of thing.

With a raised, strained voice, Pandora says, "You do nothing, and we do everything.'

A guy speaks back to her with equal force. "Everything you do makes no sense."

Pandora storms away and grabs a stick, and I suspect she will hit him with it, but she tosses it into the fire. "There," she says, "You could at least keep the fire going."

"You're wasting wood," he asserts.

They stand bare-naked in front of each other, and the guy does nothing to cover his family jewels. He has a poorly done Polynesian-style tattoo on his left shoulder.

Frank films the encounter, and he grins.

I tiptoe to the edge of the campsite and wait. Coco comes next to me and quietly sits.

Pandora looks up, sees me, and exclaims, "Bookie, what are you doing here."

"Standing. Watching," I say.

"I thought you tapped out."

"Where is everyone," I ask.

"Foraging."

"How is it going?"

"If you think you will get a meal around here, you can just forget it. These so-called experienced survivalists are worthless."

Frank aims his camera at us.

"You mean you've had nothing to eat?" I ask.

"Just some muscles and snails from the rocks, but that gets old quick."

"Then, what have you been doing?"

"I've been coordinating, choosing the site, starting the fire, building our shelters, and purifying water. Others do nothing. What is that?" She asks, pointing at Coco.

"A dog."

"I can see that," she exclaims. "Where did you get it?"

"He joined me." I decide to keep details to a minimum.

Coco sits attentively, and Pandora approaches him with her hand held out. The dog bares his fangs and growls. I've never seen Coco do that. "Careful, he's mean," I say while thinking it's more like he is a good judge of character.

Pandora takes two steps back. "We don't need that thing here."

I smile. "The dog has a mind of his own."

The guy arguing with Pandora says, "My name is Roger. I guess you are Bookie. We heard about you."

Roger is about six foot two, my height, and I'd guess he is in his late thirties. He has thick arms and shoulders, built like a football linebacker gaining a belly. He must outweigh me by twenty-five pounds or more.

"The name is Bartholomew."

"It's a weird name," Pandora interjects. "Call him Bookie. He is a bookkeeper for the Naked Fear film company, and they lost their marbles by sending him here."

"What's your survival experience?" Roger asks.

"I'm learning," I reply. I know Roger from watching the Naked Fear show he was on. He drove his partner to tears, and she tapped out after fifteen days. She did the lion's share of the work, building the shelter, finding food, and everything else. But he wore her down. Roger and Pandora make an interesting pair, and I understand why they were chosen for this challenge. The producers knew the dynamics between these two would be explosive.

Roger asserts, "Bookie, this challenge is not a place to learn. We are all tested and proven survivors. From what Pandora told us, you will become a burden. We are on day four and haven't had a decent meal since we've been here. The rest of the team is in the forest looking for food, and if they find it, we certainly can't share it with you."

"Why aren't you out in the jungle with them," I ask.

"Someone needs to man the camp and keep the fire going."

"Two of you?"

Roger bursts out, "Pandora should be out there with them rather than staying here and barking out empty orders,"

"It's not me," she counters. "You've done nothing and should be helping the others."

"My strategy is to conserve calories," he shouts.

"You're a fat pig," she charges.

"That was the plan to bring my food supply along with me." Then, with his thick hand, he pats his ample stomach. "You need to think ahead."

Frank grins behind the camera. The TV audience will love this.

There is movement behind the encampment, and the other team members appear. It's Ada, another naked woman, and a naked man. June and another cameraman named Bob follow them. The naked woman and man are familiar from seeing them on previous Naked Fear shows. They are hardcore personalities that would make Atilla the Hun uncomfortable. The guy's name is Harry, and the woman is Wilma, and they both drove their partners insane. Wilma holds a small dead snake in her left hand, resembling a short, skinny rope.

Harry is about the same age and build as Roger, and the name fits him. He is a gruff, hairy bear of a man who looks like he could bend steel in his bare hands. The combined physical force of these two men could lift a truck.

Wilma is around thirty years old and attractive like the other women in this show. When picking candidates, the producers must have had beauty and the female form at the top of the criteria list. Besides her beauty, Wilma's main distinguishing characteristic is bright purple hair. It's doubtful a professional hairdresser had anything to do with that. It was probably the result of experimentation in the bathroom sink with a friend. She has five earrings spread along the edge of her left ear but non on her right. In her previous twenty-one-day Naked Fear challenge, her partner described her in endless ways, like self-centered, egotistical, and a witch. Many other terms were bleeped out. Her dialogue on the show also had its fair share of bleeping. Thousands of people on social media called it the "Bleeping Episode."

Why did the producers put Ada in this mix? It's probably to place at least one sheep among the wolves, and I suspect that's what they did by sending me down here.

Ada sees me, smiles, walks over, and hugs me, this time not discretely sideways but as though she appreciates seeing me. Again, the tender touch of her body leaves an impression. "Bartholomew, I'm glad you are still here," she says.

Ada's makeup from day one is gone, her hair is tangled, and her eyes are drawn. No matter. I find her to be lovely.

"I'm okay," I say. Coco didn't growl when Ada approached me as he did with Pandora. The dog is somehow a good judge of character and is cautious of psychos.

"Is this your bookkeeper, guy?" Harry asks.

"That's him," Pandora replies.

"Where have you been?" Ada asks.

"Wandering around and admiring the beauty," I reply, realizing that Pandora, Roger, and Harry stare at Coco with drooling eyes. I suspect they see him as a meal.

Pandora says, "See what I told you. Bookie is lost in a dream world. He doesn't have what it takes to survive twenty-eight days on a jungle island." She turns to Wilma. "What did you get?"

"Ada found it," Wilma states, holding the dead snake in the air as though raising a trophy. "Protein," she proudly proclaims.

With the snake held high above her bright purple hair, I have the image of a sorcerer ready to mix a magical potion. Or perhaps she resembles a villain superhero ready to strike lightning on our heads.

The attention of the group focuses on the small snake. After skinning and gutting it, Harry puts the skinny snake on a long stick and places it above the fire. The snake wiggles as the fire's heat penetrates muscles and nerves.

June catches my eye and tilts her head toward the jungle. "We need to talk," she whispers.

Coco and I follow her along a path, and five minutes later, we arrive at the campsite of the production crew. They have set up four large tents. Two sizeable solar panels sit by one tent, and a satellite dish points to the sky. Inside one tent are film and communication equipment tables with cameras, computers, and radios. The three remaining tents have cots and sleeping bags. A green tarp covers an area with cooking equipment, tables, and comfortable camping chairs.

This is quite a setup for the film crew, including Diego and Carlos, two Panamanian men hired for this production. Diego is the speedboat skipper, Carlos is a medic, and they cook for the staff.

June says, "I was worried about you. How did it go?"

"As I said the other day, I wanted to check out the island, and I kept my promise to be here in three days."

"We regret we didn't get any of your adventures on video. Did you record it with your diary-cam?"

"How does it work?"

She rolls her eyes. "That's a pity. We now need you in the camp here."

"Why is that?"

"A new personality needs to be injected into the group. It will help the dynamics and storyline."

"You mean you need a candidate for mobbing."

"Well, not exactly."

"I'm not up for it." They can't force us to do anything. That is in their standard contract, which I never signed because procedures were forgotten during the frantic rush to get me to the airport.

She pauses as though considering options. "So, what will you do, tap out?"

"Our bosses said I should last five days minimum. That's tomorrow, so I'll be headed home."

"What?" she exclaims. "Please don't do that."

I pause, shift my weight from one leg to the other, and give it some thought. My camp here is better than my desk in Hollywood. Then, knowing that in Guyana, we negotiated everything, I ask, "Do you have any incentive for me to stay?"

"What do you mean?"

"Why should I stay on the island?"

"To interact with the survivalists. The longer we have bodies here, the more interesting it becomes. You need to be living with these people."

"Never. I'd consider staying in my camp on the other side of the bluff and occasionally coming over for a visit. And that's it."

June takes a deep breath, hesitates, looks in both directions, and whispers, "Come with me."

We go into a tent with many boxes piled on each other. They contain food supplies, enough to last more than twenty-eight days.

"Take your pick," she says.

I pick out several items, a couple bags of rice, spaghetti noodles, and four cans of mixed vegetables. "That should do it for now, except why not throw in one of those portable camping chairs. And then I'll stick around for a while."

"Giving you the food is already too much. I can't give the chair."

"Fine. Call the pilot to come and pick me up in two days."

June looks defeated and nods her head. "Okay, you can have the chair, but don't forget to come here daily."

"Maybe every other day."

In desperation, she murmurs, "Alright, alright."

June gave in too quickly. Where I grew up, there would be much more back-and-forth discussion before making a deal. She puts my food items in a cardboard box, and I am in a dilemma. I can't very well carry this in front of the other participants. "Can you get this to me?" I ask.

"Where are you camping?"

That question sets me back. I surely don't want them to see my camp, with everything collected yesterday from the fisherman's boat. So, the best option is to set up a fake camp to lead them away from the real one.

I say, "On the other side of the bluff is a beach and a small lagoon. At the end of the beach is a large pile of driftwood. That's where I've set up camp."

"We have a boat in the harbor, so we can take everything to you. And that allows us to take some footage of your camp for the show."

"That's fine with me, but deliver it later this afternoon because I first want to wander around and check out some jungle flowers." So that gives me time to get back and build a simple camp.

June and I walk back to the survivors' encampment, Coco sticking close to my side. When I get there, the five participants sit in a circle around the fire pit, allowing much space between each other. Each holds a small piece of snake meat. Unfortunately, some meat looks burned, and other parts are raw.

Roger takes a bit of burned meat and says, "This is great, but find a bigger snake next time."

"You find the snake," Pandora says. She sees me. "Well, it looks like you lost out, Bookie boy. We saw you go with June. The rules are you can't speak with them. Were you tapping out?"

"Thinking about it," I say. "Maybe soon."

"You can stick around and watch our feast."

My eyes scan the participants sitting on the dirt. Their skin is dirty, and Roger and Harry crouch like animals. It's an image of two hyenas ready to snatch food from each other.

"I'm heading out," I state.

"Where to?"

"There is much of the island to explore, and I like the jungle flowers, the sounds of birds, and the wonder of evening sunsets. See you around."

"Loser," Pandora says.

Roger, Harry, and Wilma laugh.

Ada peers up at me, and I feel compassion for her being stuck with these creatures. I nod to her and then slip into the forest, my mind somehow taking a mental snapshot of her physical outline and sweet demeanor. But she's no softy. I suspect her mental willpower will outlast all those nasty freaks.

Hurrying over the bluff, there's a task needing urgent attention, the need to construct a fake camp.

* * *

At my main camp, I collect my archery bow and homemade fire starter and head to the driftwood pile at the end of the beach. Then, I get busy. Because of the abundance of driftwood, it is easy to quickly build a lean-to. I form a square fire pit with logs and start a large fire with my bow drill. I spread dry grass and reeds from the lagoon's edge to make a bed inside the shelter. The camp must appear to be used.

Then I return to my main shelter, satisfied it is well secluded, hidden behind palm trees and jungle vegetation. Someone can walk within fifteen feet of the place and not know it is there.

I use the time to stretch the sail of the fishing boat across the top of my unfinished shelter. The large size of the sail gives me an idea to expand the shelter's walls. Collecting more bamboo poles, I quickly construct the walls, and it's becoming a proper jungle hut.

Before finishing the last wall of the hut, I hear a boat motor in the distance. So, Coco and I sprint to my fake camp, arriving just as a boat approaches the breakers. It's a twenty-four-foot fiberglass speedboat with a powerful outboard motor, the same one that met me when I came here.

The long outcrop of rocks protruding into the water forms a natural jetty where a boat can come close to the shore. Otherwise, it means navigating through waves breaking toward the beach, although they are small.

Frank and June ride in the boat driven by Diego, the same dark-skinned Panamanian man who took me down the island's east coast on the day I arrived. He knows his way around the sea. The boat swings close to the outcrop of rocks, avoiding the breakers, and continues up to the shore. June waves to me and smiles as Diego cuts the motor.

Frank and June jump off the boat into knee-deep water and walk to dry sand, and Diego gets out and holds a long rope fixed to the boat's bow. Frank carries a box containing my food, and his ever-present camera is strapped over his shoulder. I wonder if he sleeps with the thing? June has the camping chair.

Tail wagging, Coco runs down to greet them.

"Welcome to my palace," I say.

"This is highly unusual bringing you this food, and I disapprove,"

Frank says. "You should be over there with the others."

"I'm not sure the more I think about it," June says. "This provides an interesting contrast, one group struggling together and a loner who barely survives for an extended period on his own. But, of course, at some point, Bartholomew's situation will become intolerable because of hunger and loneliness, and he can then join the others." She turns to me. "Then we can create a drama, and you can tap out."

Who says these shows are not scripted?

"Still, I don't like it," Frank says. "Providing food and comforts isn't exactly according to the rules."

He would croak if he knew about my stuff from the beached sailboat.

June laughs. "We have done much worse than this. It's what the viewers believe that counts."

"Okay," Frank says. "Let's get this show started. Move the box and chair out of the scene, and Bookie, move over by your primitive shelter. Then, June, ask him some questions."

I move over, sit on a driftwood log next to my simple shelter, and ensure the burlap bag is appropriately positioned below the beltline.

June asks, "So, Bartholomew, how long have you been here."

"A while."

"On your own?"

"Uh, huh."

"Why don't you join the group?"

"It's good here?"

"Do you feel they ran you out?"

"Nope."

June turns to Frank. "Turn that thing off. This isn't going anywhere."

She looks at me. "You've got to make longer dialogues, and need to describe your experience, how you survive, and your feelings. That's what viewers are interested in. It should be a monologue, not a dialogue where I ask questions. My voice doesn't show up in the final cut. Can you do that?"

"I guess."

"Okay, let's try again."

Frank starts filming, and June asks, "Tell us about how you came to this spot."

"I walked here."

"No, tell us all the details about your adventure."

"Uh, I left you up there a few days ago and came down here."

"Did you go anywhere else?"

"Not so much, just here and there."

"Bartholomew, we need to work on this. Tell us what you're thinking."

"What I'm thinking? Like now?"

"Yes, please explain it," June pleads.

"Okay. I'm wondering if you enjoy filming a bunch of naked people?"

"That's enough," Frank exclaims, hanging his camera to his side.

June looks at me, puzzled, and says, "Bartholomew, I know you did not receive proper coaching before this challenge. And, talking in front of a camera may not be easy for you."

"Talking with anyone isn't easy."

Frank rolls his eyes upward.

"I understand," June says. "Perhaps the producers were too quick in sending you here."

"It was a mistake," I respond, knowing I'm enjoying myself.

She raises her hands and asks, "What should we do?"

I sway back and forth, look upward for a few seconds as if thinking, and say, "I got an idea, so I'll tell you what. In two days, I'll come over to the camp, and we'll see what happens. Maybe you get a good scene, and maybe not, but that's a possibility I can offer."

Frank and June look at each other and nod their heads, and Frank immediately heads to the boat. I suspect there is more exciting action at the other camp, for he is getting little from me.

June turns to me and says, "Bartholomew, please be careful. You now have some basic food to last a few days, but I worry about you being out on your own, someone new to this sort of thing. Wandering around and looking at flowers will not enable you to survive."

"I've got a dog," I proclaim.

"Well, that's a start, but it needs to be fed."

"We will manage. Could I ask something?"

"What's that?"

"How do you put up with Frank?"

She glances at the boat, then back at me, and says, "You are certainly direct." She hesitates and then almost whispers. "Confidentially, between you and me, twenty-eight days with someone like him is too long."

I smile. "Tap out, or come over here, relax, and enjoy the sunset with me."

She smiles. "Tap out? I don't think so because I need the job. Although, I wouldn't mind watching sunsets with you. Bartholomew, you are an interesting person but not made for this, and I fear you won't survive. Your PSR is very low."

"PSR?"

"Your Primitive Survival Rating. Look at your shelter. The next storm coming through here will blow it away. I regret the producers pulled you into this."

"Don't worry about me. Think about yourself."

Frank yells from the boat, "We need to get going."

June slightly shakes her head, slowly walks down to the water's edge, and gets in the speedboat. A minute later, they are heading south beyond the breakers, back to their camp.

Sitting in the comfortable camping chair, I watch them go. The chair is saucer-shaped with a high back and padded seat. It has a cup holder that will come in handy for my tea when I sit here in the evenings to watch the sunsets.

As expected, the filming session with Frank was a disaster, and I may have messed with their heads in that their expectations were not met. Frank seems frustrated that the neophyte survivalist is not over at the other camp being mobbed by a group of hardcore assassins. On the other hand, June has a different plan, this wanderlust dreamer floating in and out of the camp to bring a different narrative to the story. Unfortunately for them, they will get neither.

The more I'm around June, the more I wonder what she is doing here? As she said, this job pays the bills, but she seems capable of much more. And it's like she is trying to do a good job, but her heart isn't into it.

I'm now committed to a few more days of being here, which I don't mind. This is a thousand times better than sitting behind my paper-cluttered desk back at the office. Moreover, I have a good setup with my secluded camp in the forest. So why rush getting out of here?

Being here may also give me a unique opportunity to think about my next move in life. I fell into the bookkeeping job by chance, and it's not for me in the long and short run. Only what's next? I know what my missionary parents would say. Trust the Maker of heaven and earth. But, unfortunately, it's not always that easy.

The conflict in the camp on the other side of the bluff isn't appealing. They are only four days into this adventure, and the survivalists are already going at each other's throats. Hunger, despair, and desperation will set in, and tensions will rise. Is cannibalism a possibility? That's not for me.

I am now an outsider, and they will likely turn on me, so I must be careful around them. Besides the survivors, the thought of the bullet holes and dried blood on the fisherman's boat is troubling. I now possess all the drug runner's items on the sailboat or whoever he was. His dog is now curled up, sleeping not far from me. That feels strange to be using his things, but one must be pragmatic and not let emotions get in the way of survival.

The bullet holes in the boat are a concern as they came from a powerful weapon. But would the person who fired that gun revisit this island? Probably not.

If I can stay clear of the nonsense in the other camp, everything should go okay, but what about Ada? Her image rests in my mind. She is different than the others. As those brutes turn on each other, will they also turn on her? Is there any way I can help?

DAY 5

A light streak of gray appears in the eastern sky, and I rise from my bed and stretch my back. The bed is anything but a memory foam mattress, but I'm getting acclimated. A mat would help, but where would one acquire such a thing?

The mosquito repellent from the fishing boat was a good find. And the fireplace ashes sprinkled around the bedposts repelled the bugs attacking from ground level. So far, I have very few insect bites, but I need more sage and eucalyptus leaves to scatter in the hut.

Having decided to stay here a few more days, I need to add to my food supply. Yet, the question is how much effort to invest in this? Early morning is the best time to hunt, and there is an open area on the other side of the small lagoon where I spotted animal tracks. There they come to drink.

I possess three weapons: the hunting knife, the archery bow, and the .38 pistol from the fishing boat. The gun is left behind because one booming shot would scare the animals away for a long time.

It takes patience to convince Coco to stay at the camp, but he finally understands and curls up in the sandy dirt near the hut. There is no need to tie him up.

Going down to the sea, I dive in, and the water is refreshing and makes me feel alive and alert. Then, on the beach, I rub sand over my body to wash away the human smell.

Still wet with water, I walk cautiously, skirting the lagoon's edge. Our tribal hunters taught us how to move with stealth, slow, quiet, almost unseen, taking notice of every sound and movement. Noises around the lagoon signal that the day is alive. Birds chirp out their morning calls. Some are familiar, whereas others are not.

I slide behind a bush near the clearing, take the bow, and ready an arrow. Then, crouching down, I wait. Ten patient minutes later, I sense movement in the forest. A deer cautiously moves into the clearing, a small buck. He stops, raises his nose, smells the air, and looks around. It is a beautiful animal.

He walks to the water's edge, bends down, and drinks. And I slowly pull back the string and release the arrow. It is a perfect shot, in the side near the heart, and he takes a lurching step back from the water and falls to the ground. The chirping birds go silent.

It is a Central American Red Brocket deer, or *mazama temama*, ranging from southern Mexico through Central America to northwestern Colombia. It is like the *mazama Americana* deer we have in Guyana, which can weigh up to forty-five pounds. Trophy-sized Mule Deer in North America are much larger, weighing around four hundred and fifty pounds. The one I shot is young and will provide enough meat for many days.

I lift the deer to my shoulders, carry it to a grassy place near the beach, and take out my hunting knife. Then I skin it and eventually prepare cuts, mainly small strips, for smoking. Some bones are kept for making soup, and less brittle ones for Coco. Then I pack the meat in the deerskin and carry it back to camp.

Coco is quite interested when I arrive and more than happy when I give him a bone. So that will keep him occupied for a while.

Some chunks of meat go into the pan to cook, and the rest is hung high above the fire on horizontal bamboo stalks. Then I enclose the chimney with a wall of long bamboo stalks, so it has four sides to better contain the smoke. The trick is to keep the fire low so the meat dries but doesn't cook. The smoke also keeps flies away.

I take a slice of cooked meat from the pan, which is delicious. Many people in Guyana prefer Capybara meat, but I like venison. When I moved to California, I was amazed at how many people could not stand the thought of hunting an animal for food. Yet, they were happy to eat a juicy steak or hamburger, not considering the source or the process of how it got on their plate. In my town of Mabaruma in Guyana, every kid participated in hunting and preparing meals.

At noon I eat a healthy portion of venison accompanied by rice given by June. Then I prepare a venison stew, including heart of palm, young bamboo shoots, and roots from an edible plant that tastes like yams. It will cook all day, and I will have it for dinner.

Drifting into a lazy afternoon, I relax at my beach camp by the driftwood pile and then sleep in the shade of the hut. After the nap, I take a long swim past the breakers, and when coming back to shore, Coco meets me with a stick in his mouth. I take it from him, flip it into the water, and he splashes in to retrieve it. It's incredible how Coco has changed, gaining weight and energy in a few days. He is still on the skinny side but doing better.

Sitting on the comfortable camping chair, with feet in the sand, the sun warms my body. I spend time weaving a hat from bamboo leaves, a skill learned from the women in my village. It's great to have the dog for company, but is that enough? No. It would be better to have someone to share the day with and the night. And the future. Not having that person leaves an empty spot in my being, meaning my perfect day could be better.

Far out in the water, several cargo ships pass by. Then, a large catamaran sails from the north and eventually turns around the south of our island. To better observe these vessels, I must remember to bring binoculars.

Pleased to wear the bamboo hat, I relax, letting my mind wander, realizing how quickly I adapted from the office world back to nature. Running around without clothing is not a new thing for me. As little kids in the village, we all went naked, but there came a time when we put on pants and t-shirts. Now, in some way, it feels like reverting to childhood innocence. Being like this gives an incredible feeling of freedom.

Still, to be filmed nude on the Naked Fear TV program makes me uneasy, especially knowing this is seen by millions of people. It makes me wonder if our culture has drifted into a twisted form of voyeurism.

After another swim, I return to my campsite and put more wood on the fire. Smoke wafts up through the chimney where the meat is being cured. I stretch the deerskin tying it between poles, and scrape away any remaining fat. Inside the hut, I arrange the food from June and the items from the fishing boat. The .38 pistol is hidden in a place just inside the hut entrance. It feels good to put things away, and it feels like home. Maybe I should stick around for a few more days? I'm still on the film production company's payroll, and what better way to make a living than this?

Although, I'm not doing what was asked of me, to fake pain and tap out. Until now, they hardly have me on film. I promised Frank and June to go back to their camp tomorrow to do some filming. They want drama, but that's not my plan. I will stroll in, say hello, and head out. Getting caught up in the hostilities over there is not for me.

Anyway, the survivalists don't want me in their camp. Who cares? After an enjoyable day like today, I'm happy to be an outcast.

DAY 6

It's a warm day and I'm glad to wear my woven bamboo hat. Polynesians would laugh to see such poor craftsmanship, but at least it does the job.

After loading my backpack with a bottle of water and a plastic bag full of venison jerky, I climb up the narrow trail to the top of the bluff. Coco friskily scampers ahead of me, sniffing here and there. In the distance I see the lagoon and beyond that is the survivalists' camp. This would be a good place to spy on them with my binoculars, except I decided not to take them today. The binoculars would raise all kinds of questions if discovered by the other campers.

While not explicitly stated in the contract between the Naked Fear film company and the participants, it is considered taboo to use any "props." That means any modern tools or devices to simplify the challenge. I now have a hut full of helpful devices, almost what one would find in a simple household. Then again, I didn't sign a contract to be on this adventure, as my bosses were frantic to quickly get me to the airport.

My goal is to show up at the camp, interact with people a tiny bit, and get out. I'm not ready to fake misery, as requested by the producers, nor to get into battles with Pandora or anyone else.

There is no movement in the camp, but a few trees block my view, so I can't be sure anyone is there. Winding my way down the risky trail, Coco and I go around the lagoon, cross the narrow stream, and head into the jungle. From there, we move slowly.

Ahead of us, I hear voices and crouch down and put my hand on Coco's neck and pull him close to me. "Quiet," I whisper, gently patting him. He seems to get the jest of the word, which is pretty good for a dog that lived in a Spanish speaking world.

On the path are Harry and Wilma, and she says, "We've got to find food."

"You make too much noise," Harry accuses. "You scare the animals."

"So, what. You can't catch anything."

"We have to keep trying."

"Your traps are worthless. Those pigs are too strong and break the traps to pieces."

"We need to make them stronger," Harry exclaims.

"I think the others found food and are not sharing."

"We need to keep an eye on Pandora and Roger. They can't be trusted."

Harry and Wilma continue into the jungle. Her purple florescent hair is like a neon sign announcing her presence. Or, maybe more like an alien landing on earth and terrifying the wildlife on this island.

I wait until the sound of their conversation disappears in the distance and then pull my hand away from Coco's neck. He's an intelligent dog, responsive to my commands.

Moving down a trail different than the one Harry and Wilma took, I hear noise, like leaves moving or softwood breaking. Putting my hand out, I signal for Coco to walk behind me. Slowly I move toward the sound.

Just ahead, I see Ada crouched down near a decaying log pulling off strips of rotten bark. After each strip is removed, she carefully peers at what's underneath.

I quietly approach her and, when twenty feet away, whisper, "Hello."

She jerks up and sees me.

"Hi," I say. "I didn't want to scare you."

She smiles. "You did, but I'm getting nervous about everything now." She looks at my head and says, "Nice hat. How did you know how to make it?"

I grin. "Trial and error. It's primitive, but it keeps the sun off the face. Are you looking for grubs?" I ask.

"Yes. Grubs, worms, and anything else. That's not the most delightful meal, but I need protein, and anything will do."

"What have you eaten so far?"

"Besides the snake, I caught five small crabs, but they didn't go far with five hungry people,"

"Has anyone else found food?"

"No. They spend more time discussing than doing."

"Don't you mean arguing?"

She nods. "That's more descriptive." She pauses. "Why are you here?"

"I came to check in with June."

"Are you tapping out? That's the rumor."

Ada rises from her crouched position and sits on the old log, moving slowly as though conserving energy. Her hair is tangled, and red insect bites are on her legs. The mosquito net functions at night, but staying protected during the day and evenings is impossible.

"Tapping out? I've been thinking about it, but not today. I made a promise to check in every couple of days."

"Why don't you join the group here?"

I smile, hesitate, and say, "I like being on my own." That's one reason, but not the only one. "How are you holding out? What I mean is, how are you holding out with the others?"

Ada takes a breath. "It's not easy. It looks like someone purposely chose difficult personalities for this challenge."

Nodding, I say, "I'm assuming you are hungry." I wait a moment, look around to ensure no one is watching, and reach into my bag. "This might help." I bring out a strip of jerky.

She looks at it in disbelief, then raises her hand and takes it. "What is it?" She asks.

"Venison."

"I can't believe it." She takes a bite and chews slowly. "It's delicious. Where did you get it?"

"Wandering around."

"Oh, come on. Where did it come from? Did you meet some hikers in the jungle?"

"Not exactly, but I'd rather not say."

"Bartholomew, you surprise me." She concentrates on the jerky, taking each bite slowly. For several minutes, nothing is said.

Removing the plastic bottle of water from my bag, I hand it to her. "It's safe. Drink it. I scavenged several empty bottles from the beach."

She takes a sip and then liberally drinks a third of the water. "This is like a five-star restaurant."

"Can we keep a secret?"

"What's that?"

I reach into my bag, take out the plastic bag containing the jerky, and hand it to her. Her eyes open wide. I say, "Keep the water and hide this in the forest somewhere safe where insects and animals can't get to it. Eat a piece when needed, but please don't tell the others. I don't want to be on their radar. Can you do that?"

"Is that fair to the others?"

"Are they fair with you?" I ask.

"No, but I'd rather set an example."

"They are not ready for examples, at least not yet. If you show up with this, it will cause too many questions. I'd prefer not to face them until the right time. So, please put it in a hiding place and don't say anything."

"Okay, I can do that, and thank you. I don't know what to think."

"Don't think. Just eat. I need to go to the camp."

I walk away and head for a path leading toward the beach, and Coco walks beside me. I turn around, and Ada sits on the log holding the bag of venison jerky. She looks at me and smiles, and somehow, I perceive something is clicking behind those clear blue eyes. It appears like more than an appreciation for what I gave her. It's a look of curiosity, puzzlement, or perhaps a realization that the jungle wanderer is capable of more than just looking at flowers. Or, was that a look of attraction?

I was stricken by Ada the first time I saw her in that clearing a few days ago. For sure it was physical because she is a stunning young woman. Seeing her like that in her natural state definitely made an impression. However, there's more to her. I've realized that she is kind and resourceful and has many positive qualities. So, to think she might feel an attraction to me is too much to believe. Or is this just my imagination taking me down a futile path. In any case, my brain needs to focus on survival rather than dealing with ambiguous relationships.

This is not what I expected when agreeing to go on this insane adventure.

* * *

As I walk into the camp, Pandora and Roger argue about something.

48

Frank films them while June stands to the side with her clipboard. June sees me and smiles, but she quickly turns to the filmed action.

Roger sits on the ground, and Carlos, the medic, bends down and wraps Roger's hand with white gauze.

Roger looks over at Pandora and says, "This is your fault. With all your constant jabbering, I lost focus and cut my hand. You don't know how to keep quiet."

"For a so-called experienced survivalist, you are pitiful at doing the simplest tasks. It's a miracle you didn't whack off your hand," Pandora mocks.

"It's a miracle the fire keeps going. I'd expect it to be extinguished with all the hot air out of your mouth."

"You cut yourself on purpose and are nothing more than a big crybaby because of your little scratch, and now everyone else will end up doing all the work. So why don't you tap out, you lazy bum?"

"Talk about laziness. You are the most hopeless excuse for a female I have ever seen."

"If you were in Seattle, I'd sue you for sexual harassment. You can't talk to a woman like that."

"I'll sue you for calling me a bum. Vagrants, tramps, drifters, and hobos have rights as much as anyone else. Society should not discriminate against them, and that's what you are doing, and we have it recorded on video. I'll see you in court."

Frank grins. This is the type of scene they like on Naked Fear, that tense conflict with stressful music shown just before the commercial break.

They see me, and the argument stops.

Pandora turns and says, "Hey, look who's here, the wanderlust, Bookie with a crazy-looking hat. Did you bring any food?

"No."

"Ha, still talkative as always. When are you tapping out?"

"Maybe tomorrow." I quickly glance at June, who looks down at a paper on her clipboard. June slightly shakes her head. Perhaps she wrote me into the script.

Pandora points at Coco and exclaims, "You still have that mangy thing."

"Yes."

"He must be starving as you are starving."

I smile. "I don't know because the dog and I are not the greatest conversationalists." Then, shifting my weight, I glance toward the jungle and say, "Well, I better go. See you."

June rolls her eyes upward. They got all of two minutes of me on film.

I turn to leave, and Pandora yells out. "Bookie, where is that archery bow you had?"

Looking back at her, I ask, "Why?"

"I need it."

"Why is that?"

"We have been trying to catch a wild pig, but it breaks our trap. So I want to shoot it."

"The bow is mine," I say.

"You think wrong," Pandora shouts. "In survival communities, we share, and it should be in the hands of the best hunter."

"Is that you?"

'Of course."

"Let's go," I say to Coco. We take a few steps toward a path.

"Where are you going?" Pandora asks.

"Wandering." I certainly don't want them to know the direction of my camp.

The argument between Pandora and Roger quickly restarts. I hear rapid footsteps behind me when I'm fifty feet down the path. Turning, I'm surprised to see June.

She says, "Bartholomew, stop, please. I need to talk with you."

"What's up?"

"I want you to know I appreciate you coming into camp. That was a good scene between Pandora and Roger, and then with you coming in, it enhanced it. You bring a new dynamic. Can you please not tap out?"

"Why shouldn't I? The bosses said I should stay five days. We are now on day six. So, what do I get out of it, that is, if I stick around?"

"Do you want more food?"

"I don't need more food."

"Then, what do you want?"

There is nothing I want from them, but I do have a curiosity. So, not knowing how to express it, I say, "I'm somewhat perplexed."

"What do you mean?"

"It has to do with you. I have questions and want to know something about you."

"What?"

"Exactly what I said."

"What is it?" She impatiently asks.

"I've been thinking about you."

"Ask me now."

"No. There's too much to it."

"That's weird."

"Maybe, but come to my place, and we can watch the sunset and talk. Leave Frank behind and bring another one of those camping chairs."

She looks down the path and back at me, hesitates as though her mind is racing at full speed, and concedes, "Okay, but it will have to be tomorrow evening. This evening I need to compile some of the footage."

"See you then. Get there before sunset, and we can have a bite to eat."

* * *

The sun goes down, day six ends, and I relax in the camping chair at my beach camp while enjoying venison stew as Coco chews on a bone. The day wasn't that productive, but it was interesting, to say the least. The meeting with Ada on the jungle path was something to ponder, and I'm attracted to her. But does she feel the same? I'm not sure how to get an answer to that.

It was revealing to overhear the discussion between Harry and Wilma when they walked on the trail, as it looks like subgroups are forming. They distrust the other survivalists, and tensions are evident. Naturally, the Naked Fear producers want as much of that as possible.

The argument between Pandora and Roger was bizarre, and no observant person would ever call those two a cohesive subgroup. Both are obstinate and volatile, and I'm sure that's one of the reasons the producers proclaimed this to be the best show ever. With Harry and Wilma in the mix, the dynamics become explosive.

What is concerning is Pandora demanding the archery bow. It's not just a weapon for providing food but also a symbol of power, and she wants as much power as possible. My Amerindian elders had weapons, and sometimes they shared them with others. Still, respect and gratitude was always shown when using another person's weapon. Pandora showed no regard for me. Right now, I own the bow. They may eventually attempt to take it away from me by force, but it will only be loaned on my terms.

In any case, I didn't achieve the objectives for the day, to visit the camp and get out without experiencing conflict. Pandora's challenge causes concern. How far will she go to take the bow from me? That takes away my tranquility.

Just as I finish my stew, I notice something. Far out on the ocean, the same large catamaran appears from the north and sails south. At one point, the sails are lowered, and the boat becomes stationary in the water. Then, using the binoculars, I see a speed boat come in from the south with two men. The speedboat slows and comes alongside the catamaran, but on the opposite side from where I am looking. Therefore, I cannot see what is going on.

After fifteen minutes, the two boats drift apart, and the speedboat accelerates and heads south. Then, the catamaran's sails are raised, and it goes south and circles around the bottom of our island. It is far away, but I see the name painted on the back, *Sueño del Mar*, which means the Sea Dream.

What was that meeting of the two boats all about? There could be many reasons, but the encounter seemed odd.

DAY 7

The day begins as usual by putting wood on the fire, boiling water in the tea kettle taken from the beached sailboat and making coffee. The venison jerky hanging in the chimney smoker is well-dried, so I put it in plastic bags, keep a strip for myself, and give Coco three pieces. He instantly becomes focused on his food.

I have several projects for the day. First, it's critical to improve my hut. Yesterday I noticed that the white sail, now used as a roof covering, was partially visible from the beach. Someone might notice it, which wouldn't be good. So, the plan is to remove it and build a thatched roof to better blend with the environment. That may take several days, but I will start today.

Second, I'm curious about the abandoned, dilapidated house in the clearing north of the small lagoon, wanting to check it out in more detail. There could be usable things in the ruins, or I might discover something about the previous owner.

And finally, June arrives before sunset, if she even comes.

I question whether it's worth spending energy on the roof? I'm beyond my five-day commitment, but my bosses said to stay longer if possible. I feel uneasy that I have not done all they requested, such as, to fake misery. Maybe they want me to go to the survivor's camp, and roll around in the dirt, moaning and groaning. Naw, that's not for me.

Artificial drama is not for me, and I discovered that much of the spectacle here is planned, first by choosing the right characters, and then creating an environment where they fail. When will they start handing out scripts where actors memorize their lines?

Do I want to be part of their story? No way. Making my own unique story independent of Naked Fear is preferable.

Apart from the production, I'm feeling exhilarated by this

experience. And honestly, I don't want to return to my desk at the office in Hollywood. Hanging out here is much more challenging and fun.

Is this the change I seek? Should I escape civilization and exist like Tarzan? It's tempting, but people need other people. But I dread going back to my pile of paper in Hollywood. June might have some advice, so I look forward to this evening.

After removing the sail from the hut's roof, I spend a couple of hours cutting long bamboo stalks and placing them across the rooftop. Then, when the structure is solid, I cut leaves from palm trees and other jungle plants to lay across the rafters.

The roof construction went much faster than expected, and it is finished, and I go down to the ocean for a short swim to cool off and then take the path up to the old house ruins. It is at the end of a large clearing. A long rectangle of rocks is laid out beyond the house, which seems to have been a garden. I'm pleased to notice the familiar green leaves of Yacón growing among the garden weeds. These perennial plants produce edible roots which resemble sweet potatoes. After digging with my hands, I pull out eight hand-sized tubers. There are probably enough Yacón plants here to last me several months. Yacón is traditionally grown from Colombia to Argentina, so it is likely the owner of this house may have originated from South America.

Inside the house, the fallen, crumbled roof covers the floor, and there is evidence of mice making this place their home. There is nothing of use inside the ruins. I'm guessing the occupant left this place at least five years ago, but it's hard to tell. Why he left is unknown, but did the loneliness get to him if he was here on his own? Or, perhaps the previous owner of the island asked him to leave.

There is another clearing to the north of the house, and I'm surprised to find a few fruit trees uncared for, two orange trees, and two lemon trees. It is the end of the growing season, and all the trees are covered with fruit.

I pick an orange, peel it, and take a bite. It is juicy and sweet. So, I put six oranges and four lemons in my bag.

Twenty steps behind the fruit trees is a small grove of banana plants and, surprisingly, two large avocado trees. Whoever lived here had the right idea. Taking a small bunch of bananas and four avocados, I carry a weighty load back to my hut, like bringing shopping bags back from the supermarket. When approaching my campsite, I see that my jungle hut blends with the trees and bushes, no longer visible because of the white sail.

Lunch consists of venison stew, and dessert is a banana and avocado. Life is good.

After a short nap, I take the fishing gear found on the sailboat, go down to the ocean, and head to the rocky jetty. Attaching hooks and a sinker to a line, I use rock muscles as bait and lower the line into a deep pool with a sandy bottom.

A few minutes later, there is tugging on the line, and I pull up a sea bass about twelve inches long. I run a nylon line through the fish's gills and mouth and put the fish back in the water, where it will stay alive and fresh.

An hour later, I have three more similar-sized fish.

I do easy work the rest of the day, like strengthening the driftwood roof on my beach hut. It needs to look lived in to give it authenticity when June arrives. Then, using my hunting knife, I make two plates from flat pieces of driftwood and then carve primitive spoons and forks.

As the sun descends, I realize June will soon be arriving, so I start the fire in the firepit next to the pile of driftwood.

For the meal, first, I wash the Yacón tubers found at the abandoned house, wrap them in palm leaves and place them around the fire. Then, after cleaning each fish, I wrap them in palm leaves, each in a separate package, and put them further away from the fire, where they will slowly cook.

Taking my bar of soap and razor, I wash and shave in the lagoon. Just as I am finished, the sound of a boat motor churns away in the distance.

* * *

June waves at me from the boat as Diego navigates along the jetty toward the shore. Then, carrying a camping chair, she jumps onto the sand and says to Diego, "Please pick me up in two hours."

I push the boat back into deeper water, and it speeds away, and we walk up to my beach camp. I say, "Welcome to my home." I make sure my brown bag hangs low to cover the essentials.

June places her chair next to mine and says, "This is highly against the rules to socialize with a participant, but I'm intrigued why you asked me here."

"Kindly relax," I say. "We both work for the same company, so consider that two colleagues are having a business meeting."

She laughs. "I guess that's one way of looking at it."

Coco walks over to sniff June's leg and wags his tail. She rubs him behind the ears, and he heads over to my fake hut, curls up, and shuts his eyes.

"Please take a seat. We have been here for a week, so I thought you might enjoy an evening out. Putting up with those guys for twenty-eight days without a break might result in serious burnout."

She grins and glances my way. "Bartholomew, you are observant. While you may not be the most experienced survivalist, at least you have an eye for people."

"Are you hungry?" I ask. I notice her hair is not tied back in her perpetual ponytail but flows free, held on one side by a stylish hair clip. Unfortunately, I'm not the greatest at knowing the terms for women's hairstyles.

She says, "I'm famished, being so busy that I hardly ate anything all day. What do you have, the rice I gave you the other day?"

"Something else," I say.

I go to the firepit, take the cooked Yacón tubers and fish, open the palm leaf wrappings, and put them on the homemade wooden plates. Then, after sprinkling sea salt on the fish and squeezing half a lemon on each one, I give the food and homemade forks to June. "Bon appetite," I say.

"This is amazing," she says. "Did you catch these?"

"No, I bought them at the local fish market."

She laughs. "But the lemons. Where did you get them?"

"Wandering around."

"You seem good at that." She takes a bite of fish, slowly chews, and says, "This is delicious. I've been eating canned food for a week. This is in a different class. Where did you learn to cook fish like that?"

"One becomes creative."

"It's more than that. You are innovative."

"I guess."

"And are these potatoes?"

"Something like that."

She takes a bite and says, "They are sweet with hints of apple and celery. What are they called?"

I pause, not sure how much to tell her. "They are called Yacón, which comes from the Inca language meaning water root, and they are rich in electrolytes if you are into stuff like that."

She stops eating, stares at me, and says, "How do you know all this?"

I shrug my shoulders and raise my eyebrows. "Just wandering around."

"Yeah. Do you think I believe you? There's more to it."

"Not much." I point at her food and command, "Now, eat."

We savor the fish and Yacón in silence, and when finished, I hand her a banana and orange for dessert. It might be overkill if I offered avocado. For now, I keep that secret to myself.

June stares at the fruit in her hand, slightly shakes her head back and forth, and says, "I won't ask anything."

The sun reaches the horizon, and streaks of red and yellow fill the western sky. I put tea leaves into a boiling kettle on the fire. The leaves were removed from the teabags; otherwise, June might believe there is a supermarket on this island. Next, I add *suma* leaves to the teapot to give it a unique taste. Suma is a calming tea, and some say it is an aphrodisiac, but I'm not sure about that. Then I pour the tea into the two ceramic mugs and hand one to her.

"Thank you," she says. "What is it? And where did you get the mugs?"

"It's jungle tea, and the mugs were found near the beach."

She sips it. "This is amazing." Then, taking a deep breath, she says, "You were right. I need to relax."

The magnificent orange sunset illuminates her olive skin with a lovely radiance, like she's meant to be the centerpiece in this splendid God made scene.

We quietly watch the sun become a red ball and then disappear into the sea with a final pinpoint flicker, like a candle extinguishing.

June glances at me and says, "Bartholomew, you are clean, shaved, and smell like soap. How did you do that?"

"There are things around here with pleasant fragrances to wash with." I avoid mentioning how I shaved.

"As I said, you are ingenious. Unfortunately, most people on these adventures get extremely dirty, almost beastlike. In such dire conditions, they lose respect for their bodies. However, this experience doesn't seem to impact you. You are fit, and your body tone seems great."

"I don't have an explanation."

"Well, it's a pleasure, as there are few clean men on this side of the island."

"But isn't it weird to watch sunsets with a clean naked man, except for this silly brown bag acting as clothing?"

She glances at me. "Yes, it is unusual. I've become accustomed to it, although it sometimes gets to your head."

"Honestly, it's weird to stand like this in front of the camera. It's not my thing, and you've got to understand."

"I've sensed that, but if you knew you would be uncomfortable, why did you sign up?"

I laugh. "Pressure from the bosses and a stupid momentary impulse, but let me ask you something. Would you be a contestant on this show?"

She grins. "It depends on the pay, but no, never."

"After a few days here, I would say the same thing, but it's too late. I jumped into this thing way too quickly without understanding the implications."

"No participant does, as the conditions can be so extreme. I've seen that each survivor is different, but this experience breaks down social façades. It exposes people for who they are, becoming naked to the world in many ways."

I peer down at the brown bag in my lap. "Definitely, we are exposed." Then, pointing at the bag, I say, "Sitting here like this next to you puts me at a disadvantage. It feels weird."

"I suppose it does." She pauses and grins again. "Hey, wait a second. Are you suggesting I should conform to your attire?"

I laugh. "Absolutely not. I was just sharing my feelings."

"That's appreciated. So, what is this mystery why you invited me here?"

I wait a few seconds. "Several reasons. First, let's start with you."

"With me?"

"I've been watching you, and something is puzzling that I would like to know about. You are very good at what you do, coordinating all the disjointed pieces of this show. But it somehow asks if this work really suits you? May I ask a blunt question?"

"Sure, go ahead."

"At the bottom of your heart, is this what you want? It's one of those things nibbling in my mind."

June takes a deep breath. "Wow, that's a first. I've been on these challenges for two years, and no one ever asked that, neither the participants nor the production team. Most of the time, everyone is wrapped up in themselves. Frankly, I'm taken back."

"Is my question relevant?"

"Yes, but it's difficult to answer. To be honest, I came to Hollywood with high expectations, and then the system beat me down with lies and abuses along the way. For women, it is tough, although realistically, few people make it to the top of the entertainment world. So finally, I quit attending auditions, as the rejections were too painful. Eventually, I took this job of traveling to dirty mosquito-infested places while watching people suffer. It pays the bills, but it's not satisfying."

"Is this what you really want?"

June pauses, her eyes fixed for a moment on the sea and then glancing back at me. "Your question takes me to an uncomfortable zone. The simple answer is this doesn't fulfill me."

"Do you know what would?"

"I'm not sure."

"What would make you sure? That is, what would give you enough confidence to walk away from your current life routines."

She smiles. "Bartholomew, you are asking hard questions. This surprises me, for I didn't know you thought at this level, as I assumed you were just wandering in your fanciful world of flowers in the jungle. To be honest, I don't have an answer to your question, but it's a good one and needs consideration."

I nod. "Maybe I can switch gears and ask something different, totally unrelated to the question about you."

"Okay,"

"Should I tap out or stick around a bit longer."

"I don't know. Before coming here this evening, I would have asked you not to leave because the show needs you. You bring a unique dynamic, this mysterious nomad drifting in and out of camp at unpredictable times. But what is best for you? Truthfully, our producers don't care about you as a person, nor any of the participants. They are more concerned about ratings than what this experience does to people physically and mentally. So, I'll ask you a question. Are you getting anything out of this? If yes, then stay. If not, then leave."

I look at her, the glow of the last light reflecting on her face. What she said made sense. "We are asking each other similar questions. So, I'll stay, at least for a while. This gives me a rare time to think, so I'm not doing this for Naked Fear."

"It's your decision, but I'd be interested to know what you discover during your thinking time," she says.

"It looks like we both have things to consider."

The motorboat's sound rumbles in the distance and is quickly seen speeding along the coast beyond the breakers. It slows as it passes by the rocky jetty.

"He's early," June says, "Unfortunately."

June stands up, turns around, and lifts her chair to take it away.

"Why don't you leave that here?" I suggest.

She looks at me, laughs, and puts the chair back on the sand. "Is that an offer for another sunset meal?"

"Absolutely, with pleasure."

"Bartholomew, thank you for this evening. It was very much needed in many ways."

I smile, "A meal with a naked man?"

She grins. "The meal was fabulous. Thank you. What can I say? You are female eye candy."

The boat approaches the shore, and Diego, the skipper, yells out, "Senorita June, there is a big problem back at camp. They need you urgent."

"What's wrong?" She cries out.

"It is a big problem. Senor Frank said to get you quick."

June runs to the boat, hops in, and sits down just as I wade into the water and push the boat backward. Diego revs the motor, and he heads it to deeper water. June waves to me as they speed away to the south.

* * *

When the motorboat disappears, I go behind my beach hut, retrieve hidden clothing, and put on a t-shirt, long cotton pants, and an army jacket. Everything is tight but functional. I suppose they can be called 'mine,' as creepy as it sounds. The owner of the sailboat has no more need for them, so I assume. Back in the chair, I listen to the sound of the surf. Coco comes out of the hut and sits beside me until I pat him on the neck, then he lies beside the chair.

I reflect on the time with June and wonder what she is thinking. I'm sure this experience was out of the ordinary for her to spend an evening alone with one of the participants. Even more so, what does she think about the question I asked? It feels like there is something out of sync in her life. I'm not the one to fix it because I am in a similar place of uncertainty. But perhaps I can be a catalyst.

Somehow my thoughts switch to Ada and the others, and I'm convinced the camp pressures will increase. They will likely turn on her because Ada has a different character than the others. Do I leave her to the wolves?

My decision is to stay a few days longer, for I might help Ada and June in some small way. Perhaps I can do something for them.

Why did June have to urgently go back to camp? Tomorrow I'll head over there to see what's going on. It sounded serious.

DAY 8

It is mid-morning, and Coco and I quietly stand behind a bush near the survivors' camp. As usual, an argument is going on, and this time it's between Roger and Harry.

"This fool should be sent home," Roger exclaims. "He could have killed everyone."

"Who's the fool," Harry counters. "I didn't start this thing."

"Sure, you did. I didn't take your food."

"It was just a tiny piece of a crab thrown into the fire. It didn't have your name on it."

"That's the problem with you, no respect for others."

"What are you talking about. You have no respect for anyone. Look at this place and what you've done."

"You had a hand in it too, buddy."

While the camp could never have been described as orderly, now it is a mess. Two of the shelters resemble wood piles more than living quarters. Harry's wickiup is on its side, and Roger's lean-to has crumbled to the ground.

Harry sits on a rock as Carlos, the medic, puts disinfectant across Harry's forehead. Roger stands fifteen feet away while pressing his right hand against has ribs, and it looks like he will charge any minute. June stands between them as though she is there to stop a fight, but these guys would run over her like steamrollers.

The two cameramen, Frank and Bob are at the edge of the clearing with their cameras lowered. They can't film the action with June in the picture. Ada, Pandora, and Wilma stand beside the cameramen.

I silently drift to the side of the clearing, and Coco follows.

Pandora sees me and shouts, "Bookie, this is not for you. It's between the core survivors."

"What happened?" I ask.

"None of your business. Just leave. We don't need you here."

I wryly say, "It seems like the wind was strong last night, some kind of storm."

"You're not funny," Pandora shouts.

"Did anyone get hurt?" I ask. Harry and Roger have swelling under their eyes, now turning blackish-blue. They see through slits on both their right and left eyes. It's impossible to know which man won the bout, so it was likely a draw. I bet it was exciting to watch, but I wonder about the women's safety. I grin and ask, "Will there be further rounds?"

Pandora shrieks, "I said you're not funny. Look at them. If they had followed my orders, we wouldn't be in this chaos. Everything has got to be rebuilt."

June speaks up. "It's not normal for the production staff to speak with the participants except in unusual circumstances, but this goes against all the rules. Physical violence is taboo and a cause to terminate the challenge for those involved. Harry and Roger, is that what you want?"

"I want it for him," Roger sneers, pointing at Harry. "Make him disappear."

"You were both involved. Unless there is an agreement between you two to refrain from this behavior, you will have to go home."

"You can send that moron home," Harry mutters. "Better yet, drop him off a cliff. He's useless."

"What I said is final. Can you two agree to continue this challenge without violence?"

Roger looks at Harry and says, "I can, but he better respect other people's food. Or else."

"Or else what?"

Roger sneers. "Don't worry. No matter what the knucklehead over there does, I'll stick to your ridiculous rules, but he better stay away from me."

"Okay," June states. "And you, Harry. What do you say?"

"No violence, but I'm setting up my camp in another place. I can survive just fine without that peckerwood."

"That's your right," June says. "Now, let's move on. Frank and Bob, you can get back to filming."

June glances at me and raises her hands in desperation. Harry stands up, walks over to the fallen wickiup, takes an armload of fallen poles, and heads into the jungle. Wilma joins him as Bob follows them with his camera. This wonderfully cohesive team of survivalists has just become two smaller competitive teams. That should keep the cameramen busy and only amplify June's workload.

"Good riddance," Pandora remarks.

Wilma turns back and gives Pandora a look that would make evil monsters cower.

Pandora snickers, "That mess on your head looks like a purple mop, freak woman."

I imagine another rumble in the jungle will break out, only this time between the two women.

Wilma sneers at Pandora and follows Harry down the path. While he has a large load, Wilma carries nothing.

Ada stays still, like a jungle cat watching every move and carefully considering every word. Eventually, she walks to me and lightly says, "You got here too late to miss the excitement."

I nod. "It looks like there was a hurricane."

"More than that. You should have seen it yesterday evening. They got into an argument over a small crab's leg. I doubt if there was any meat in it at all. In fact, it wasn't the crab. For some time, this has been brewing, two alpha males that can't get along."

"What happened to the shelters?"

"The wickiup belongs to Harry, and the lean-to is Roger's. They threatened to throw each other out of camp, and it escalated, and they eventually destroyed each other's shelters. Then a mixed martial arts bout began. They were rolling all over the campsite, pounding each other's brains into the ground. Finally, Bob, Diego, and Carlos pulled them apart."

"What did Frank do?"

"He hid behind his camera and filmed the entire thing. He seems to think the camera gives him impenetrable superpowers."

"Where were you?" I ask.

"In the bushes with the other women, watching. Those two brutes could shred us. I was terrified, although Pandora seemed to enjoy it."

For sure she did. That fight only strengthens her position as leader. "And your shelter?"

64

"It is still intact. I was afraid they would tear up my mosquito netting."

I pause and say, "Be careful. This is not resolved. Those two have short fuses, and as the hunger increases, so will their irrationality. Big men like that need a lot of calories, and they are not getting them."

The Naked Fear participants are carefully chosen, not only with conflicting personality types but also with specific physical characteristics and needs. Denying food from these two men only leads to conflict. Certainly, the casting crew knew this would happen.

Ada whispers. "I've kept our secret."

I smile. "That's good. I brought you more. Let's take a stroll into the jungle."

Ada leads me to a place next to a small clearing with a pile of logs and rocks. She removes several dry stones from the pile and pulls out her jerky bag. She has one piece left, so I transfer more jerky to it.

"You don't have to do this. It feels like cheating," She replaces the stones over the plastic bag.

"Cheating? No way. It's called survival." I pause and say, "It's not nice to see you suffer."

She takes a deep breath. "Thank you, Bartholomew. That jerky keeps me going. But, of course, anything I forage is shared with the others, which isn't much."

She looks me in the eyes as though searching deeper. "Bartholomew, may I ask what you are doing out there on your own?"

"Do you mean in the jungle or beyond that in the big wide world?"

Ada grins. "I meant the jungle, but now that you say it, the question can be expanded."

"I suppose I've been wandering. Perhaps looking for something fixed that gives meaning and purpose, but not yet finding it." It's difficult for me to talk and not get sidetracked by surveying her lovely form.

"When do you know you will find it?"

"That's a good question. Maybe I'm getting there or finding the path to get there."

She smiles. "Keep faith, and something will emerge."

"I hope so. And you," I ask. "Have you been wandering?"

"Not exactly. In my case, sometimes, I feel constrained in what I'm able to accomplish. I'd like to do more for the world."

In the forest, there is a crash, and Pandora appears. "Hey, what are you two doing? We need to get busy. Unless someone looks for food, we'll starve, and the camp needs to be rebuilt. Roger isn't in the best shape and needs help, so take your pick."

Coco growls.

I smile. "Pandora, relax. You need to conserve energy."

She frowns. "How can I conserve energy when I have to motivate this useless heap of humanity."

"Do you?"

"Do I what?"

"Why do you have to assume the responsibility for everyone?"

"Who else will do it?"

"That doesn't answer my question. What makes you feel you must take on this responsibility? What's the origin?"

"I don't know what you're talking about. This is wasting my time. And you better bring that bow to camp."

"What bow?" I ask.

Pandora grumbles something unintelligible, turns, and charges back toward the campsite.

Looking at Ada, I say, "You shouldn't go back right now."

"I don't intend to, but she's right. I need to go look for food. Otherwise, things will get worse."

I ask, "Where are you going?"

"There are a lot of rocks in the sea over by that natural harbor. Maybe I'll find some crabs or muscles."

Should I go with her? Hesitating, I say, "Good luck."

"Be careful, Bartholomew." She leans forward and kisses my cheek. "Thank you for everything."

As she disappears down the path, my cheek burns from the touch of her soft lips. I regret that Pandora interrupted us. We couldn't go deeper in our conversation about my wandering and what Ada wants to accomplish in the world.

I also think about the inability of these survivors to find food. The producers of Naked Fear would have known about this group when they were chosen that they were not the best hunters. In some of the Naked Fear episodes, the survivalists are excellent at setting traps and catching fish and wild game. But, this group was chosen because of dysfunctional personalities rather than survival abilities. Because of that, I understand why they would call this "the best show ever," at least in their eyes.

Is there more conflict to come, only more severe?

DAY 9

When the body lacks nourishment, it searches internally for energy, taking what it can from fat and muscles. Body metabolism slows down to conserve energy, and each task becomes a burden, whether collecting wood, boiling water, or searching for food. It requires extraordinary willpower to overcome this. Those over at the survivalists' camp have gone through this before, knowing what they face. Only this time, it is longer than twenty-one days.

Why people put themselves on Naked Fear is a mystery. Perhaps it's for bragging rights or some masochistic desire to punish oneself. Maybe it's for the recognition, to say, "I've been on this extreme reality show." And some are hooked on the challenge. But, of course, having done this once, the next time will be easier, so they think. Unfortunately, from what I saw yesterday, those experienced survivalists still lack skills. Someone chose them because of their physical looks and short-tempered personalities rather than their abilities to survive in the wild.

Now, I remember overhearing a discussion at the office in Hollywood. One of the producers said, "Let's go extreme and put together a group of strong personalities, so they make each other suffer." They successfully achieved that goal, although I'm not sure they expected a brawl. No matter what, the television viewers will love this, that is, if the producers add that footage into the final cut. Have we reverted to Roman times when crowds flocked to coliseums to cheer gladiators fighting to the death?

Going hungry is not for me, nor is being caught up in the torment of dysfunctional relationships between campers. I'm focused on enjoying this experience. Of course, I've been fortunate. An archery bow and fishing line certainly makes life easier. Knowing how to use them is also a plus. Even with an archery bow, many people would starve. It's essential to master the tools one has in their life.

While the bow is extremely helpful, I know at least a dozen ways to construct effective animal traps. Those incompetent blockheads have failed. Any teenage kid in my village of Mabaruma could out-survive these so-called experts.

There was also the luck of finding many usable items in the beached sailboat. I can thank Coco for that, who led me there. And then, discovering the fruit trees behind the derelict house was remarkable.

But it fits my philosophy to broaden one's horizons and venture out, which makes me guilty of hypocrisy. For months I hunkered down behind a desk in a Hollywood office while logging expense reports. The routine of going to the gym in the evenings and running on the beach on Saturday mornings has not exactly expanded my life. It's been nothing more than a holding pattern; something must change, and I need to get out of my rut.

Thinking about the fight between Roger and Harry, that combat benefits me. Their noisy commotion certainly frightened away much of the animal life, which migrated to my side of the buff. Still, I already had plenty of wild animals here. And that defines my main task for the day, to add to the food stockpile.

I could spend the day fishing but decide to hunt, so I get up before sunrise and head up the trail where I first spotted wild javelinas. Coco stays behind, happy to sleep.

After creeping through the forest for fifteen minutes, I hear rustling and grunting sounds. Peering around a tree, I see six full-grown peccaries. Raising the bow, I pick out a sizeable male peccary and release the arrow. When the arrow hits the pig, it immediately falls over, and the others scamper away.

It's preferable to skin and butcher the pig where it lies. These animals have fleas, and fleas have nasty parasites. Carrying this thing in its current state for several hundred yards back to my campsite would leave me covered with horrid bites. No thanks.

After butchering the animal, I carry the meat to my campsite and put a couple pounds in a pot for stew. The rest is cut into strips and hung in the smoker. It would have been best to soak the meat in a brine before going in the smoker, but one must be pragmatic and work with what is at hand. This one pig will provide a significant amount of jerky, enough to last a week or more, especially when supplemented with other food. Coco is excited to get a bone.

I clean my hunting knife at the beach and go for a swim and use soap to wash the pig smell off my body. Cleaning javelina is a messy business and tiring. However, one of the benefits of going nude is no clothing to wash.

Now, I have a dilemma. Should I take some jerky to the survivors' campsite? To do so will open all kinds of questions. In my opinion, none of them are great hunters, so even if they used the bow, they would likely miss their target. While they have some skills in building shelters and starting fires, their trapping skills are limited. It's uncertain if anyone knows how to use a bow and arrow, so I risk it might be ruined or the arrows lost.

But I am in a predicament. While I'd like to help, it would likely become a full-time job if I became the primary food supplier to those unhappy campers. And, who knows what kind of criticisms and pressure would mount against me? Pandora and her little army of complainers will likely mob me, and I don't need to add that to my peaceful life.

Twenty-eight days is a long time without food, and some will tap out. So, with fewer mouths to feed, it simplifies the equation. Am I being self-centered or selfish in thinking this way?

After hunting and working all morning, I am hungry. Adding sea salt, chopped orange, and orange rind to the javelina stew makes a delicious lunch. But, while trying to enjoy the meal, my mind continues to drift to the others. Except for Ada, most of them are a sorry lot, but then I wonder if that is the right way to think? My parents taught me that all lives are of value, and they demonstrated that when working at their clinic in Mabaruma. But that principle also applies to everyone on the other side of the bluff.

I'll give it a day and go over there tomorrow to evaluate the situation. Maybe there is a way to help.

After lunch, I add more wood to the fire to keep the smoker going and then nap. Afternoons on this island can be hot and humid. However, Coco is content to lie directly in the sun. His tongue hangs out from his mouth, and he pants like sprinting a mile. Lying in the hot sun must be a great pleasure for a dog, for the dogs in Guyana did the same.

After the nap, I put more wood on the fire. Smoking javelina is trickier than deer, and the temperature must be kept low and steady. It will take eight hours or even more until the meat is cured correctly, chewy but tender.

One project I have in mind is to attempt to refloat the fishing boat stranded on the beach. With some digging and a good high tide, it might be possible to put it back in the water. But unfortunately, that project will have to wait because I need to stay around the camp to keep the smoker going.

Instead of refloating the boat, I spend the afternoon adding palm branches to the roof of my hut, tying them with pieces of nylon rope found on the beach. The roof now has enough slant for the rain to run off. March is a dry month, but this is a tropical island, and storms are unpredictable. When finished, I push on one of the corner posts. The structure is solid, and I am satisfied.

At the end of the afternoon, I go to my driftwood hut at the beach, sit in a camping chair and watch the sunset. Boats are in the distance, including the *Sueño del Mar*, the Sea Dream, the large catamaran that often passes by.

The other chair is empty next to me, and I think of the pleasant evening with June, hoping she will return. I feel an unexplainable emptiness, like a vacuum to fill, knowing it's not my thing to be a hermit existing on my own.

My experience with the opposite sex has not been a resounding success. First, there was no opportunity for girlfriends when stationed on a Marine base in the Middle East. Then in university, I dated, but studies got in the way. Or maybe they were an excuse. Relationships didn't work, and how could they? Here you have this weirdo guy from a jungle village in Guyana attempting to relate with California girls. Culturally we were light-years apart. After university, I worked, saved money, and traveled, which didn't help fill the emptiness. The vacuum is still there.

The grandeur of the sunset makes me feel small and insignificant. The Creator of this beauty is a magnificent artist. My parents claim that the Creator can lead our lives on a good path. That's fine, but is God interested in finding me the right life partner? Somehow, I feel He has other things to worry about.

When evening comes, Coco and I return to our camp. Again, I ensure the fire is low, so the meat will cure through the night and be ready in the morning.

After rubbing a few drops of mosquito repellent over my body, I put on a t-shirt and pair of cotton pants and lie on my bed. The pants, taken from the sailboat, are short and tight but helpful for sleeping. The hut is now solid and secure, Coco sleeps near the open door, and a .38 pistol is hidden nearby. That's another project, to build a door.

With the infrastructure I'm building in my camp, I could stay here for a long time. It's starting to feel comfortable. Whereas, when thinking about the Naked Fear show, I have no desire to spend more time in front of the camera. Being on the show has little to do with what I want out of life, at least for what is essential.

It was a productive and satisfying day, although probably with too much introspection. It can happen when one is on their own, overanalyzing everything. I was taught to think that way. The tribal leaders in my village drilled something into us, which I suppose is now a part of my psychological makeup. Never become complacent, stay tuned to your surroundings, and don't lower your guard, for dangers come in many forms.

Of course, if you push that too far, it becomes an anxiety disorder.

DAY 10

After breakfast and feeding Coco, the day's first task is to remove the jerky from the smoker and put it in plastic bags. The meat is cooked to perfection. Next, I put the bags in the large plastic box from the sailboat.

That causes me to think about refloating the boat. So, after housekeeping, Coco and I walk along the beach to the sailboat. Coco sprints ahead, excited, tail wagging. I'm sure the dog misses his owner, whoever he was?

Approaching the boat, I see something that concerns me. There is the indent of a boat's bow on the sand not far from the sailboat, and footprints are everywhere. Most are depressions in the soft sand, but a few are clearly distinguishable, showing two different shoe sizes.

This perplexes me. Did someone sail up the coast, see the boat on the beach, and stop for a look? I had taken just about everything from inside the sailboat, so there were no treasures to find, but there is something I hadn't noticed before. One side of a wooden seat is open, revealing a hidden compartment. Inside, I see the telltale white powder.

This reveals that whoever came here explicitly looked for this boat, and they knew where to find hidden drugs. That's a concern, for the Naked Fear participants and film team are exposed to drug runners. The bullet holes in this boat are a reminder that someone has a dangerous weapon. Is there any cause for these drug runners to cause us harm? It is unlikely, but one never knows.

There is one thing for sure. My tracks need to be better covered wherever I go, a skill learned in the jungles of Guyana. I don't want anyone following me back to my campsite.

I walk around the boat and believe it is possible to put it back in the water but is it wise? The sailboat seems to be known, and if I go sailing around in it, would malefactors ask questions? It's best to stay clear of them, whoever they are.

Deciding to visit the survivors' camp, I put on the pair of shorts taken from the sailboat, as I no longer choose to stand nude in front of Frank or Bob and their cameras. After putting javelina jerky in a plastic bag, Coco and I walk to the top of the bluff and over to the other side.

Making a silent approach, I see that the survivors' camp is quiet. No apparent arguments. Everyone must be out foraging for food. Harry's wickiup is gone, so he has set up in another location.

I go down to the beach and see Roger sitting under a palm, attempting to open a coconut with a machete. Each time he strikes the thick coconut husk, he loudly grunts.

Approaching him, I ask, "How's it going?"

Startled, he turns and says, "Not good. What are you doing here?"

"Checking in. Coconuts are tough to crack."

He looks at the coconut in his left hand. "You better believe it, and this is killing me."

"Why's that?"

"Carlos suspects I have a couple of broken ribs, and cracking coconuts is not fun. He suggested that I tap out, but I refuse."

"Let me try it for you."

"You? What does a bookkeeper know about anything?"

"I might get lucky."

He hands me the coconut and machete, and says, "Go for it."

I take the coconut, and with a few quick cuts, I remove the thick husk, and with one swift movement, the top of the coconut is chopped off."

"Here, drink," I say.

Roger's eyes are wide. He questions, "How did you learn to do that?"

"You learn a lot on the internet."

Roger drinks the coconut juice, emptying it in one go.

I take the coconut shell back from him, break it into several small pieces, deftly dig out the coconut flesh, and then hand it all back to him. He pops a large chunk of coconut in his mouth and rapidly chews.

"Oh, man, I needed this. It's really good," he says. Then he stops chewing for a second and says, "Where'd you get the pants?"

"Found them."

"It ain't exactly Naked Fear."

"Maybe not, but it keeps the bugs from crawling in your private parts."

He laughs.

"How are things over here?" I ask.

"Not so good. Everyone is tired and cranky. You getting anything to eat?"

"A little. Muscles, crabs, grubs, and stuff like that."

"That's good. Maybe you did the right thing by not hanging with us. I should probably do like you. Sometimes it's living hell around here."

"Pandora?"

He smiles. "She's quite a woman, ain't she?"

"You mean she makes life interesting?"

"You got it. That woman is a pain, but something is magnetic about her."

"If you say so." I pause. "Could I ask a question?"

"Sure."

"Have you seen any boats come by here in the last day or two?"

Roger scratches his head while chewing coconut. "Every day, there are some ships out there."

"I mean a smaller boat that may have come closer to shore."

"A large catamaran sometimes swings north to south, around the island's southern tip."

"Anything other than that??"

"Come to think of it, yesterday, a fancy speedboat with two gigantic outboard motors came by just beyond the breakers. It slowed and stopped for a while just out there. Someone with binoculars was looking at us, probably getting their kicks by looking at nude chicks. Then they went on."

"So, it didn't come into the harbor or anything like that."

"No. Why are you asking?"

"I'm just being careful. If you see anything suspicious, please let me know."

"You sound scary. What could be suspicious?"

"That's it. I'm not sure." Do I tell him that drug runners might be passing this island? Am I overreacting to what I saw on the beached sailboat? At this point, it seems best he doesn't know. Roger has enough to worry about with broken ribs, hunger, and confrontations with Pandora.

"Whatever," Roger says. He looks at my shorts. "The film crew ain't gonna like that you got civilized."

I smile. "Who cares? Have you seen June?"

"She's out in the jungle with Frank and Bob, filming the ladies."

"Is there anyone else around?"

"I think Carlos and Diego are over at the production crew camp."

"Okay, when you see June, could you tell her I was around?"

"For sure. By the way, we need the bow and arrows."

Here it comes. It feels like Roger is on the same track as Pandora. "Have you seen any animals?" I ask.

"Not really. Only some tracks, which means they are there."

"When you see an animal worth shooting, let me know."

"Bookie, we want the bow. I will take it from you if I must."

"And how would you do that?"

He pauses, glares at me like an alpha male staring down someone in a bar, and states, "I'd break you like a pencil."

"Try it," I say, "anytime." I glance down at the machete in my right hand and then back at him.

Roger stops chewing the coconut as fear covers his face, realizing someone close holds a dangerous weapon. But, with the pain from broken ribs, he can't do much.

I raise the machete above me like an executioner, and Roger hunkers down with his hands above his head. Then, with a swift motion, I swing the machete and throw it twenty feet away near the water's edge.

"Anytime," I say again. "So, see you around."

I nod at him, take a few steps toward the jungle path, then stop and turn around and see Roger sitting on the sand, perfectly still, while holding the coconut pieces. He stares at me with wide, frightened eyes.

* * *

A fierce wind comes off the sea during the night, followed by a thunderstorm, like being targeted by enemy bombs. Then, sheets of rain beat against my hut. Coco comes closer to my bed, curls up, and whimpers every time lightning and thunder occur. The hut shutters in the wind and stays intact, leaking in a few places. I cover Coco and myself with the boat's sail, and we remain dry and warm.

DAY 11

In the morning, the rain lets up, and I wear the rain jacket from the sailboat while fixing the leaking roof and restarting the fire. The storm reminded me of the need to put a door on the hut.

During breaks in the rain, I work on the door while Coco stays curled up in a dry place inside the hut. The storm brought cooler temperatures, making me wonder how the survivalists are doing. I imagine they had a miserable night. While I might have a morbid joy in this, I don't. The thought of Ada's suffering is not pleasant. And strangely, I sympathize with the others, even Pandora and Roger.

Yesterday Roger threatened me, which was distasteful, and I hope he got the message that I won't be intimidated. The archery bow is significant in their minds, but they haven't even seen any wild game. Even having the bow, they would waste time in the forest when they should concentrate on other ways to source food. There are many techniques they have not fully explored.

Building the door doesn't take long, and it is now made up of a primitive frame of bamboo stalks with nylon loops acting as hinges. The next project for the day is to attempt to refloat the sailboat, as it might be fun to use it for fishing in deeper water or even exploring the island.

Coco and I head to the beach and walk north toward the boat. At the pile of driftwood next to my beach camp, I find a flat board that can function as a shovel, and when arriving at the sailboat, I take a closer look. Currently, it is low tide, and the entire boat is surrounded by sand, yet the tide is moving in. With the flat board, I shovel around the boat's sides. It is hard going, and the sand is wet and heavy because of the storm. Eventually, I dug a moat around it.

Finding a plastic bottle on the shore, I use it to remove all the rainwater inside the boat. Then, I wait.

An hour later, the tide comes in, and it seems higher than on other days, and I assume it is from the storm that still churns up the sea or maybe from the moon's pull. Then, seawater fills the moat, and I continue rapidly shoveling under the boat, and it budges. Another large wave empties into the shore, and when it retreats, I push on the vessel, and it shifts a few inches. With the next wave, the boat moves more. Then with the next wave, I strain myself pushing with full force against the bow, and the sailboat floats and slides into knee-deep water. I rotate the boat, face it toward the sea, hop in, pull the starter rope on the motor, and it putters away. Sitting on the bench at the back, I navigate it into the open sea. There is gas in a tank near the motor, but I must remember to bring back the jerrycan of gas now at my hut.

Coco barks from the shore and does not want to be abandoned. It tells me he is at ease in the boat.

Once past the miniature breakers, I move the vessel south a hundred yards around the rocky jetty and tie it to a rock at the large pool where I had caught the sea bass. The shifting sea knocks the boat against the rocks, so I use the anchor to keep the boat in deeper water.

Coco and I return to our camp, and at noon I eat stew and give some javelina jerky to Coco.

With so much spinning in my mind, I make a definitive decision. I no longer want to participate in the Naked Fear show. But I won't leave the island just yet. So I take off my necklace with the bead-like microphone, remove the transmitter and diary cam from the brown bag, and leave them in the hut. Then, wearing shorts and a t-shirt, I grab my archery bow and walk over the bluff to the survivors' camp.

When carefully approaching the camp, I see Ada and Pandora slowly moving like robots whose batteries have given out. They add sticks and palm leaves to the top of their round shelter. Roger is bent over, leaning one hand against a palm tree and, with the other, holding a palm branch. He limps over to his lean-to, places the palm branch on the roof, and then groans, putting his hand on his ribs.

Having a grin on his face, Frank films their misery.

Walking into the camp, I say, "How are you all doing?"

The three survivalists stop and look at me with drawn faces, like zombies staring into a void. Roger looks at me with wary eyes, like facing an enemy and having no weapon.

"How does it look like we are doing?" Pandora snaps.

"This reminds me of one of those home renovation shows," I comment.

"Very funny," Pandora sneers. She notices my shorts. "Bookie, where did you get those?"

"At the clothing store."

Frank lowers his camera, points at me, and yells. "Hey, I'm not getting a signal from you."

"Maybe the lightning zapped the electronics."

"And you are not wearing your microphone."

"It was lost in the storm."

"It's against the rules to wear clothing unless you make them. The name of the show is Naked Fear."

"Sorry, Frank, but I didn't read that anywhere. We are supposed to be resourceful, and who says I didn't make these shorts.'"

"I wish I had clothing," Pandora exclaims. "Last night was living hell. I didn't think we would make it."

I remark, "That storm was like being in a war zone."

Pandora nods and then hangs her head. "I don't think we will make it if a similar storm hits this island. And we are running on fumes. Where did you sleep last night?"

"There are places," I answer.

Her eyes fix on my bow. "Bookie, we need food."

"What have you eaten?"

Ada speaks. "They have had little. Bartholomew, can you help?"

Her plea touches me. I intend not to become their food provider, but I ask, "Roger and Pandora, have you seen any wild game?"

Roger answers. "No, but there are tracks."

"Coco, stay here," I command. "Ada, can you look out for him?"

"Yes, gladly," she says.

I turn and slip off into the jungle.

* * *

Following the small river inland from the lagoon, I slowly move along a well-used animal path. The rain will have washed scents from the air, which works in my favor. Deep in the jungle, I spot a small deer, but it moves away, and there are too many branches and tangles to go after it.

Further down the trail, I hear familiar rustling-grunting sounds, so I ready my bow with an arrow. Then, cautiously, I approach a group of three javelinas intent on finding food in the jungle undergrowth.

Releasing the arrow, it hits one of the javelinas, which takes three steps and falls. The two remaining javelinas speed away.

After finding some dry eucalyptus leaves, I start a fire with my bow drill and roll the javelina to remove the fleas. Then I take the javelina back to the survivors' camp. This one is slightly smaller than the one I shot the other day.

Walking into the camp, I drop the javelina and ask, "Do you know how to prepare this?"

Ada says, "Yes, I can do it."

Roger drops to his knees while holding a palm branch, and tears come to Pandora's eyes. Frank films the action, but there is displeasure on his face. He attempts to avoid me with his camera.

"Make sure you share it with Harry and Wilma," I command.

Calling Coco, I turn and walk away.

Before getting to the jungle trail, Pandora calls out, "Don't you want some food?"

"No thanks," I say, continuing toward the path.

* * *

Back at my campsite, I question what I've done by supplying food to that inept group of zanies. Does that mean I am now their provider? But I must admit feeling pleasure when dropping the javelina in their camp. The relief on the faces of the inefficient campers was one thing.

Still, there was even more satisfaction in seeing the disappointed look on Frank's face. Frank gets perverse joy in filming misery in others, and the more agony there is, the greater his delight. Combined with that, the constant focus of his camera on the women shows where his mind is at, and it's more than appreciating the female form and beauty. He seems to like it when women are tormented. It makes one wonder if some viewers of Naked Fear are like Frank?

The show's entire premise increasingly makes me uneasy. To watch agonizing naked people on television is one thing, but to experience this is at an entirely different level. The risk taken by participants is high in terms of the impact on their physical and mental health. It confirms my decision to not participate in this show according to their rules. Instead, I will live on this island on my terms.

They now have food, so I won't go back to their camp for a day or two. I have another plan.

In the morning, the rain lets up, and I wear the rain jacket from the sailboat while fixing the leaking roof and restarting the fire. The storm reminded me of the need to put a door on the hut.

During breaks in the rain, I work on the door while Coco stays curled up in a dry place inside the hut. The storm brought cooler temperatures, making me wonder how the survivalists are doing. I imagine they had a miserable night. While I might have a morbid joy in this, I don't. The thought of Ada's suffering is not pleasant. And strangely, I sympathize with the others, even Pandora and Roger.

Yesterday Roger threatened me, which was distasteful, and I hope he got the message that I won't be intimidated. The archery bow is significant in their minds, but they haven't even seen any wild game. Even having the bow, they would waste time in the forest when they should concentrate on other ways to source food. There are many techniques they have not fully explored.

Building the door doesn't take long, and it is now made up of a primitive frame of bamboo stalks with nylon loops acting as hinges. The next project for the day is to attempt to refloat the sailboat, as it might be fun to use it for fishing in deeper water or even exploring the island.

Coco and I head to the beach and walk north toward the boat. At the pile of driftwood next to my beach camp, I find a flat board that can function as a shovel, and when arriving at the sailboat, I take a closer look. Currently, it is low tide, and the entire boat is surrounded by sand, yet the tide is moving in. With the flat board, I shovel around the boat's sides. It is hard going, and the sand is wet and heavy because of the storm. Eventually, I dug a moat around it.

Finding a plastic bottle on the shore, I use it to remove all the rainwater inside the boat. Then, I wait.

An hour later, the tide comes in, and it seems higher than on other days, and I assume it is from the storm that still churns up the sea or maybe from the moon's pull. Then, seawater fills the moat, and I continue rapidly shoveling under the boat, and it budges. Another large wave empties into the shore, and when it retreats, I push on the vessel, and it shifts a few inches. With the next wave, the boat moves more. Then with the next wave, I strain myself pushing with full force against the bow, and the sailboat floats and slides into knee-deep water. I rotate the boat, face it toward the sea, hop in, pull the starter rope on the motor, and it putters away. Sitting on the bench at the back, I navigate it into the open sea. There is gas in a tank near the motor, but I must remember to bring back the jerrycan of gas now at my hut.

Coco barks from the shore and does not want to be abandoned. It tells me he is at ease in the boat.

Once past the miniature breakers, I move the vessel south a hundred yards around the rocky jetty and tie it to a rock at the large pool where I had caught the sea bass. The shifting sea knocks the boat against the rocks, so I use the anchor to keep the boat in deeper water.

Coco and I return to our camp, and at noon I eat stew and give some javelina jerky to Coco.

With so much spinning in my mind, I make a definitive decision. I no longer want to participate in the Naked Fear show. But I won't leave the island just yet. So I take off my necklace with the bead-like microphone, remove the transmitter and diary cam from the brown bag, and leave them in the hut. Then, wearing shorts and a t-shirt, I grab my archery bow and walk over the bluff to the survivors' camp.

When carefully approaching the camp, I see Ada and Pandora slowly moving like robots whose batteries have given out. They add sticks and palm leaves to the top of their round shelter. Roger is bent over, leaning one hand against a palm tree and, with the other, holding a palm branch. He limps over to his lean-to, places the palm branch on the roof, and then groans, putting his hand on his ribs.

Having a grin on his face, Frank films their misery.

Walking into the camp, I say, "How are you all doing?"

The three survivalists stop and look at me with drawn faces, like zombies staring into a void. Roger looks at me with wary eyes, like facing an enemy and having no weapon.

"How does it look like we are doing?" Pandora snaps.

"This reminds me of one of those home renovation shows," I comment.

"Very funny," Pandora sneers. She notices my shorts. "Bookie, where did you get those?"

"At the clothing store."

Frank lowers his camera, points at me, and yells. "Hey, I'm not getting a signal from you."

"Maybe the lightning zapped the electronics."

"And you are not wearing your microphone."

"It was lost in the storm."

"It's against the rules to wear clothing unless you make them. The name of the show is Naked Fear."

"Sorry, Frank, but I didn't read that anywhere. We are supposed to be resourceful, and who says I didn't make these shorts.'"

"I wish I had clothing," Pandora exclaims. "Last night was living hell. I didn't think we would make it."

I remark, "That storm was like being in a war zone."

Pandora nods and then hangs her head. "I don't think we will make it if a similar storm hits this island. And we are running on fumes. Where did you sleep last night?"

"There are places," I answer.

Her eyes fix on my bow. "Bookie, we need food."

"What have you eaten?"

Ada speaks. "They have had little. Bartholomew, can you help?"

Her plea touches me. I intend not to become their food provider, but I ask, "Roger and Pandora, have you seen any wild game?"

Roger answers. "No, but there are tracks."

"Coco, stay here," I command. "Ada, can you look out for him?"

"Yes, gladly," she says.

I turn and slip off into the jungle.

* * *

Following the small river inland from the lagoon, I slowly move along a well-used animal path. The rain will have washed scents from the air, which works in my favor. Deep in the jungle, I spot a small deer, but it moves away, and there are too many branches and tangles to go after it.

Further down the trail, I hear familiar rustling-grunting sounds, so I ready my bow with an arrow. Then, cautiously, I approach a group of three javelinas intent on finding food in the jungle undergrowth.

Releasing the arrow, it hits one of the javelinas, which takes three steps and falls. The two remaining javelinas speed away.

After finding some dry eucalyptus leaves, I start a fire with my bow drill and roll the javelina to remove the fleas. Then I take the javelina back to the survivors' camp. This one is slightly smaller than the one I shot the other day.

Walking into the camp, I drop the javelina and ask, "Do you know how to prepare this?"

Ada says, "Yes, I can do it."

Roger drops to his knees while holding a palm branch, and tears come to Pandora's eyes. Frank films the action, but there is displeasure on his face. He attempts to avoid me with his camera.

"Make sure you share it with Harry and Wilma," I command.

Calling Coco, I turn and walk away.

Before getting to the jungle trail, Pandora calls out, "Don't you want some food?"

"No thanks," I say, continuing toward the path.

* * *

Back at my campsite, I question what I've done by supplying food to that inept group of zanies. Does that mean I am now their provider? But I must admit feeling pleasure when dropping the javelina in their camp. The relief on the faces of the inefficient campers was one thing.

Still, there was even more satisfaction in seeing the disappointed look on Frank's face. Frank gets perverse joy in filming misery in others, and the more agony there is, the greater his delight. Combined with that, the constant focus of his camera on the women shows where his mind is at, and it's more than appreciating the female form and beauty. He seems to like it when women are tormented. It makes one wonder if some viewers of Naked Fear are like Frank?

The show's entire premise increasingly makes me uneasy. To watch agonizing naked people on television is one thing, but to experience this is at an entirely different level. The risk taken by participants is high in terms of the impact on their physical and mental health. It confirms my decision to not participate in this show according to their rules. Instead, I will live on this island on my terms.

They now have food, so I won't go back to their camp for a day or two. I have another plan.

85

DAY 12

I leave our island, the Isla San José, around five in the morning, at least according to my rough calculation of the Big Dipper's position in the sky. Instead of sailing south to round the bottom side of the island where I might be seen by the survivalists, I stay on the west to catch a stronger wind coming directly off the ocean. At the top of our island, I head northeast toward the Isle del Rey. From the nautical map found in the sailboat, it appears to be the largest island in the Pearl Island archipelago.

A solid and steady breeze pushes the boat at a good pace, perhaps five or six miles per hour. It cuts through the water quite well for an old wooden boat, and I'm quickly relearning my sailing skills acquired as a teenager. It's risky to sail in the dark because of potential rocky shallows around the island, so I'm happy when the first gray light appears in the east. And I'm glad to be out in deeper water.

Besides carrying the nautical map on the sailboat, I have jerky, drinking water, and binoculars. And I have five hundred dollars from the money found on the boat. In the back is the ten-liter jerrycan of gas to be used if the wind dies down and the motor is necessary to get back to our island. I left Coco back at the camp because he might be known at my destination. If I am delayed in returning, he's smart enough to go to the survivors' camp. He warmed up to June, and I'm sure she will take care of him. My plan is to be back by nightfall, but one never knows.

My destination is San Miguel, marked with an X on the map, which I'm assuming is a town. The goal is to ask a few questions to gather information, if possible, and buy a few things to take back to my camp. Why was that town singled out by the drug runner owner of this boat? San Miguel is on the north side of the Island of Rey.

It's a pleasant morning, and I feel free as the wind pushes the sail. The boat is sturdy and could manage a much stronger wind and rougher sea. After eleven days on the island, it's good to be out on the water. While our island is a paradise, being around the survivors' camp isn't satisfying. The living condition there could be better. Having helped the participants by providing the javelina, I believe there is more I can do. Going to San Miguel gives me ideas that Frank will not like. The survivalists need some "accessories."

Care must be taken, for this boat shouldn't be seen in San Miguel. There are probably hundreds of sailboats like it along this coast, but someone knew this boat, came to it, opened a secret compartment, and removed drugs. If it is noticed, it will raise curiosity to be avoided.

Rounding the top of the Isle del Rey, the wind dies down, and the sail flops against the mast. I start the motor and putter along the coastline and see a town far ahead. Before getting to the town, I navigate the boat into a small inlet surrounded by mangroves. A path leads down to the water, so I tie the boat to a sturdy mangrove branch and put the binoculars, jerky, and water in one of the secret compartments in the sailboat. After putting the money in the front pocket of my tight shorts, I hop knee-deep into the water and wade up to the path. I head up the trail, wearing the small flip-flops initially found on the boat and a tight t-shirt. I wonder if anyone will notice that I am wearing undersized clothing?

It is about a fourth of a mile to the town, having tightly packed houses of various shapes and sizes. Most are wooden with tin roofs.

Walking to the harbor, I see a sign that says '*La Barca Ferry*.' A small ticket office is near a dock, whereas small posters and ads are stuck in every available place on the outside walls of the small structure. A few signs advertise charter boats to take people to other islands.

Then, I see a poster for the catamaran that regularly passes by our island, the *Sueño del Mar*, the Sea Dream. It is available for individual charter. The poster is old and faded, as though it was put up ages ago. Is it still valid, for seeing it almost every day in front of my beach camp certainly doesn't seem the boat is chartered?

Dozens of boats are beached on the sand and anchored in the water, everything from small wooden paddle boats to a few large yachts anchored in deeper water. A few restaurants are at the top of the sandy beach, with tables and chairs on the sand.

I go to a coffee bar, take a chair and table outside, and order a coffee, orange juice, and an omelet. After asking the server the time, he says it is ten o'clock, so it has taken me about five hours to get to San Miguel. It might take six or seven hours to return, as I will be tacking against the wind.

When the man brings my food, I ask him, "Do you know the *Sueño del Mar*, and how could I find out about chartering it?"

He says, "Look at the poster on the ticket office."

"Does it ever come to San Miguel?"

"In the past, it came once a week, but it has not been seen here for many months."

"Do you know who owns the boat?"

He glances up and down the beach, then says, "*No lo se.*" Then he walks away.

It seems his "I don't know" has more to it, like, it's best not to ask. This is strange territory for me, so. I shouldn't push it. But at least I understand there is something ominous about the Sueño del Mar with the locals.

The omelet comes, and it is out of this world, cooked with onions, peppers, and cheese. I enjoy every bite. Living on a jerky diet can get old, although jerky would be a feast for the Naked Fear participants back on the island.

The server accepts Dollars for payment of the meal, and then I take a street heading into the center of town. It is the main shopping street with tourist shops, small food markets, and a hardware shop geared toward tools and parts for boat maintenance and repair.

At a tourist shop, I buy a small backpack. While the brown burlap Naked Fear bag is helpful, the backpack will be more useful.

At a market, I get a kilo of dried beans, cans of tomatoes, chili peppers, and a dozen tortillas. Next, I add spaghetti noodles, a bar of soap, a bottle of shampoo, two bottles of water, and a large bag of dry dog food.

I also buy a thin beach mat and a sizeable two-people beach towel. It's just what's needed to make my bed more comfortable and provide a light blanket.

It's a heavy load, and I carry it back on the path, arriving at the boat and packing everything in the secret compartments.

Then, returning to town, I stop at a tourist shop to buy a long-sleeved colorful shirt, better-fitting shorts, and a pair of long pants. The shop has leather sandals that fit my large feet, so I take them along with a Panama hat and sunglasses. Then, I have an idea. Approximating the sizes of the survivalists, I pick out clothing items.

Knowing the boat requires work, at the hardware shop, I purchase two large cans of waterproof paint, a small can of white paint, a couple of paintbrushes, and turpentine. I see a need to transform the boat, so it won't be recognized. I also buy a cheap watch.

Carrying this second load of goods back to my sailboat, I start the motor and head west around the island's north, and when sensing a breeze, I raise the sail. The Panama hat protects my face from the bright sun, and I wear my new long-sleeved shirt to avoid sunburn.

Tacking into the wind, as expected, the return trip to our island takes longer, and I make it back in six hours. I secure the boat at the deep pool by the rocky jetty and carry everything from the sailboat back to my campsite. Coco is thrilled to see me and even happier when I give him a generous portion of dried dog food. Even the dog is getting tired of jerky.

The sun drops below the horizon at 6:28 pm. I eat stew with a couple of tortillas, feeling satisfied with the day's accomplishments. I now know the time by having a watch, but is that such a good thing? I take a plastic water bottle, cut off the top, and add a cup of dried beans with water to let them soak overnight. Tomorrow, I'll cook the beans with the remaining stew in my pot and add the chili powder bought from the store.

Exhausted, I'm in bed at nine o'clock. The beach mat and large beach towel provide comfort, warmth, and protection from insects.

Before going to sleep, a couple of things are on my mind. First, the javelina given to the survivors should last several days. Hopefully, it helped their overall mood, but one can't be sure with that group. The Naked Fear casting department put together a bunch of flawed personalities. Even if they were not suffering from hunger, there would still be conflict.

If I am now the provider for that group, that increases my workload and stress, and my paradise here may no longer exist. Yet, somehow in some strange way, it gives me satisfaction if I can undermine the objectives of the Naked Fear production company. My bosses live a rich, comfortable life in Hollywood, yet they make their fortune off the suffering of others. That financial model doesn't make sense.

Another thing stays on my mind. At the harbor restaurant in San Miguel, I asked the server about the *Sueño del Mar* and if he knew of the owners. He seemed troubled by that question and quickly turned away from me. What does that mean?

DAY 13

At sunrise, I decide the project for the day is to transform the sailboat.

First, before going to the beach, I add the soaked beans and chili powder into the javelina meat pot to slow cook above the fire. Then, Coco and I walk to the sailboat, and I move it from its place of anchorage to the sand. Using small wooden plugs, I pound them into the bullet holes in the boat and then smooth them off with my hunting knife. After opening a can of paint bought at the shop in San Miguel, I dip the paintbrush and spread a bright blue color on the boat's trim. It perfectly covers the weathered yellow, and the bullet holes are impossible to see.

With the second can of paint, I cover the boat's interior in dark blue, hiding the grim bloodstains. That includes painting the secret hiding places, so all traces of the white powder are gone. Finally, tilting the boat on its side, I paint the mast.

Then, I carefully inspect the paint job to ensure every bit of yellow is covered. No registration numbers are on the boat, so no work is needed to change numbers. Then, I take the small can of white paint bought in San Miguel, and near the bow, above the waterline, I write '*Luz*,' meaning light, a somewhat common name for girls in Spanish-speaking countries. I'm guessing other boats might have that name.

The paint job took four hours, and the sailboat is now unrecognizable from its previous state.

Waiting for the tide to come in and the paint to dry, I swim in the sea, throw sticks to Coco, and sit on the sandy beach enjoying the day. The warm sun quickly dries the paint.

When the boat freely floats, I sail north about two hundred yards and squeeze the *Luz* between a gap in a patch of mangroves and into a small creek. After tying it up, Coco and I walk back to our camp.

The sailboat will give freedom to sail around the islands. And, if anyone asks, I'm just a tourist who hired it from someone on the mainland. There are plenty of companies over there renting all kinds of vessels, from paddle canoes to luxury yachts. Yet, I do have worries. In the past, the boat was used for despicable purposes, so I assume it could still be recognized and questions asked.

Returning to my campsite, I find that the beans are perfectly cooked with the meat, and I enjoy a chili bean lunch with tortillas. Then Coco and I make our way over the ridge to the survivors' camp.

This time I circle the camp and come in from the south side, using a different approach to avoid anyone backtracking me.

Today, I'm wearing the clothing bought at the shop in San Miguel, a colorful shirt, proper-fitting shorts, leather sandals, the Panama hat, and colored glasses. Instead of carrying the brown bag, my backpack is looped over one shoulder. In the pack are the items for the survivors, that is, if they want them.

Silently sliding next to a palm tree at the edge of the camp, I stand and watch a heated discussion. Coco sits beside me. Frank and Bob film the action.

"Don't eat everything," Pandora yells. She faces Roger.

"Chewing on a rib bone isn't everything," Roger counters.

"We need to stretch this out over many days," Pandora claims.

Parts of the javelina still hang over the fire, mostly bones with little meat. Some small bones stick out of the cooking pot to make brothy soup

Harry stands away from Roger, chews on a rib bone, and the two men stare at each other like antagonists before a bar fight. Their eyes are still swollen and black and blue. Because of the javelina bones, Coco watches them with great interest.

Pandora says, "This is day thirteen, and we still have fifteen days to go. So, this may be your last meal, knowing you guys never find food. Until this javelina, Ada provided our meals, which wasn't much."

"What about you," Roger counters. "How much did you deliver."

"Some sea snails, which is more than you."

"What can I do with a busted rib," Roger moans.

Harry smiles.

"Think ahead," Pandora says. "If we want to eat, we need the bow and arrows."

Stepping around the tree, I move forward and with a soft voice, ask, "How many wild animals did you see in the jungle."

They all turn and look at me, and the camp becomes utterly quiet, as though a time machine froze everyone in their place. It's as though they don't recognize me.

"What happened?" Pandora asks.

"What do you mean?" I ask.

"You have clothing."

"A bit," I respond.

"Where'd you get it?"

"Wandering around."

Frank lowers his camera and screeches, "You can't do that. It's not part of the script."

"What script?" I ask. "On Naked Fear, we are supposed to survive, and that's what I'm doing."

"But not like that?" He points a finger at me and almost drops his camera.

June says, "Wait a second. We can adapt the storyline." She pauses. "Bartholomew, where did you get that clothing? There is no store on this island, and the only habitation is the guesthouse. You came here with no money. Did you steal that clothing from someone at the guesthouse? If so, we are in trouble. We told the island's owner that we would stay in the south to not bother the wealthy guests over there."

"I'm not even sure where the guesthouse is," I state.

"You took that stuff from campers," Pandora howls.

It's challenging to know which one is more annoying, Frank or Pandora. So I wait a moment and then calmly ask, "Have any of you seen any campers on this island? I certainly haven't."

Not having an answer, the survivalists and film crew return to silent mode. After waiting a minute, I say, "Does anyone want stuff?"

"Like what?" Pandora asks.

I remove the backpack from my shoulder and take out a red t-shirt. On the front is the image of a palm tree. Holding it up so everyone can see, I throw it on the ground halfway between the survivalists and myself.

Pandora doesn't hesitate. She sprints to the t-shirt, picks it up, and presses it between her breasts like a precious treasure needing protection.

"Who else wants one," I ask.

The hands of the remaining survivalists go up.

Taking out two blue t-shirts with symbols of fish on the front. I say, "Two times extra-large for Roger and Harry."

Harry quickly walks to me, takes the t-shirts, and returns to his spot near the firepit. He flips one to Roger, and they both put them on.

I take out two remaining t-shirts, green with parrot images on the front, and Wilma and Ada come to me and take them.

"Thank you," Ada says. She puts it on, and while the t-shirt is slightly too large, it magically transforms her into a civilized human."

Wilma puts on her t-shirt. It's surprising to see how her faded purple hair and the green t-shirt complement each other. I hadn't noticed something striking about her before. She's an alluring woman.

"I have something else," I say, reaching into the backpack and taking out five pairs of shorts and belts. I hand them to the five people according to my guess of sizes. They quickly put them on. The shorts are slightly too big on all of them, but that doesn't bother them. Instead, they have new looks on their faces, a mix of joy and relief, like stepping out of a dungeon.

Then, turning toward the path, I say, "Let's go, Coco."

"Hey, wait, you can't do this," Frank cries out, "It ruins everything."

Coco and I swiftly disappear into the jungle. I'm glad they accepted the clothing and even more satisfied that Frank's female film subjects are less interesting according to his lusty worldview. I wonder what the Naked Fear company back in Hollywood will think of this. I may lose my job, but it doesn't matter. It's one thing to watch this show on TV, but to live it in real life is entirely different. Why revel in human torture? Isn't the show's premise absurd and demeaning when you think about it? I'm determined not to be a part of this deviant production anymore.

* * *

While Coco sleeps in a sandy area at the hut's entrance, I lie on my bamboo bed and listen to palm trees moving in the gentle ocean breeze. The relaxing sound of the surf is in the background.

My mind wanders to the moment when the survivors put on their clothing and the delightful looks on their faces. Receiving something so simple made a difference in their lives.

Putting people in such primitive conditions makes excellent TV entertainment. But is it demeaning?

It was a pleasure to see the relief on the survivors' faces this afternoon. Something changed. They gained dignity, which was meaningful, making me think that more things could be done to improve the lives of needy people, starting with those survivalists.

Somehow, this experience is causing me to see the world at a new level. It may not be a big deal to others, but it is for me.

DAY 14

The morning starts early, and my first thoughts are about yesterday's visit to the survivors' camp. I wish I were a psychologist to better understand everyone there.

Because of my upbringing in a remote town in a jungle in South America, I've often felt uneasy around people, especially those at the Naked Fear headquarters in Hollywood. I don't fit in. I've heard them talking about me, even calling me a weirdo. My colleagues always put themselves first over others, and their identity seems to rest on what they own. My perspective is different.

With my villagers in Mabaruma, faith, family, community, and personal responsibility come first. Honestly, those values might be helpful for those over at the survivors' camp. But, except for Ada, their self-centeredness works against them.

To see Pandora rush forward and grab the t-shirt for herself was an example. The battle between Roger and Harry is another, and I'm not sure those two could ever get along. Wilma affronts you with purple hair as though making a statement she doesn't care what society thinks, but I think she has internal struggles. She and Pandora established boundaries between themselves. In some ways, it seems Wilma depends on Harry and follows him, but I sense she controls their odd relationship. Roger would never follow Pandora in a million years. However, it was strange the other day when he expressed admiration for her.

Ada is different, quiet, observant, and thoughtful and has constantly done things to help the team, even when they didn't deserve it. Even in this primitive state, she is beautiful with messy hair and a dirty body. When Ada put on the t-shirt, she was the only one that thanked me.

June questioned where I got the clothing, and rightfully so. It must have been a great shock to see me show up with sandals, a Panama hat, and sunglasses. She suggested I stole my clothing from the guesthouse, but I have never been there. I saw it from the air when we approached the island's airport and from the boat when we went from the airport to the beach when we started this challenge.

From what I remember, the guesthouse was more like a small hotel, with several large bungalows spread out along the beach and a larger building with a swimming pool. There seemed to be other structures behind the main building, maybe a warehouse or housing for the staff.

The guesthouse intrigues me, and I want to check it out. Who knows, maybe there is something of interest over there?

On my nautical map, there is not much detail about our island. A short line going east to west must be the airport, and a tiny square by the beach south of the airport is probably the guesthouse. A road goes from the guesthouse to the airport, and another line, perhaps a road, heads south, ending in the jungle. And that's about it.

It seems to be a two or three-mile walk from my camp to the guesthouse, and on a straight flat road, I could make it in less than an hour. It will take longer on jungle paths.

Putting the hunting knife, matches, jerky, a bottle of water, a t-shirt, and binoculars in my backpack, I head up the trail to the large clearing where we camped on day one. Coco runs ahead, stopping to sniff bushes and occasionally leave his scent. It is nice to have comfortable sandals and shorts. The day is pleasant, and it takes thirty minutes to reach the clearing. The small shelter where Ada and Pandora camped on day one is still there.

Instead of following our original trail down to the sea, I go north to the edge of the clearing and am happy to find a narrow road. It must be the one on the map leading to the guesthouse. After an hour of easy walking, I notice a building. Instead of going there, I take a jungle path and circle to the east, eventually coming to a small hill with a good view of the guesthouse.

Crouching low behind a pile of rocks, I use my binoculars to survey the place. It's evident it was built for luxury. The main building has a peaked roof extending out on a teak terrace, like the style one might see on a Polynesian island. A large deck seems to be a place to eat meals or drink. Next to that building is a big swimming pool. Around the pool are a few wooden lounge chairs covered with white cushions. A long dock goes from the beach to deeper water. Tied to the dock is a speedboat with two large outboard motors.

Four large bungalows spread out to the north of the main building. They are built in the same style as the main building, each with a wooden terrace from which you can step directly onto the white sandy beach. An abundance of palm trees gives a tropical feeling. It seems designed for wealthy holidaymakers looking for a place of solitude and relaxation.

Behind the main building are other structures, which I assume are living quarters for the staff. Beyond that is a building that looks like an oversized garage covered with solar panels. Next to the garage is a sizeable high-end SUV, which must transfer guests and supplies from the airport to the guesthouse.

At our office back in Hollywood, I remember someone saying that a multi-billionaire recently purchased the island. It seems the previous owner was the one who gave permission for Naked Fear to use the island, and there were negotiations with the new owner, as he didn't want our team here. However, he eventually agreed we could film on the island if we stayed in a defined area in the south.

Having seen the place, I can't think it will provide anything of use during the next fourteen days, that is, if I decide to stay that long. But I'm glad I came here to check it out.

Then, I turn to the right and see a boat approaching the land. It is a large catamaran, and the sail is lowered when it is a hundred yards from the end of the dock. The motor starts, and the catamaran slowly navigates toward the beach, turns, and ties up at the dock. On the back, I see the name the *Sueño del Mar*, the Sea Dream, the same catamaran that often meets a high-speed boat to the west of our island. However, the speedboat tied to the dock below is not the same one that meets the *Sueño del Mar*.

Getting a closer view, I see that it is a magnificent vessel, perhaps fifty-eight feet long. There are two crew members aboard it. One crew member jumps onto the dock, lifts a small ramp, and fixes it between the pier and the boat.

An electric golf cart with a driver appears from the side of the main house. Then, the crew members unload eight medium-sized cardboard boxes from the boat and put them on the back of the golf cart. Next, the driver turns the golf cart around, heads back toward the beach, and goes into the oversized garage. At the dock, one of the crew members unties the ropes of the catamaran, and it motors to deeper water, and then with sails raised, it catches the wind and glides away.

Then, I notice Coco, who has been waiting patiently beside me. He raises his nose, it twitches, and then he charges down the hill.

My first instinct is to run after him, but I don't want anyone to see me. There was an agreement that the Naked Fear production should not bother anyone at the guesthouse.

Coco speeds past the main building like a greyhound chasing a mechanical rabbit at the racetrack. He heads back toward the warehouse, disappears inside, and starts barking. Then there are quick, short growls, and someone yells, "*ayhee*", like in pain., followed by rapid high, pitched Spanish. There is a crashing noise, and a moment later, a loud bang like a gunshot, and I fear for Coco until I see him running from the building. The golf cart driver appears, shaking his right hand with blood on it. It seems that Coco bit him. He holds an automatic pistol in his left hand and raises it, yet refrains from shooting because of the other buildings in his line of fire. Or maybe its because he is holding it with the wrong hand.

I whistle for Coco, which is a mistake, for the driver looks up in my direction. I crouch down, and shortly after, Coco bounds up the hill, and I whisper, "Let's get out of here."

Coco and I sprint toward a narrow, root-tangled trail.

* * *

Zigzagging along twisted paths, Coco and I run for five minutes. In a way, it feels like playing in the jungle with my friends when I was a kid, only that gunshot at Coco wasn't a game. The gun was unsettling. It reminded me of my time in the military when targeted by a sniper when the reality of an actual bullet took on a different meaning than a video game.

My question is, why did Coco run down there in the first place? It seemed he caught a whiff of something, a familiar scent that made him aggressive, immediately charging to the warehouse. Is that place known to him?

Coco is happy to keep running in front of me, but I can't keep his pace forever, so I slow down when arriving at the road heading south. He stays with me, and we walk for five minutes, and then there is the sound of a car motor behind us.

I say, "Come," and Coco follows me into the jungle, where I crouch behind a patch of chest-high jungle palms. Then, the large SUV slowly joggles down the bumpy road. Holding Coco at my side, I peer through the undergrowth and see the man who drove the golf cart now driving the SUV. His right hand is wrapped in a white cloth. Another man with a large black mustache and dark green baseball hat is on the rider's side. He holds a rifle of some kind, pointing it out the open window.

Now, I wish I had the .38 pistol back at my hut.

The SUV passes, and I turn away from the road, walking through the thick jungle vegetation, going to the island's west side. It will take more than two hours of snaking around bushes and stepping over the slippery roots of trees before returning to my campsite. Still, it's undoubtedly better than meeting the SUV. They will return on this road.

I'm perplexed. Why did Coco attack and bite the man? More worrying, did they hear my whistle for Coco? Perhaps they were instructed to keep people away from the luxurious guesthouse and are merely doing their job. Yet surely they must know a film production crew is here?

Those gunshots add a new reality to my idyllic tropical island getaway.

DAY 15

It's day fifteen, and I spend the morning constructing a small veranda next to my hut. It provides a shady place to sit. Having the veranda is unnecessary but working on it gives me time to think about yesterday. The event at the guesthouse was unsettling, and I'm unable to get my head around it. Why would those men be so intent on finding Coco?

If a dog made mischief in villages in Guyana, it would be shooed away, and people would continue with their lives. Finding Coco seemed important to them. The only explanation I have is that Coco belonged to a drug trafficker. And I'm pretty sure that man was shot.

Did those men in the SUV believe that Coco's owner was still alive? Maybe those men are guards keeping drug runners away from the guesthouse and island. What other reason could there be?

In any case, I don't want to make assumptions, and from now on will be more cautious. I'll take different trails, cover my tracks, and always carry the .38 pistol. This may be an overreaction, but the sound of that gunshot and seeing the rifle with the man in the SUV was not imagination.

I'm also torn between tapping out or staying longer on the island. Defending the survivalists against two men with high-powered rifles seems unrealistic. Still, if our team is in danger, I might be able to give an early warning. And then, I think of Ada, and my decision is evident. I will stay on the island until everyone is safe.

After finishing the veranda construction, I swim in the sea to wash off. Then, I put on a t-shirt, shorts, sandals, and my Panama hat. Taking my backpack, I load it with jerky, a water bottle, gifts, and the .38 pistol.

Taking the trail to the top of the bluff, Coco cautiously goes ahead of me. The backpack is heavier than usual because of the added weight of the pistol and handouts for the survivalists

I'm more at ease going up the narrow trail, knowing where to step and what to avoid. One slip, and it would be a long, painful way down. Once on the other side of the bluff, I circle the lagoon and walk into the jungle, wanting to approach the survivors' camp from the east.

One hundred yards away from their campsite, I see movement, so I slide behind a tree, but Coco raises his nose, gets a scent, and bounds ahead.

A familiar voice asks, "Coco, what are you doing here?"

I walk down the path and see Ada leaning down, and scratching Coco's neck while the dog wildly wags its tail. Approaching her I say, "It seems you found a buddy."

She stands and grins. "This is a very friendly dog." Ada is wearing the shorts and t-shirt I gave her.

"Coco picks who he likes, and you are on the good side."

"It appears he's doing better than the first time I saw him."

"He's put on weight, unlike most Naked Fear survivalists who put themselves on a bizarre weight loss program."

Ada smiles, but I can see the reality of my statement in her tired eyes.

"How is everyone doing at the camp?" I ask.

"Somehow, the mood is more tranquil. Pandora and Roger don't argue much and even went swimming together. It's like a transformation, not one hundred percent, but certainly different than before."

"Frank must love that," I state. "With him, the more conflict, the better. How is June holding out?"

"She seems okay but somewhat detached, as though her head is not into the production of Naked Fear."

"So, what happened?"

"First of all, we have food, thanks to you. That made people less edgy. And the clothing did wonders. It made everyone more comfortable, and the t-shirts helped us sleep better. I don't know where you found this clothing."

"In a shop," I say.

She pauses as though searching for words. "Bartholomew, you are a mystery."

"What do you mean?"

"You are so aloof, and even though rejected by the other

survivalists, you look out for them. They're not sure what to think. In fact, they are afraid of you."

"What do you mean?"

"Roger said you almost cut off his head with a machete."

"He's imagining things."

"Wilma said you are not human, the way you come ghostlike into the camp and then disappear. No one knows where you go or what you do."

"I like to roam around."

"It's more than that."

I wait a moment and ask, "How are you doing?"

"See, there you go, looking out for others. But to answer your question, after receiving the food and clothing, what could be better."

"Why are you on this Naked Fear challenge?"

Her eyes open, "What do you mean?"

"I saw the Naked Fear episode where you lasted twenty-one days without a partner. It seemed a harrowing experience, so why go through it again."

"Probably stupidity and unfounded expectations."

"Why's that?"

"Three years ago, I started a site on social media and gained a following. Then, after going on my first Naked Fear show, my following skyrocketed. So, I thought that going again would further help the numbers. Money from advertising helps pay the bills."

"Are you one of those social influencers, whatever that is?"

"That's what they call me. In my case, I try and influence for good."

"What's that mean?"

"My following is younger women, and I speak about values and identity and what is right and making good decisions. Unfortunately, too many social influencers set a bad example, and when people copy them, lives are hurt."

"So, you go on a nude show?"

Ada nods her head. "I know. The show is about fortitude and survival, which are good qualities to exhibit. But there are inconsistencies, and I struggle with that. Being here this time confirms this is not what I want to do. I guess I'm a slow learner."

"Will you continue with social media when you return to the other world?"

"If I can do good."

"Is there anything else you'd like to do besides posting on the internet?" I guess my question might sound condescending.

She pauses as though I touched a sensitive spot. "I'd like to do more for people, although it isn't clear what that is. And personally, I'd like to see more of the world, not just for my own pleasure, but to learn how people live and what they think. So, I need to broaden my experience and then use it for the right cause."

"I like that. It sounds like a noble objective."

"Can I ask you a question?"

"Go ahead."

"I've wondered about you. You seem to be a loner, a mystery, yet thoughtful of others. I've wondered if you are in a relationship. Can you share anything about your life?"

I smile. "My job is quite boring, as a bookkeeper, and it allows me to save money until I figure out the next step. But no, I don't have a significant other. Women find me different, and that perplexes them."

"Indeed, you are different but attractive."

"To you?" I ask.

She looks me in the eyes. "I see you as a kind and considerate person walking a unique path. That's a powerful combination, and this may be the wrong word, but I find you appealing."

I'm not sure how to respond, and for some reason, our conversation stops. We become quiet and look at each other like tuning into a rare wavelength. There's no other way to describe it.

Eventually, she asks, "What will you do when this filming ends?" It's like she is attempting to lighten the moment.

"Go back to Hollywood, make a bit more money, travel, and settle down when I find the right place."

"I like that, to travel."

I grin. "Where do you want to go?"

She laughs. "Is that an offer?"

"Just curious."

"I want to see countries around the Mediterranean, from Spain to Israel."

"It's something to dream about," I say. I take the backpack from my shoulder, open it, and hand her the gifts for the survivalists. "This is something I thought you all might enjoy using." It's a bar of soap and a bottle of shampoo.

Ada takes the bottle, opens the top, smells it, and tears come to her eyes. "This means just as much as the clothing, even more. Thank you."

"Can we talk again sometime?" I nervously ask.

"Yes. Please let me know when."

Something in me wants to say now, today and forever, but all I can say is, "Soon," whatever that means. So much for precision.

Ada smiles but looks puzzled.

I turn, and head into the jungle, and Coco follows.

* * *

Back at my beach camp, I sit in the camping chair and watch the sun disappear. For some weird reason, the colors seem more vibrant this evening.

The discussion with Ada was unusual, and I'm not sure what to think about it. During our discourse, she expressed her desire to see the world. Her wish is to explore the Mediterranean from Spain to Israel. It's a pleasant thought to do that with her. So, what's next after this Naked Fear film shoot ends? Is it to go back to my desk in Hollywood?

Behind all the questions and uncertainties, there is something I can't escape. A lovely young woman like Ada leaves an impression. It's an alluring thought to go through life with her, but I am a loner and drifter with little to offer. So realistically, we will go separately when this Naked Fear film shoot is finished. Then, she will head back to her social media influencing and me on to the next event, whatever that means.

Yet, she said she finds me appealing, and I could kick myself, for, at that moment, I could have expressed my feelings for her.

And besides the encounter with Ada, I keep thinking about that incident at the guesthouse. I'm curious to know more. Not having specific plans for tomorrow, I decide to do research. I want to learn more about this island, the guesthouse, and the Sueño del Mar catamaran.

106

DAY 16

Two hours before daybreak I walk on a drk jungle path to the Luz. Coco raised his head when I left and quickly went back to sleep. I imagine he thinks this is no time for a sensible dog to be out. It takes some minutes for my eyes to adjust to the night, but there is just enough light from a half-moon to give visibility.

The men at the guesthouse are a worry. My Amerindian mentors said to always understand your environment and know your enemy. The same thing was taught in the Marines. So, who are those men, and more importantly, who are they working for? I can't rest until having answers.

I aim to learn more about this island to understand what our Naked Fear team might face. To do that, I can't go strolling into the guesthouse and ask, "Who owns this island, and why are you getting so frazzled over a silly dog?" My research must be done from another place where I can freely talk with people or access the internet. I'm going to try and get to Panama City on the mainland. That's a long sailing journey for a small boat like the Luz, so alternative transportation may exist.

Sliding the Luz away from its hiding place in the mangroves, I start the motor, navigate beyond the coastal surf, and then cut the engine and raise the sail. There are rarely big waves hitting the island. Since we have been here, the sea has been relatively calm, except when that storm came through.

Turning north, I head for a closer island, the Isla Pedro Gonzalez. On my nautical map, it appears to be six to eight miles beyond the top of our island. It seems to have several small towns and an airport.

Sailing in the dark can get you into trouble, especially when traveling without running lights. If I stay too close to the shore, I can crash on rocks. On the other hand, going out too far has the danger of cargo ships going to and from the Panama Canal. A half-moon gives enough light to see the shoreline. Eventually, after rounding the top of our island, the morning light appears, which calms my nerves, for I can now see far ahead.

I am in open water for an hour, then approach the south of Pedro Gonzalez Island and skirt around it to the west. Sailing for twenty minutes, I pass a harbor with a breakwater. It seems newly built, where a few yachts are docked. The Luz would stick out with that crowd. Along the beach is a massive, beautifully constructed hotel with bungalows. It's sad to see how modernization for tourism destroys the pristine jungle.

Further along the coast is a small town with around fifteen boats anchored in a bay. There is a long dock, like the one in the village of San Miguel. Many boats here are like the Luz, so my sailboat fits right in.

Some boats are anchored close to the sand, so I do the same with the Luz. Rolling up my pants, I hop into ankle-deep water and step onto the shore, carrying my sandals and backpack. In the backpack is eight hundred dollars from the money found on the Luz, I'm wearing the long pants, colorful shirt, Panama hat, and colored glasses bought in San Miguel, just a typical tourist.

The .38 pistol is stored in one of the secret hiding places of the sailboat.

It is early morning, the sun is low in the sky to the East, and the town is quiet. Walking along the beach, I come to a ticketing hut like in San Miguel. It is covered with publicity posters for boat rides and diving excursions. However, after finding the ferry schedule, my heart drops when I see that it only runs three times a week, and today is not the day.

I'm disappointed and will need to come back tomorrow. Instead, the day's plan shifts, and I will buy some supplies when the stores open and head back to my campsite.

Then, I get an idea. On the nautical map, there is an airport on this island. Perhaps an airline provides regular transportation servicing the large hotel down the coast. Walking through the small town, I see a faded road sign with an arrow. It says, 'Fernando Eleta Airport – 1 kilómetro.'

That's not far, less than three-quarters of a mile, so I walk along the side of the two-lane road. After five minutes of walking, a car approaches and slows down, stopping beside me. A window goes down, and the driver says in Spanish, *"¿Vas al aeropuerto?"*, Are you going to the airport?

I reply, *"Sí, ¿está lejos?"*, Is it far? My Spanish is not fluent, but adequate. I learned it from Colombian gold miners that regularly came across the border to our village in Guyana. So while Guyana is an English-speaking country, we had plenty of opportunities to learn Spanish.

"Not at all, but may I give you a ride?"

He switched to English, which is a sign my Spanish needs improvement. "Yes, please," I answer.

Once I'm in the car, he asks, "Where are you going?" He has a full head of gray hair and kind brown eyes. I'm guessing he is in his early sixties.

"Anywhere with the internet," I say.

"Doesn't your hotel have one?"

"It's not working, and I need to check my portfolio." Of course, that's not exactly the whole truth. While the internet is nonexistent at my campsite, I do have a small mutual fund portfolio. And a person must check their finances from time to time.

He says, "The regular airline flights only come here once a week, on Saturdays, so I'm afraid you can't take it today."

Again, my heart drops. "That's too bad. I was hoping to get to Panama City or someplace on the mainland to use the internet and do a little tourism."

"How did you get onto Pedro Gonzalez Island?"

"I have a small sailboat, but it would take forever to get to the mainland. It's much quicker to fly."

He hesitates, looks me over like anyone who picks up a hitchhiker, and says, "I have an idea, but I need your help."

"I'm open," I reply.

"You can fly with me to Panama City."

We arrive at the small airport, and he parks the car next to a row of hangers. At one of them, he takes a key and opens two large doors. Inside is a four-seater single-engine airplane, and it looks new.

"This is my hobby," he says. "I'm semi-retired but fly to Panama City twice a week. If you help me push it out, I'll take you over there, and you can return with me if you want. I'll be leaving there at four o'clock this afternoon. The flight is about twenty to twenty-five minutes each way."

He gets behind one wing, and I get behind the other, and we push the plane out of the hanger, and then he locks the doors. We both get in the airplane, and he starts the engine, and soon we are up over the water, heading east. It's a strange feeling to be in the air in a small airplane piloted by a guy you don't know. He certainly got us off the ground, and now the flight is smooth. The day is glorious, and the view of the surrounding islands with sandy beaches and turquoise bays is outstanding.

The man shares about himself over the noise of the plane's motor. His name is Enrique Colon. Colon translated in English is Columbus. He explains that he is a lawyer and owns a Panama City fiduciary company specializing in trusts, foundations, and offshore companies. He stays active in his company, as he is not yet ready to sit on the beach and do nothing.

I have a terrible thought when we are fifteen minutes in the air. I have no identification, a passport, or a driver's license. The Naked Fear production team holds my passport and the clothing I had arrived with.

"I'm sorry, but I forgot my passport. What can I do?"

He smiles. "Don't worry. We are not flying into Panama City International Airport, where they would check your papers, but into Albrook Airport, almost in the middle of the city. It is used by private planes for domestic flights, and there is no need to show your identity. Albrook was an air force base but turned over for general use."

That's a big relief because I could see myself sitting in the airplane all day to avoid going through customs.

We fly past Panama City, and it's a fantastic sight, made up of dozens of tall modern buildings. It's very different from Georgetown, Guyana's capital. Georgetown is a beautiful city full of older historical buildings. Still, Panama City is totally different with its modern, stylish high-rises.

"That city is amazing," I remark.

He replies, "The economy is good in Panama, with many international companies having offices here. We have a thriving financial industry of banks and fiduciaries, like mine, and we have revenue from the Panama Canal. Of course, we are more fortunate than our neighboring countries and better at business." He laughs.

After landing and parking the plane, we share a taxi to the center of Panama City, which is only ten minutes away. The streets are broad, and traffic flows. The taxi stops in front of a tall building, and I offer to pay for the cab, but Enrique refuses. He has an ongoing deal with the taxi company. He offers to take me to see his office, but I graciously decline, as I want to get busy with my research.

Besides banks and financial companies, Panama City is full of hotels with recognizable hotel chain names. I'm tempted to stay in one for a night as a needed change from my jungle hut, but returning to my island tomorrow would be problematic.

Eventually, I find an electronics shop and go in and pick out a low-priced large-screen smartphone. After paying for it, the seller directs me to a coffee shop with free Wi-Fi.

Finding the shop, I go to the counter, order a coffee, a sandwich, and a plate of cookies, and take a table in the back. While waiting for my order, I take out my phone and realize it needs a charge, so I ask permission from the barista to use a power plug in the wall close to my table. He says, "No problem," and heads off to serve a client.

After plugging in the phone, it takes a few minutes to go through the setup instructions in Spanish. Then, finally, I log onto the internet and quickly look up our island, Isla San José. Like backtracking a trail in the jungle, I find out that the island is owned by a company in Panama that is owned by Olsen Holding, a Florida company. Olson Holding is owned by Jim Olsen, who bought the island two months ago.

Doing more research, I discover that Jim Olson is a multi-billionaire who made a fortune in a startup technology company. Then he made even more money in venture capital and the stock market. He is fifty years old, known for philanthropy, and his wife died three years ago from an incurable disease. One news article quotes him, saying, "Wealth may give a person the false impression they are invincible, to be like a god. But events happen over which we have absolutely no control. It makes you humble. I lost the most important person in my life, and I could do nothing about it."

There are photos of Jim Olsen on the internet. A bio website says he is 6'1", stays fit, and runs a half marathon twice a year. He looks tan and healthy, but there is sadness in his eyes. He has no children.

It's amazing what one can learn about people on the internet. Jim Olsen seems transparent about who he is and what he does. While not egotistically promoting himself by attending every tuxedo social event, he is not a recluse. Instead, he comes across as a good guy.

Then, I research the *Sueño del Mar* catamaran. A tourism company owns it, and surprisingly, when following the ownership chain, it works back to Jim Olsen. That's a big surprise.

This raises questions, and I see a couple of opposing scenarios. One is that the guesthouse on our island is a clean operation. The two men in the SUV are Jim Olsen employees, perhaps so far down his management structure that he doesn't know them. They were probably out for a joy ride to find Coco, having been told to keep invasive animals off the island. With one being bitten by Coco, it seems normal that they might want to eliminate the dog.

The other version is that everything one sees about Jim Olsen on the internet is a front. Crime bosses hide behind legitimate businesses to give them respectability. So his fortune might be made in the drug trade.

Neither scenario is conclusive, so on our island. I need to be cautious, keeping the archery bow and pistol close. With this uncertainty about Jim Olsen and the two men on the island, I feel responsible for protecting the Naked Fear participants and film crew. They have no idea about the bullet holes and traces of drugs in my boat and the uncertainties about the caretakers with guns at the guesthouse. Then again, this might be nothing more than a self-concocted, unfounded Bartholomew conspiracy theory.

Nevertheless, and unfortunately for me, it means spending more time at the survivors' camp, which I don't fully desire. Although in thinking about it, there is one attraction at the camp. Ada is there, and I'd like to know her better.

My food order comes, and the coffee is out of this world. The beef sandwich is delicious, with layers of thin-sliced meat, cheese, lettuce, and a pickle on the side. It's a treat to eat something different than camp-cooked food.

Ordering another coffee, I eat the plate of cookies. The server tells me the cookies are called *Cocadas* and made of coconut. They are delicious little cookies that remind me of macaroons. The server said they are made with sweetened condensed milk instead of eggs. I'll need to get some to take back to my camp.

The coffee is called *Geisha*, which first came from Geisha, Ethiopia. It grows exceptionally well in the tropical weather of Panama, and it is not as sour or bitter as regular coffee.

Leaving the coffee shop, it's a nice feeling to be in civilization, and I find my heart pulled in two directions. On the one hand, I love the jungle, for it gives me a sense of freedom. And the diversity of plant and animal life and the magnificent sunsets make me appreciate creation's wonder. But I also like the city, especially a city like this that is clean with all the amenities to make life pleasant and comfortable.

Having discovered more about Isla San José and its owner, I enjoy Panama City for the rest of my time. At a tourist shop, I buy five light blue t-shirts for the survivalists. They have images of a large red heart and 'I' and 'Panama' written on either side of the heart, meaning, "I Love Panama." They will look good on the Naked Fear participants, and I can already picture Frank's reaction.

I buy Cuban cigars for Roger and Harry and individually gift-wrapped hairbrushes for Ada, Pandora, and Wilma. For June, I pick out a mini bottle of Eau de Perfume and have it gift wrapped. I purchase a kilo bag of Geisha coffee and a French coffee press, so I won't have to put coffee in a boiling pan anymore. The coffee is expensive. At a pastry shop, I purchase a large box of Cocadas cookies. All the shops accept U.S. Dollars.

After meeting Enrique Colon at the airport at four in the afternoon, we fly back to Pedro Gonzalez Island. He is happy to see that I enjoyed Panama City. Still, most of our conversation on the way back is about trusts and foundations and their various uses. One of my university business courses covered this topic. He is surprised to learn that I have a business degree and am a "Controller" for a film company in Hollywood. What it really means is logging expense receipts. I offer to pay for the plane ride, but he refuses. After landing and putting the airplane back in its hangar, he drives me to town, and before going away, he gives me his business card.

It is nice to meet an intelligent, cultured man who enjoys life. He gives me something to aspire to.

The town shops are still open, so I purchase more basics, including dried beans and spaghetti noodles. I pick out eggs, bags of yams, onions, garlic, green peppers, and hot peppers. Also, I get spices, six one-liter bottles of water, and two boxes of laundry soap, one for me and one for the survivalists. I'm thinking of making a meal for them, as I may spend more time in their camp. As an alternative, I may just give them the ingredients and let them prepare their food.

The sailboat is as I left it; I load it with my purchases and sail away. The crossing back to Isla San José is smooth, and I enjoy a stunning sunset. It's a thrilling experience to sail on a peaceful sea. It makes me understand that humans are tiny in the vastness of the universe.

With the dimming light of day, I slip the boat into its hiding place in the mangroves. It's a job to lug all the items back to my camp, and I'm tired from a long day. But, on the other hand, it's delightful to be met by a happy, overly enthusiastic dog who has been alone for many hours. I eat jerky while Coco devours dry dog food, and I realize the meat supply is getting low, so I decide to go on another hunting trip in the morning.

After feeding Coco, I shut the door to my hut and try to sleep, but my brain is charged up from the day's adventures. While I immensely enjoyed meeting Enrique Colon and seeing Panama City, I wish I had discovered more about our island. Indeed, I found out about the owner, but the guesthouse is still mysterious. Maybe I'm making a big deal out of nothing, but a nagging feeling tells me there is something more to take care of.

Eventually, I sleep.

DAY 17

My plan for the day is to treat the survivalists, as I'm tired of seeing them suffer and could care less about what Frank or the Producers back in Hollywood might say.

After an early morning visit to my hunting spot, I have venison cut into strips and hanging in my smoker by mid-morning. And, above my fire, a pot of venison stew simmers. I've added onions, garlic, peppers, and spices to it. Of course, Coco is thrilled to get a fresh bone with some meat.

When the stew is ready, in my backpack, I place a bag of rice, plastic plates and forks, a box of laundry soap, and the t-shirts and other gifts bought yesterday in Panama City. On top, I carefully put the .38 pistol.

Then, I carry the pot and backpack to the survivors' camp. When approaching them, I stop behind a tree as usual to get the camp's mood. Today, there is laughter. It's Pandora and Roger.

With a happy voice, Pandora exclaims, "I think you will domesticate me."

"That's impossible," Roger replies. "But there's no need. We love you as you are."

"Roger, I think you're a fool to be on this camping trip with me."

"A lucky fool."

Their combined laugh rumbles through the campsite.

I creep into the camp, and Pandora sees me.

"Hey, Bookie. Welcome to Paradise Cove." They are wearing the t-shirts and shorts I gave them.

"Paradise Cove?"

"It's the new name of our place. What do you have there?"

"Something I cooked up. Can you boil half a pot of water?"

"What for?" She asks.

"Just do as I say," I command.

"Yes, sir." She leaves carrying an empty cooking pot.

"That's quite a lady, ain't she?" Roger states. He carries three pieces of wood and places them near the fire.

"You bet," I agree. "How are your ribs."

"Each day better."

"I see you are moving more freely."

"I decided to be responsible for the fire, so I plan to look for wood in the jungle each morning."

"I noticed some driftwood past the lagoon."

"We did too. It's heavy, so Harry will help me with it."

That's a new one. Mortal enemies are at least working together. "Anything else happening around here?"

"We got a bit organized with everyone taking on specific tasks, like looking for seafood and forest food, fire maintenance, construction, preparing drinking water, and stuff like that."

"That's good."

Pandora returns with a half pot of water, and I take the rice bag from my backpack, pour it into the metal pot, and place it over the fire alongside the pot of stew.

Pandora asks, "Where'd you get the rice?"

"Wandering around."

She says, "I don't know what to think about your wandering and how you find the things you do, but that food is appreciated."

The remaining three survivalists appear from the jungle, followed by Frank and Bob. They carry their cameras at their sides. June walks behind them with her clipboard. Ada and Wilma wear their t-shirts and shorts, whereas Harry wears shorts but no shirt, his massive chest resembling a furry blanket. The time given to filming seems minimal, as fully dressed participants don't precisely meet Naked Fear standards.

Harry approaches the fire and exclaims, "Something sure smells good."

"Bookie brought it," Pandora says.

I nod to everyone and then look at Ada, who smiles. It gives me a pleasant feeling, like the first warmth of the morning sun. There's a change with Ada and Pandora, and Wilma. Their hair is clean and doesn't look so dull. It seems the fluorescence returned to Wilma's hair.

I say, "I brought something for you." Then, reaching into my bag, I pull out the new t-shirts and hand one to each participant. "See if they fit."

The three women turn away, take off their t-shirts, and put the new ones on, as the men put on their extra-large t-shirts. Finally, the women turn around, and the entire group laughs when realizing all shirts are identical with the large bright red heart on the front and 'I' and 'Panama' above and below the heart.

Frank swings his camera as though swatting flies and says, "They can't do that. It is totally against the show. It's a mockery. Bookie is ruining everything. This is becoming like a beach holiday resort."

Frank storms off toward the production crew camp. Bob hangs his camera next to his side, turns to June, and asks, "What should we do?"

"Take a break," she says.

Bob turns and walks down the same path as Frank.

June smiles. "As Harry said, something smells good."

"Join us," I say.

"It's not exactly according to the rules," June says.

"Why let Naked Fear producers ruin a good meal?" I ask.

June hesitates, grins, and says, "I'd be pleased to join you."

Using a split piece of bamboo as a spoon, I serve rice and stew on plastic plates, handing one dish to each person. They sit on large logs, and everyone gets focused without any conversation. After a liberal second portion is given to each person, the two cooking pots are empty.

Roger says, "We can now truly call this Paradise Cove because that was heaven. What was in it?"

"Venison, onions, garlic, peppers, and spices," I reply.

"Where's you find all that?" He asks.

"Here and there. The venison is fresh from this morning."

"And the other stuff?"

"From wandering around."

The others stay quiet as though they do not know what to say. Eventually, I reach into my bag and pull out three gift-wrapped packages. "These are for Ada, Pandora, and Wilma." I hand one gift to each woman.

They hesitate as though holding a fragile crystal vase. Then they delicately open the colorful wrapping paper to not damage it. The contrast between the primitive jungle campsite versus the delicate, bright paper is remarkable. Slowly each woman removes the hairbrushes from the wrapping. When Pandora sees the hairbrush, she slightly groans, holds back a cough, and tears flow from her eyes. The eyes of Ada and Wilma are red.

"Thank you, thank you," Pandora whispers. "This means so much. My moppy, messy hair needs this."

Pandora has thick, curly red hair, which has become a rat's nest since coming here. Ada and Wilma also thank me.

"And now, for the men," I say. I take out the two cigars and hand them to Roger and Harry.

They both laugh.

Roger says, "Every once in a while, this is what a man needs. Those are some of the best Cuban cigars you can find."

"No stinky cigar smoke around here," Pandora states.

"Don't worry. This is a man thing. Harry and I will sit by the beach and enjoy the sunset. What do you say, Harry?"

Harry nods. "That's right. Just you and me, peckerwood."

They bump fists and laugh.

"One more thing," I say. Reaching into my bag, I take out the small box of laundry soap. "This is for the clothing when it's needed. Use it sparingly."

I say, "Let's go, Coco, " taking my empty cooking pot."

The dog gets up, and we walk down the jungle path. Behind me, I hear footsteps, and when turning around, June rushes toward me.

"Bartholomew, can you wait a second."

"Sure."

"Can I come to your camp to talk?"

"I'd be pleased to have you. Come over for a simple meal this evening, and we can watch the sunset. What do you want to talk about?"

"This."

"This what?"

"What you are doing to this show. I don't know what to make of it."

* * *

In the evening, June and I sit in the camp chairs near my beach camp.

Coco chases seagulls along the water's edge.

Our dinner was venison steak and a side dish of avocado halves. We drank two bottles of the fizzy water I got on Pedro Gonzalez Island.

I get up from my chair and prepare coffee with my new French press and the Panamanian Geiza coffee. After handing a mug of coffee to June, I get the box from the Panama City pastry shop, open it, and offer the *Cocadas* coconut cookies.

June picks one out, takes a bite, and says, "That's delicious."

"Try the coffee," I say.

She takes a sip. "Amazing."

We savor the cookie and coffee flavors for several minutes while relaxing in anticipation of the approaching sunset. Our conversation has been about the weather and the beauty of the sea, but I'm sure that isn't why June wanted to see me.

I say, "You wanted to talk with me."

She takes a deep breath. "My job is to keep the Naked Fear production on track, that is, to stay within the storyline. But now, we are far outside it, and I don't know what to do. Frank is beyond depressed. It's like he's losing his mind. He argues that you destroyed the authenticity of the show."

"You mean he can no longer watch naked women suffering."

June nods. "Yes, he is a concern. I can't stand the guy but must put up with him."

"So, what happened to the show?"

"We are far from what our producers expect, so much so that I'm not sure it can be brought back on track."

"Why is that?"

She laughs. "Is it normal for participants on a Naked Fear show to wear t-shirts saying "I Love Panama" with big red hearts? That doesn't exactly fit the pain and agony expected. And now, they are running around like happy campers. Of course, when the Producers see the footage, they will go berserk."

"Back in Hollywood, I heard one of them say this would be the best show ever. He spoke about the divergence of personalities and the conflict to come."

She smiles. "That's a good one, the best show ever. It's the weirdest show ever. While not explicitly stated, we aren't supposed to have all the props.'

"Props?" I ask.

"Yes, props. Clothing, shampoo, hairbrushes, soap, cigars. What's next? They are supposed to survive on what they find. It's called survival skills."

"Isn't that what's happening?"

"What do you mean?"

"As a group, we are surviving on what we find."

"You mean, surviving on what you find. I can't believe how you operate. Somehow like magic, you appear out of nowhere with beautifully wrapped gifts and a fancy box with wonderful cookies from a pastry shop in Panama City. Do you have superpowers?"

"No. I'm just surviving like we were asked."

"It's impossible what you do. Are you getting things from the guesthouse?"

"Not at all, although I'll be honest with you. I went over there one time to check it out. I was watching the place from a small hill just to the south. Then, suddenly, Coco went crazy and ran down to the guesthouse and started barking at a couple of the workers. One of them grabbed a gun and took a shot at Coco. I whistled for Coco, and the guy took a shot at me, and we sprinted for the jungle. The two guys drove an SUV on the road through the jungle looking for us, and we disappeared. Honestly, that's all I had to do with the guesthouse." I left out the part about Coco chomping on the guy's hand.

"That's a frightening story."

"I told you that story for your safety. If the workers from the guesthouse come to your camp, please be careful. Something doesn't seem to be right."

"What is it? What isn't right?"

"I can't put my finger on it."

She pauses, sips her coffee, and says, "Still, you haven't explained where these things come from. A coffee press?"

I grin. "Honestly, they have come from foraging on a larger scale than normal, but I'd rather not say more. Let's admit that I'm surviving, exactly what the show expects."

"You've gone beyond the rules."

"Not really, but does it matter?"

The sun meets the horizon, and June gazes across the sea. She states, "I've been thinking about that."

120

"About what?"

"That question, does it matter? When coming here the last time, you said unusual things, profound, and they stuck with me. You asked what I want to do, and I've concluded that it isn't Naked Fear."

"What do you enjoy doing?"

She looks at me with lovely brown eyes that belong in a romance movie. "I get the most joy when helping people. So, for a change from the weekly film production, I go to the Salvation Army kitchen in Los Angeles and help cook and serve needy people on Saturday mornings. There's something deep and meaningful in doing that, much more than what I get from this show. But volunteering on Saturday mornings doesn't pay the bills."

"I know the dilemma. I also like the idea of helping people. It's redemptive."

"Hollywood is not a redemptive place, and I want this to be my last gig with Naked Fear. But what comes next, I don't know?"

I wait for a moment. "Any current relationships?"

She shakes her head. "Not for some time. I was married for three years to someone whose identity was Hollywood, and to make it worse, he strayed."

"I'm sorry to hear that."

"So, relationships are difficult for me, and of course, I want someone to share life with. But we need to be on the same page. And that goes back to the question of what to do next?"

How do you reply to that?. I'm not so much into feelings, but I understand June. I'm kind of in the same boat. But then, I look at the magnificent sunset filling the sky and think of the artist behind it. At times like this, one feels small, and only one thing comes to mind. "Perhaps there is someone with a greater plan. Have you ever considered that?"

"You mean God?"

"Yes. Don't laugh, but from a broad perspective about the meaning of life and all that, I see two options. First, human life has little significance because we are tiny, finite specks in the grand scheme. Or, life has meaning because it matters to the one designing this sunset. If the second one applies, isn't He able to lead you to the next gig in your life, as you called it, and the right relationship?"

June sighs. "Thank you, Bartholomew. Are you sure you aren't a magical angel?"

I laugh. "Anything but that, as the same applies to me." Hesitating, I say, "I have a suggestion."

"What's that?"

"Why not let this show evolve without trying to shoehorn it into a storyline. Don't worry if it's outside the norm. That takes off all the pressure."

She reflects for a moment as though caught between duty and creative freedom. Then, "Great idea. I can do that."

"And as far as your future, look at the evolving colors in this magnificent sunset. Can't the artist paint the same beauty in your life?" Perhaps I should be feeling like a philosopher or poet. Still, I feel like a hypocrite when saying this because it's easier to preach it than live it.

She glances at me and nods. "As I said, you are an angel. That's comforting."

"I'd like to make a deal," I say.

"What's that?"

"When we get back to Hollywood, we write resignation letters."

June laughs. "You mean to trust the Artist for the next step?"

"Absolutely."

"It's risky," she states.

"Maybe, and maybe not."

June sticks out her hand, and I shake it. She takes another cookie and sips her coffee with a smile.

"There's one other thing," I state. I get up and go into my beach hut and come back with a gift and give it to June. "It's for you."

She looks baffled and takes a moment before removing the pink ribbon and removing the colorful paper. "It's Eau de Perfume," she remarks.

"To remind yourself that there is more to life than dusty survivors' camps."

June sprays perfume on her wrist and smells it, and with tears in her eyes she delicately applies it to her cheeks and neck. Searching for words, she stammers, "How? . . . Why? . . . Where did you find, ah?" She laughs. "Never mind. I know your answer. But even so, I am mystified."

As the sun meets the horizon, the sweet smell of perfume drifts through the air. We reflect in quietness. Most city dwellers would never experience this, and I should be filled with awe and wonder. But instead, I think about the deal we just made, and I consider what might happen once my source of income, bookkeeping for Naked Fear, has been flushed down the toilet? And so much for trusting the One who can put beauty in your life.

DAY 18

Day eighteen starts lazily with a breakfast of venison stew and a long swim in the sea. The weather is perfect, a warm tropical day, with clear turquoise water and a slight breeze moving the palm trees.

There's not much to do around the camp, so I go fishing. This afternoon I plan to head to the survivalists' camp and take them a couple bags of beans, some yams, and jerky. They ate all the stew and rice yesterday, so they have nothing left today and will be hungry. In the meantime, I wouldn't mind having fish for lunch.

Using muscles from the rocks as bait, I lower my fishing line into the same bottomless pool used previously and then go to the shore and sit in one of the camping chairs. Now I have time to daydream and think. The last few days were busy, and I pushed myself, but I'm glad for all I accomplished. It's time to relax.

The time with June last night was delightful, and we had a chance to talk at more than a superficial level. We both made an important decision, for, with a shake of hands, we agreed to leave our jobs at the Naked Fear film company in Hollywood. I knew it would happen at some point, for that is just a place to earn money and gain experience. But what comes next?

I don't have a clue in the world about how to answer that question.

Yesterday evening I challenged June, saying that the Artist who paints beautiful sunsets could create the same beauty in her life. Do I believe that?' Can He do the same thing for me?

My upbringing taught me that the ultimate spiritual being, who is all-powerful and loving, cares and looks out for us if we let Him. My parents live that way, and many of my Amerindian friends believe the same.

Living in a village in Guyana was a wonderful experience. And that formed my worldview, which is different from someone growing up in California or New York. That created a gap between them and me that couldn't be filled. My perspective includes a spiritual realm with an almighty God. Their viewpoint tends to be secular, defined by the material, where everything is one. That means I have a basis for determining what is absolute. For them, there is no fixed right or wrong, and everything is relative. Everyone makes their own flexible truth. I have a changeless truth. Therefore, we have a divergence. They think I am weird, and I think they are strange. Which perspective is better? I just know I will never fit in.

One complicated thing is that the California and Hollywood world teaches diversity and acceptance, but when one is divergent from Hollywood's core beliefs, then diversity means nothing.

Maybe that's one reason our producers were so quick to throw me into this adventure. They didn't like my difference. Sending me here might be punishment for the weirdo guy who counts expenses over in the corner. Or an experiment? They know I exist outside their beliefs but don't understand why. Maybe they expect me to come back beaten down and repentant? I will never conform to their worldview, for I find it narrow and constricting.

So, in planning my next step, I need to go my own way and not be too concerned about them and their values.

My parents gave me a model to live by. They are medical doctors and could have stayed in Kansas and lived comfortably. In staying there, money would not have been a problem, yet they gave up material things like cars and houses and went to a place where they lived simply. The small hospital where they work lacks equipment and medical supplies. Yet, helping poor people gives a much greater reward than chasing material possessions.

I'm not a doctor and can't follow their profession. While medicine is fascinating, my interests are in other areas. But it would be nice to aid people in some way. My wish would be to help people like my parents, but how?

In some ways, June's desire is like mine. And we face the same issue. Her joy is to assist those in need, but leaving her current job means no funding. This dilemma seems impossible to solve. Unfortunately, sitting on a tropical island beach won't provide a solution, so I'll need to work out my next step when I return to

California.

I'm glad about the improved conditions of the survivalists. They are no longer hungry, and the clothing makes them feel more human. I feel good about that and laugh when thinking about Frank. He is odd, and while I shouldn't think wrong of anyone, I was satisfied to see him storm out of the camp.

What gives greater enjoyment is to know that this Naked Fear film shoot is way outside the storyline? The producers in Hollywood will go bonkers when they see the footage. It doesn't fit the other episodes that TV viewers expect. Now, we have a bunch of 'happy campers,' as June called them. It's not supposed to be that way. Viewers prefer seeing suffering naked people groveling in the dirt, shivering at night, and crawling with bug bites. This show is ruined.

Yes, there is a sense of satisfaction.

I pull in my fishing line and have caught two large sea bass. I clean them, take them back to camp, and grill them over the fire. Then, with a sprinkling of lemon, I have an excellent meal.

I rest for an hour, and then Coco and I head over the bluff to the survivors' camp.

* * *

When getting close to the camp, I hear voices arguing. Then, winding around some low palm branches, I see Frank and Ada facing each other.

Frank shrills, "You need to play the game."

Ada stares at him and quietly states, "I don't need your game."

"You agreed to come on this show, so act appropriately." He points a long skinny finger at her.

"I'm not doing this."

"Do it or no reward," Frank yells.

I approach them and say, "What's going on?"

Frank glares at me and says, "You don't belong here. Leave now."

"What do you mean?" I ask.

"You destroy everything. The show is a failure because of what you've done. I'm getting it back on track, and you aren't part of it."

"That's okay," I say, knowing the show means little to me.

His eyes glare. "What do you mean, okay?"

"If that's your wish, I'm not part of the show."

126

"That's not a constructive attitude, but fine. Just stay away."

Frank storms off, carrying his camera.

I turn to Ada and ask, "What happened?"

"Like a crazy man, Frank charged into camp this morning and told everyone that we are not respecting the contract. Repeatedly, he kept screaming, "Naked Fear, Naked Fear, Naked Fear. That's the name of the show." He said the contract states we can't use props, and clothing is props. And we can't be eating store-bought food, which he said you are bringing."

"So, I assume he wants everyone to take off their clothes."

"That's correct."

"Did they?"

Ada nods. "Yes, except me."

"Why?"

"Frank says they won't be paid, and he threatened them."

"What was the threat?"

"Breach of contract. The producers will take them to court. He said millions have been spent to make this show, and now that money is lost. The survivors will be forced to pay back every penny."

"And, I suppose everyone stripped down, and everything is back to normal, or should I say, back to abnormal?"

"They reluctantly did what Frank asked."

"And, what about you?"

"As I said, I'm not playing that game."

"Let's see what's going on," I say.

We walk into camp, and Roger, Pandora, Harry, and Wilma stand naked around the fire pit. The brown bags cover their lower parts, and their faces are drawn. A javelina is on a thick pole hung on supports over the fire.

"Where'd that come from?" I whisper.

"Diego, the boat skipper, shot it this morning, and Frank and Bob filmed a scene making it look like Pandora caught it and butchered it. After that, it was Diego and Carlos who butchered it."

"So, Frank's way of getting the show back on track is by orchestrating the story. But, of course, it's fake, and the viewers will think it is real."

Ada nods.

Standing on one side of the campsite, Carlos, Diego, Bob, and

Frank watch the participants. Frank has a perverse smile as he stares at Pandora and Wilma.

June stands apart from the other onlookers. She sees me, raises her palms up, and rolls her eyes.

I walk over to her and ask, "What happened.?"

"Frank didn't sleep all night, ranting around the production crew site and keeping the rest of us awake. Then, in the morning, he stormed this camp. He was out of control, and I would have called 911 if possible. There was no fear that he could harm the participants because Roger and Harry would break him in two. But then he challenged them on the contract."

"What does the contract say?"

"It's vague, but with slick lawyers, the wording could be held against the participants in a court of law. However, they need the money and don't want to end up in court, so they reluctantly gave in."

"How do you feel about this?"

"Not good, but Frank may have a point, and I'd hate for the participants to not get paid. Our producers have an army of nasty lawyers, whereas these participants have probably never met one. In a court of law, they would be eaten alive."

"What are you going to do now?"

"Our discussion last night was helpful. You suggested letting the show evolve, but we never thought it would come to this."

"And our agreement? Where do we stand on that?"

She smiles. "We shook hands, and it's the right thing to do. When my work here is finished, I'm leaving Hollywood."

"Me too," I state, feeling depressed that the participants are being forced back into this against their will.

Roger and Pandora grimly look at me. Roger nods, and he and I walk to the edge of the camp outside of hearing range. He says, "I'm sorry. Having the clothing was great, and the food you brought, but I have debts to pay, and so does Pandora. But we can survive the next ten days like this. Frank is now providing the food, so at least we won't starve, although he said we must pretend we are starving." He points at the javelina above the fire. "And he wants more arguments, so I'll give him some serious drama." Roger smiles.

"If I can help, please let me know."

"I will, man. I appreciate everything you've done." He laughs and whispers. "At least the ladies won't have tangled hair. They hid the hairbrushes, shampoo, and soap."

Instead of being a bushy mess, Pandora's thick red hair is now flowing curls. Likewise, Wilma and Ada no longer have twisted birds' nests on their heads.

He heads back to the fire to tend to the javelina. I shake my head but smile. At least the women have things that will help keep their dignity. I'd hate to see them drift back to the place of despair where they were a few days ago.

Ada catches my eye, and I nod for her to join me.

Standing away from the others, I ask, "Are you going to be okay?"

"Frank can't intimidate me."

"I'll try and come by each day to see how you are doing. Then, if it becomes unbearable, you can join me."

"That would be nice, but I'll stay here to watch Frank's show. The others will need support."

"Come with me for a minute," I say.

She follows me into the jungle, where I reach into my backpack and hand over the bags of beans and yams. I say, "Hide this from Frank, and use it when the team needs a supplement to the javelina meat."

Ada puts the food in a patch of jungle palm and says, "I need to go but will come back in a few minutes before the ants find it. Thank you for everything. You are a good man."

She walks away, and I say, "Stay safe." I regret she didn't accept the offer to join me.

Frank suddenly appears on the path and passes Ada. He stops and yells at me, "Get out of here, and I don't want to see you again. We have ten days to finish filming this show, and you will not ruin it."

"How can I ruin it?" I ask.

"Viewers want to watch naked people who struggle to survive."

"How about you, Frank? Are you obsessed with watching nudes?"

"Leave," he screams. "It's Naked Fear, Naked Fear, Naked Fear. That's the name of the show. You can't break the rules."

"What kind of people made the rules?" I ask.

He glares at me. "We have a gun back there and will use it to keep you away."

"Try me," I say while patting the archery bow hung across my chest."

He has a quick look of fear in his eyes, then says, "We don't need you."

I turn and walk away as Coco sprints ahead.

* * *

It's another sunset, and I feel lonely in the camping chair. It was nice to have June here yesterday evening. But, this evening, I wish Ada was here. She is a lovely woman. I regret she didn't come here with me, for I can imagine the pressure Frank will put on her. Of course, the other participants could turn on her under Frank's direction, but I wonder about that.

Roger now seems different, somehow more grounded, for lack of a better term. His financial situation requires him to accept ten more days of being a paid actor for the Naked Fear show. I believe he will protect Ada, but the pressure coming from Frank is fierce.

Of concern is the threat made by Frank to use their gun on me. He seems to be cracking up like he is becoming a tyrant. There is no telling how his distorted mind will use this newfound power. What's the old saying? Power corrupts, and absolute power corrupts absolutely. It's uncertain if Frank knows how to use the rifle in the camp, but he could become extremely dangerous. If anyone crosses him, there is no telling what he might do.

June is the coordinator for this production, and I fear for her as I do for Ada. June has probably never faced someone like Frank, who is going off the rails. She has a strong will, and I am confident she could manage Frank in normal circumstances. But now, June desires to finish the job and get past it to move on. At the same time, June feels responsible for this production, and if Frank pushes too far, she will attempt to bring him back in line. That means conflict. At the end of the day, Roger and Harry would intervene if things were to get physical. Who could stand against a team of two overweight linebackers?

Frank's rejection of me should be discomforting, but why should I worry about this whacko? It's not like the entire camp turned against me. Roger expressed gratitude. It's just that Frank has put a sour mood into the camp. I suspect Bob will be on Frank's side regarding alignments, but who knows how Carlos, the medic, and Diego, the boat skipper, will act? They want their salary, so they are motivated to see the show through to the end. Frank will make it known that I am a person non gratis. That doesn't bother me so much, as it almost feels normal.

The question now is, what should I do over the coming days? One idea is to hop on the Luz with Coco and sail back to California. That could be a fun and fantastic adventure as there is so much to see between Panama City and Los Angeles. I'd like to visit some of Central America's old temples and historical Spanish sites. To explore the Gulf of California would be exciting to see whales and porpoises. That means I must get my passport at the production crew campsite. They also have the clothing I wore when traveling to Panama.

But, if I leave, I'm breaking a promise made to Ada. I said I would try and see her each day. And I don't like leaving her on her own with Frank. She goes against his demand to revert to the original Naked Fear dress code.

There was also that unpleasant experience with Coco and the men working at the guesthouse. I still have this niggling feeling that something isn't right.

No, I shouldn't go on a sailing trip to California, at least not right now. I need to know that Ada and June are safe and will check in over there once a day. There are ten days to go, and I don't want to live those days in gloom and doom.

Instead, I'll try and enjoy my camp, the beach, and the sailboat. Putting up with loony Frank is another matter.

DAY 19

Up early, I am out on the sea in the Luz. As usual, I left Coco behind. The dog seems to be recognized by people and is likely to be associated with this boat's previous owner. At least I'm assuming that's the case with the two guys over at the guesthouse.

Heading north, I pass the end of our island, Isla San José, and in seeing Pedro Gonzalez Island not far in the north, I head in that direction. A visit there will be nice to see people other than the dreary faces at the survivors' camp. Also, it is an opportunity to buy a few more supplies, although I do not need much.

Sailing past the east side of Pedro Gonzalez Island, I pass the fancy hotel by the beach and then arrive at the village of Pedro de Cocal. It's the same village I had visited, so I anchor the Luz close to the beach amongst similar boats. A few women sit on beach towels and engage in animated talk while small children build sandcastles.

This tranquil scene contrasts Frank's craziness.

I pass under a white arch with lettering saying, "*Bienvenido a Pedro Gonzalez.*" Then, heading into the small town, I aimlessly walk down a street with houses on either side until coming to a white church. It is simple, with no tall spire as one finds on churches in larger towns. Perhaps three or four hundred people live in this village, maybe less.

It reminds me of my village of Mabaruma in Guyana, where life is slow and simple. Everyone knows everyone else, and while not without conflicts, one finds solidarity not found in large cities. Instead, people look out for each other.

Going back to the grocery shop where I had previously been, I purchase five cheap toothbrushes and five small tubes of toothpaste.

On the way back to the Luz, I stop at a café-bar by the beach, find a chair and table in a shady spot and sit down. I order a coffee and a bottle of water. While waiting, a familiar face walks onto the large terrace looking for a table. It's Enrique Colon.

At first, I didn't recognize him, for he had worn a dark suit and tie the other day. Today, he wears a blue short-sleeved shirt, shorts, and sandals. Then, while looking around, he sees me, and I wave. And it takes him a moment to recognize me, and then he smiles.

Approaching my table, he says, "Hola. I see you came back to our island."

"I'm not needed today for the film production," I say. "Would you join me?" I point to an empty chair at my table."

"With pleasure," he says.

"Thanks again for taking me to Panama City. It was an amazing day."

He laughs. "Panama City is certainly different than this village."

"May I ask why you live here rather than there?"

"This is my village, where I grew up, and I have family here. I have a lovely house beside the sea beyond the village's edge. I have an apartment in Panama City connected to my son's house, so I stay there to see my grandchildren.

I'm unsure how familiar I should be with him or if I might ask more personal questions. There are many unknown protocols in Central and South American cultures, so one must go carefully in seeking information.

The server comes with my coffee, and then he stops and respectfully says, *"Buenos días Señor Colón."*

Enrique answers, *"Buenos días, Alfredo. Café con leche por favor."*

The waiter leaves, and I say, "I suppose you know many people in this village."

"Everyone," he laughs.

Then, he tells me details about the village, preparations for the next fiesta, and village relationships, including the ongoing power struggle between the priest and the mayor. The new hotel complex on the island's southwest side has helped the economy. The negative is the impact on the environment. Until the hotel was built, Isla Pedro Gonzalez was not visited as much as other places in the Pearl Islands.

He then tells me about his family, his three adorable grandchildren, and his son, who runs their fiduciary company in Panama City. Having a house on this island gives him an excuse to fly his airplane. In addition, he often flies to other islands and towns on the mainland.

With sadness, he tells me about the death of his wife one year ago. That loss led him to step back from direct management of his company as he went through a time of grief, knowing the tranquil life on Isla Pedro Gonzalez would help him heal.

When his coffee arrives, he asks, "Do you enjoy working for the film company?"

I had not told him I was a participant in a reality TV show. He assumes I am on the production crew. "Not really. I'm using the job to gain experience."

"Then, what comes next?"

"I'm not sure."

"What would please you?"

That sounds like a question I asked June. "I'm not sure. In my current job, I feel like something is missing. It isn't exactly changing the world." At least I can't see it as redemptive. "I'd like to do something that has a positive impact." I pause, and to redirect the topic from me, I ask. "May I ask if you enjoyed your work?"

"Oh yes, and I still do. Although I don't work at the same intensity as before. I see my job as helping people. People come to me with their problems, and I work to solve them. That can be at different levels. Sometimes it has to do with an inheritance, and we form a trust. For many reasons, people establish foundations and companies, and we oversee boat registrations. The people I've met and the diverse problems encountered make work interesting and rewarding. Being a lawyer adds another dimension: I've sometimes represented people in legal proceedings."

I smile. "I need to find a job like that."

"Join my team," he laughs.

"Thank you. I didn't mean that. I meant to find a work that helps people, but I'm not sure what it is."

He pats me on the arm. "Don't worry. It will come."

We talk about many things, and he is surprised when I tell him I grew up in Guyana. He once flew his airplane to Georgetown. We discuss Central and South American countries and their economic, social, and political conditions. It's a delight to converse with him and a welcome change from the survivors' camp.

As we talk, a speedboat enters the large bay going full blast. There must be some speed limit rules in the bay, written or unwritten. Still, the boat is far beyond safety considerations. The two large rumbling outboard motors become silent, and the boat slides to the shoreline.

Two men hop from the boat and anchor it to the sand, and when they turn, I recognize them. They were the two at the guesthouse and in the SUV on our island. One is taller than the other, and the tall one has a large black mustache and wears a dark green baseball hat. He was the one holding the rifle in the SUV. The shorter one was the golf cart driver and SUV driver, and he has a large band-aid on his hand where he was bit by Coco. Seeing them gives me a feeling of dread. They head across the beach and walk past the coffee bar.

Enrique Colon's eyes follow them, and then he slightly shakes his head.

"Do you know them?" I ask.

He tilts his head toward me and whispers, "You do not want to know them."

"Why is that?"

"Our government does everything possible to keep people like that away from this country, but unfortunately, we border a country with particular problems."

"What are the problems?"

"I'd rather not say, but those two and others like them are filth. Please be discrete, as I should not talk that way so openly."

"Who are they?"

"These men bring destruction to everything they touch. Stay clear of them. I only wish they will meet their own form of justice." He pauses, his eyes shifting to his empty cup and then to the beach. "Forget those men. Let's have another cup of coffee and continue our enjoyable conversation."

After ordering more coffee, we watch the two men, now carrying bags, return to their boat. The smaller one gets behind the steering wheel and starts the motor, while the other pushes the boat away from the edge. He hops in, and they slowly motor past the Luz, one man pointing at it, and then their boat accelerates across the bay. They speed past a small fishing boat, and their wake nearly throws the fisherman into the water.

"Swine," Enrique Colon sneers.

It's strange to hear this educated, cultured man speak like this.

We talk for fifteen minutes more, and he says he must go. I insist on paying for the drinks, and he excuses himself, thanking me for a delightful morning. He again ensures I have his business card, and then he walks down the main street with the shops. Shopkeepers and people in the street smile and nod their heads as he walks by. I see that he is respected in this small village, someone from here who went to the mainland and became successful, but he has not forsaken his roots.

I go to the Luz, motor to the middle of the bay, and then raise the sail, glad to have met Enrique Colon. The discussion gave me ideas about my future.

What gives me relief is that the two men in the speedboat are gone. They are already back at the guesthouse, with their trip only taking twenty minutes or so. On the other hand, it will take me at least two hours to sail to my camp.

* * *

Back on Isla San José, Coco and I pass over the bluff. We then approach the survivors' camp.

Frank yells, "Ada, get out of the scene. The rest of you start an argument about the javelina. Pandora, tell Roger that he is selfish and a glutton."

June says, "Frank, you are pushing it too far. I don't want this show scripted line by line."

Frank laughs. "As though it hasn't been done before."

"If you keep doing this, I will call Hollywood."

"All they care about is drama, and we will give it to them."

"Not your way." June turns to the actors. "That's enough filming for today. Why don't you get dressed? I'm sorry you've got to go through this."

"He's a pervert," Pandora accuses, pointing her finger at Frank.

"Watch it, lady," Frank says, "Just remember the show's name, and you agreed to be on it, and now you're breaching the contract. If the producers see footage of you running around in t-shirts, they will be horrified, and there's no telling what they will do. Just remember that."

"Frank, that's enough," June shouts. "Call it a day. Go back to the production camp and relax."

I walk into the clearing, and Frank sees me and shouts, "I told you not to come here. Diego, go get the rifle."

Diego, the boat skipper, stands still, not knowing what to do.

June says, "Frank, have you lost your mind? Diego, go get that rifle and hide it."

Diego sprints away. He knows that June is the ultimate boss.

Frank puts his camera on top of a log, glares, and unexpectedly charges at me like something switched in his head. When he is a few feet away, I quickly step to the side and trip him, a move I learned growing up. We spent hours wrestling with my Amerindian friends, trained by village elders. Being in the Marines added skills. Frank falls headfirst into the dirt. He stays down for a minute and then slowly rises, not having the will to charge again. His forearm and the side of his face are scratched.

"See what he is like," Frank screams. "He's dangerous. I will sue him for bodily harm. It's in the contract."

"Sorry, Frank, but I never signed a contract, and there are enough witnesses here to testify you lost your marbles and acted first."

June stares at Frank and commands, "Constrain yourself." Then, turning to Carlos, the medic, she says, "Please take care of him, although he doesn't deserve it."

Frank stumbles across the campground, sits on a log, and Carlos, the medic, puts disinfectant on Frank's arm and face.

Roger and Harry grin, then turn and disappear Roger going into his lean-to, and Harry walking into the jungle to his wickiup. A few minutes later they return wearing shorts and t-shirts. Pandora and Wilma do the same.

I catch Ada's eye and nod my head toward the jungle. We walk down a path, and when out of hearing range from the camp, I say, "Looks like the filming got tense. How are you doing?"

"I'm fine but no longer part of the show."

"What happened?"

"It was scripted that I tapped out. As I refused to go without clothing, Frank constructed a fake scenario that I was extracted to a hospital."

"So, you could leave here if you wanted."

"Yes, except I want to be around for the others. They need moral support. Working with Frank is becoming untenable."

"You are doing a good thing," I state. "I brought you something."

Reaching into my backpack, I hand over five toothbrushes and tubes of toothpaste."

Ada takes them and sighs. "This is amazing. Everyone is going to appreciate this. You are a godsend.

She takes two steps toward me and hugs me, clinging for a long time as though drawing strength from my body. She is strong but soft, that strange feminine mix. It makes me speechless, and when she releases her grip, I stutter, "And you, are if?" My mind is jumbled, and what I say doesn't make any sense.

Ada smiles. "Are you okay?"

"Yes. Please take care of yourself around Frank. He's going bonkers."

"Bonkers?"

"Loony, whacky, whatever you want to call it."

"Maybe he's been that way, but we just didn't see it," she says.

"You're probably right."

"I better sneak these back into the camp," she says, holding up the toothbrushes and toothpaste.

See you tomorrow," I say, watching her walk down the path.

Walking back to my camp, I reflect on what Ada said. That she wanted to stay to assist the other participants. I tell myself that I want to do the same thing, to look out for them because of dangers they don't know about. But it's not true. I'm sticking around because of Ada.

DAY 20

After breakfast, I take a long swim out from my beach. When treading water beyond the breakers, I look back to the island with its tall bending palm trees near the beach and lush jungle farther inland. The sea is warm, and my world is filled with a kaleidoscope of blues and greens, and I wish I were a poet to describe this.

Coco is curled up on the sand close to one of the camping chairs, like a small white ball seen from this distance. I'm glad the dog found me. He has provided welcome company over the past weeks. However, I need to figure out what to do with him when I leave the island. He certainly would not be happy if confined to my tiny studio apartment in Hollywood.

Anyway, I plan to move on once returning to California, but what to do with the dog? I need to find a good home for him.

I slowly swim back to the beach, sit in the camping chair, and dry off. Then, I put on a pair of shorts. Swimming alone without clothing is a liberating feeling. Still, it's entirely different when someone follows you with a camera.

Perhaps this is not a problem for some participants on the Naked Fear show. However, I don't like it, especially when it is someone like Frank behind the camera. Something in his warped head makes him more than a cameraman. He seems to enjoy watching suffering, and the more sorrow, the better, especially for women.

Frank isn't happy to let June coordinate the filming. And he certainly doesn't like me, even threatening to use a gun to keep me away from the camp.

His command to Diego to get the rifle was unsettling, and I'm glad June intervened, for I may have been forced to use the pistol in my backpack to defend myself. That would undoubtedly be a memorable scene in a Naked Fear episode where a participant and a film crew member shoot each other. Maybe the producers would like that, the absolute height of drama, the best Naked Fear show of all time.

I wish that tripping Frank would have knocked some sense into his head, but that is wishful thinking. The scratches on his face and forearm will be a painful reminder of what happened. It is humiliation in front of others, and the hate toward me will only grow, so I need to pay more attention to him.

Sitting in my camping chair, I think about the fun of sailing the Luz, and then I think of Ada. Would Ada enjoy going with me? Maybe I should invite her. But something tells me not to let any participants into my world. They are mystified about how I got the food and clothing, thinking someone on our island supplied them. By revealing the sailboat, it could open all kinds of unwelcome questions.

I head back to my camp, Coco running in front of me. After making an inventory of my food supplies, I have enough to last until the end of the challenge, which is in eight days. With enough clothing and cooking utensils, there is no need to go to one of the neighboring islands to buy more. My hut is well built, and the only thing missing is a bamboo chair for my table, but with only eight days to go, I decide not to make it. We will soon be leaving, so why labor in a place that will soon be abandoned?

In a way, it's sad to think of leaving my camp, for I have been happy here for the first time in a long time. It's a zillion times more satisfying than logging expenses into an accounting application on a computer. I've enjoyed finding and preparing food, building my hut, sailing, and many other things. Being in nature is a big plus. It will be sad to leave this place. I need to appreciate the next eight days as much as possible.

Having promised Ada that I would check in every day, Coco and I walk to the survivors' camp after lunch. Again, as is often the case, I hear an argument, only now it is between Frank and June. They stand under a palm tree by the beach, out of hearing range from the camp.

Frank says, "It doesn't make sense."

"What's that?" June asks.

"The participants should be losing a lot more weight. Every viewer of the show anticipates that. A show full of hardships and hunger must have weight loss."

"This time, it's different," June states.

"It can't be. You know the producers were expecting something exceptional for this show. We aren't even close. Everything has been too comfortable, and Bookie ruined it."

"I'm not sure."

"Yes, he did. The participants were chosen for a purpose."

"What purpose?"

"As the chief cameraman, I advised in the casting."

"Are you saying you chose the participants?" June asks.

"Yes, the production team relied on me because of my exceptional camera skills and ability to capture dramatic scenes. For this show, I wanted sexy women and meat-headed men. Then, we watch their world disintegrate and see them go from beautiful to ugly. Our viewers will love that."

"Did the producers let you choose these ladies?"

"Of course. The photographer is the key person in framing reality. We were on track for something special until they made that last-minute replacement by sending the idiot bookkeeper down here. There's one week left, so we need to turn up the heat. There must be more tension, becoming so bad that someone taps out. Then, some of the remaining participants must shed tears because of the loss of that person, whereas others will be joyful. Good riddance."

"You're sick," June says.

"No. You are not doing your job. This show is about naked bodies, drama, defeats, and suffering. The greatest joy for our millions of viewers is to see suffering in others. Realize that or leave."

"I'm not leaving. Don't forget that I am the coordinator."

Raising his voice, Frank says, "You're a failure."

Standing behind them, I call out, "Frank, you are warped."

Frank and June turn toward me, eyes wide, as Frank's posture stiffens. Then, like an angry dog, the right side of his upper lip turns up, and he growls, "I told you to stay away. You have no part in this film shoot anymore."

"I agree."

"Then get out of here."

"The last I checked, the Naked Fear film company has a contract to use this island. I work for that company, and they sent me down here. So, I'll wander anywhere I want."

"But not here. You are a destroyer."

I laugh. "So, now I'm a supervillain, The Incredible Island Destroyer."

"You think you're funny. A lot of money was spent on this production."

"I know. I'm the guy keeping track of expenses."

"Then, you know what's at stake."

"Why not do a different kind of show, something redemptive. But I guess you prefer to see beautiful women hurt."

Frank turns to June. "You were a moron to tell Diego to hide the rifle."

"I did the right thing, the way you are acting," June says. "You need to calm down."

"No. Not the way things are going."

Frank stomps off toward the production team camp.

"Looks like we have a problem," I say. "He despises me, undermines you, and doesn't listen to reason."

"I'm glad Roger and Harry are here. If Frank tries to get physical, they can manage him."

"Don't let him near that rifle," I state.

"It's well hidden. I asked Diego."

"What do you think about him influencing the casting crew back in Hollywood?"

"That was a surprise. Indeed, these are lovely women but also experienced survivalists."

"It seems his goal is to break them down," I state.

June takes a breath. "If you want to know the truth, some things he said made sense. While viewers like to see the survivalists overcome hardship, the show's real catch is to watch them fail. Frank wants agony more than victory."

"It's more than for the show," I state. "He personally gets a bizarre joy from this. That's why he is dangerous."

"I agree."

"Keep an eye on him," I state. "And let me know if things get serious."

"I will, but how do I find you?"

"If I'm not here, send Diego with the boat to my campsite if you need me."

"Thank you, Bartholomew."

We walk to the survivors' campsite, where everyone wears t-shirts and shorts. It seems there is a pause in filming. Less than an hour of live filming is necessary each day, which will be trimmed down to five or ten minutes in the final cut.

Pandora sees me and grins, "Hey, Bookie. You are a good man." She winks as though we share a secret.

The other survivalists laugh.

"Happy smile," she says, pointing to her teeth. "Thank you."

"I understand," I reply. "Are you getting enough to eat?"

"Javelina," Pandora says, and then whispers, "And beans."

"So, are you okay for now?"

"At least for a couple more days."

"Maybe I can help," I say.

"Bookie, you are an amazing survivalist," Pandora states.

There is swift movement at the edge of the clearing, and Coco barks as Frank charges toward us. He has a frying pan in his right hand, and when he is fifteen feet away from me, he hurls it through the air. I duck, and the frying pan just misses my head. He charges on and then loses his balance and stumbles against my chest, but I quickly spin, and he ends up under me, and his head hits a log.

Panting for breath, he moans, "You are a beast."

Roger helps me up while Harry bends down and places a large hand on Frank's chest, holding him to the ground.

Frank screams, "Naked Fear, Naked Fear, Naked Fear, that's the show's name."

June says, "Roger and Harry, could you escort Frank back to the production camp?"

Roger and Harry take Frank by the arms and walk him across the campsite. As they leave, June says, "I'm sorry, Bartholomew, he's getting out of hand."

"We better keep a close eye on him," I say, "all of us."

Everyone nods their heads.

Eventually, Roger and Harry return to the campsite and confirm that Frank is now calm and Diego is watching him.

Once the participants are together, June surprises them by declaring her desire to walk away from the entire production. But she can't, at least not yet. They all signed contracts, including her, and she would be in breach of contract to leave the production before it is finished.

"Next time, I'll read the fine print," she declares.

"Likewise, I should have done the same thing," Pandora says. "I'm conflicted. It feels demeaning, but I don't have the resources to fight the Naked Fear company in court."

Wilma says, "Frank behind that camera makes me uncomfortable. That dude is creepy."

After some discussion, the survivors agree to act their parts, but the question of Ada is raised. Frank previously said he wrote her out of the show, claiming he has enough video to artificially piece this together. Still, it's uncertain how he can accomplish this, and he may ask her for a scene or two where she taps out on camera.

Ada says, "I realize it was wrong for me to come here, and from now on I refuse to do anything in front of Frank's camera, no matter the consequences."

The others finally agree to shoot a few scenes, which will be kept to a minimum. Although, performing naked before the camera is uncomfortable because this now has a different feeling. It is beyond reality TV and more like a scripted movie. And, it's no longer about survival, as food is served by the camera crew.

I dislike how this show is evolving and feel they should stop production and everyone goes home. But I understand their fear of legal issues. They are caught in a difficult place. I'm the lucky one for not having signed a contract.

Knowing that the participants are safe from Frank, I call Coco, and we walk to our camp. I'm wondering if I should move to the survivalists' camp. Frank is volatile, and the rifle isn't the only weapon. There are hunting knives and machetes available. It doesn't seem possible he would resort to that, but my tribal elders said to always be careful. Would he attack the others? Or is it only me he despises?

DAY 21

The standard opening line for the Naked Fear show is, "One Man, One Woman, alone for twenty-one days without clothing. Can they survive?" It's a catchy introduction with dramatic music and video clips of shivering people and snakes, scorpions, rain torrents, and drought. Except, it's not exactly true. There is no way they are "alone." At least from what I've experienced, those naked, miserable men and women are surrounded by a support team of cameramen, a medic, various technical staff, and an onsite director.

In our case, it is not one man and one woman but a group of participants, and the goal of this 'XL,' or Extra-Large production, is to heighten the tension. One must agree that the stress started strong. Then I seem to have inadvertently deflated the conflict by supplying a few of the comforts of home, such as food and clothing.

Now, they are working to restore the storyline, meaning each scene is scripted and acted.

The remaining participants are beginning to enjoy this, although they are not the world's most skilled actors. In fact, they are turning this into the equivalent of a low-budget movie. While Roger and Pandora can fake conflict, it is far from the reality of their first days here. It's more like they are auditioning for a part in a late-night furniture commercial and doing a horrible job. Harry is comical at expressing agony and resembles a jolly teddy bear on a children's TV show. Wilma would fit in fine on a soap opera, especially in the hyper-dramatic scenes with jilted lovers.

June adores every minute because of the absurdity of the disjointed scenes and silly acting, and Frank is in misery. Bob should be filming Frank instead of the participants.

During the morning film shoot, I sit on the sidelines, and Frank keeps complaining about my presence. He constantly whines and blames the poor acting on me.

Finally, I call Coco, walk far down the beach, and take a swim. Then, it's jerky for lunch and a nap.

When I go back to their camp, everyone seems worried.

"We have to do something," June exclaims.

I approach her and ask, "What's going on."

"Something's wrong with Diego. He has severe stomach cramps and is vomiting."

"What did he eat?" In jungles, there are a million things that attack your stomach.

"He had lunch like the rest of the production team."

"What was it?"

"Ravioli and vegetables from cans, and crackers and tea."

"How bad is it?"

"I don't know. Carlos is with him."

June and I walk to the production team camp, and Diego is on his knees with Carlos beside him. Carlos has his hand on Diego's shoulder.

"How is he?" She asks.

"He is in great pain," Carlos says.

Diego puts his hand on his stomach, wretches, and vomits. One can see that he ate ravioli."

"Is it food poisoning?" I ask.

"How can it be? We all ate the same thing for lunch." Carlos says.

"Maybe it's amebiasis," I say. In tropical climates, amebiasis is a common disease. These are tiny parasites caused by unsanitary conditions. They attack the intestinal wall and, if left untreated, can destroy one's liver, heart, and brain. I've had it, and only antibiotics can cure it, and it's not fun.

"I don't think so," Carlos says. "He doesn't have diarrhea, at least not yet. This looks serious. We should extract him to a hospital."

I turn to June and ask, "What's the procedure?"

"I need to make a call. A medical helicopter is available in Panama City, and they will come here to pick him up."

I look at Carlos and say, "This doesn't seem right."

June goes into a tent, comes out with a satellite phone, and makes the call. When finished, she says, "Sorry to say, the helicopter is being repaired and unavailable. But they are sending an airplane and will be at

146

the airport in twenty-five minutes."

"We better get moving," I say.

Carlos takes one of Diego's arms, and I hold the other, and we walk as fast as possible to the natural harbor where the production team boat is tied up. Diego is in agony each step of the way. We should have used the stretcher in one of the tents.

We help Diego into the boat, where he curls up on a cushion in the back, and June releases the mooring ropes and she hops in. She asks, "Can anyone drive this?"

"I can," I say.

"Please get us to the airport as quick as possible," she declares.

Steering a boat is not that difficult. With the key already in the ignition, I turn on the motor, push the shift lever into Drive, press the throttle, and slowly navigate the boat out of the harbor. Once in the open sea, I push the throttle to maximum, and the boat rumbles across the water.

Frank stands on the beach with his camera pointed at us. He filmed the entire event.

After going fifteen minutes, we pass the guesthouse, and a few minutes later, we pull up on the beach at one end of the airport landing strip. The strip cuts straight into the jungle, but the east end opens to the sea.

We manage to carry Diego across the sand, and just as we reach the edge of the runway, an airplane comes in for a landing. It has the sign of a red cross, an ambulance plane. It taxis back to us and two men in white uniforms jump out with a stretcher. We put Diego on it and then carry him to the plane.

Quickly, the plane taxis to the end of the strip. It turns and accelerates down the runway and then zooms over our heads. In twenty-five minutes, Diego will be in an ambulance on his way to a hospital in Panama City.

"That was scary," June says. "I hope he makes it."

"Maybe it's appendicitis," I suggest.

Carlos says, "It's hard to tell, but I'm glad he is in the air. They have excellent hospitals in Panama City, so he is well cared for."

I navigate the boat back along the coast, and we pass by the guesthouse. All the bungalows seem closed, but someone is walking along the side of the building. It is too far away to see who it is, but the speedboat with two large motors on the back is tied to the long dock. Enrique Colon said they were terrible men. What are they doing at the guesthouse?

Piloting back at a slower speed, we eventually reach the natural harbor near the production team camp and secure the boat.

June asks, "Where did you learn to drive a speedboat?"

I smile. "First time."

"Bartholomew, you continually surprise me, and I don't believe it. You managed it like an expert."

"One learns interesting things on the internet."

She smiles, and then her face is drawn. "This sudden medical problem with Diego was unexpected and frightening. I need to report back to our company in Hollywood."

June walks to the production team tents, and I head back to the survivalists' camp, where the others are waiting. Coco is with them.

"What happened," Pandora asks.

I describe evacuating Diego and answer their questions. Then, because it's getting late, I call Coco and head toward my camp. Now they are a man short and might need my help. It's another reason to spend more time over here.

* * *

Behind me, on the path, I hear running feet and turn, and Ada rushes up to me. She says, "Bartholomew, can I ask a question?"

"Sure." I'm glad to see her, knowing she can ask as many questions as she wants from here to eternity.

"Do you think Diego will be okay?"

"He wasn't in good shape when we put him on the airplane. So before they took off, the medics were preparing an intravenous drip."

"He's a nice guy," she states.

I nod. "Let's hope for the best."

She pauses as though she does not want to return to the camp. "And how are you doing?" She asks.

"I'm doing fine, but hanging around your camp is stressful. The tension between the participants is no longer an issue. Still, this unexpected problem with Diego is bad, and of course, there are the melodramas with Frank, the lunatic. One needs to step away from that

148

and enjoy the peace and beauty of the island."

She smiles. "I agree. We should do more of that."

Suddenly, I have an idea and say, "I like the 'we.' May I suggest doing something together?"

Grinning, Ada says, "Yes. Do you have anything exciting to propose?"

"Would you like to get away?"

She looks around. "You mean a walk in the jungle."

"We could do that, go fishing, or go to a restaurant for lunch."

"What are you talking about? A restaurant sounds lovely. Are you talking about going over to the guesthouse?"

"I'd never go there."

"Why not?"

"I'll tell you sometime."

"That sounds strange. Let's go to the restaurant. Is it at your camp, and will you do the cooking?"

"I have something else in mind. What we do has to be kept a secret between us. So, no one can know until we all leave the island. Can you promise me that?"

"This sounds mysterious, but yes, of course."

"Okay. Tell June that you will spend all day tomorrow with me. Then, just before sunrise, walk north beyond the lagoon where the beach meets the bluff, and I'll meet you there. Plan to be away most of the day."

"Where are we going?"

"It's a surprise. I just have a question. Do you get seasick?"

"No. Why do you ask?"

"I just need to know. Be at the beach by the bluff at sunrise."

"See you there," Ada says. She looks down the path toward their camp, hesitates, then turns to me and hugs me.

We wrap our arms around each other, and I like her body's soft, gentle curves against mine. It's more than physical. It's metaphysical, or whatever you want to call it. We are two people brought together by chance on a wacky reality television program, and we found an attraction. Is it temporary, caused by the stresses of this challenge? Or, is it longer lasting? For now, it doesn't matter. I like who she is and how she has been different than the other participants, quiet yet standing her ground. She is perfect, at least for me.

149

Ada releases her grip, looks me in the eyes, smiles, and turns down the path.

My heart beats fast, and my head spins.

"Let's go, Coco," I say. "If you could talk, what advice would you give?"

DAY 22

Well before sunrise, I feed Coco one of the remaining cans of dog food and tell him to stay in our camp. He is happy to obey, for running through a dark jungle is not his thing. I wear shorts, a t-shirt, sandals, and my Panama hat. My backpack contains jerky, a pair of sunglasses, two bottles of water, a long-sleeved shirt, a jacket, my hunting knife, and the .38 pistol.

Taking the Luz from its hiding place in the mangroves. I sail south. There is a perfect breeze, and the sea is calm. At the end of the bluff is a rocky point going out into the water. It provides a breakwater, although today, it isn't needed because the waves are almost nonexistent. After anchoring the sailboat several feet from the shore, I wade through the sea to the beach and wait.

Shortly after, as the sky to the east turns gray, I see Ada walking along the beach in my direction.

She waves, smiles and approaches me. When seeing the sailboat, she points and asks. "What's that?"

"A boat. Are you ready for a trip?"

"Of course, I can see that it's a boat. This is crazy. Where did you get it? You came to the island with nothing."

"It's one of those things."

"What does that mean?"

"Come one, let's go."

We slosh through the water, get in the boat, and I lift the anchor. Then, after raising the sail and pivoting the boat toward deeper water, we turn north. A few minutes later, I point out my beach camp, and then we head further out from the island to catch a stronger wind as the sun rises in the east.

Turning over the boat's navigation to Ada, I see she knows how to navigate, perhaps better than me. She finds that perfect balance, that ideal harmony between wind and sail. We efficiently slide across the water, and her face is joyful.

I sit in the middle of the boat, and it's nice to have someone else doing the work. It gives me time to take in the surroundings. In the distance to the north, a large cargo boat heads toward the Panama Canal. Seagulls glide through the sky above us, and at one point, we see several dolphins rising above the water. Their speed amazes me.

I'm thrilled to be out here with Ada. She looks at me and grins, and I give her a thumbs up. So this is how it should be, one man and one woman heading together in the same direction while enjoying life. In contrast to the Naked Fear paradigm of 'one man, one woman, without clothing, suffering in a swamp.'

We leave Isla San José and traverse the open sea, eventually reaching Isla Pedro Gonzalez. Then we go around the east of the island. Finally, we enter the large bay by the village of Pedro de Cocal, and we anchor the Luz near the other boats close to the beach.

Once getting out of the boat and walking onto the sand, Ada asks, "What is this place?"

"A village."

"I can see that, but where are we?"

"Isla Pedro Gonzalez, one of the islands in the Pearl Island archipelago."

"Okay. I guess you answered my question. Have you been here before?"

"I wander around. Most people, especially Naked Fear survivalists, live in a little bubble and rarely venture out. My philosophy is to draw a larger circle. So let's go explore, but first, you need shoes."

"Shoes?"

"Shoes, sandals, whatever, something for your feet, and maybe a hat."

Ada follows me to the street with the shops, and we find one that sells clothing. Then, she picks out a pair of sandals, a feminine-style Panama hat, and sunglasses. I pay in U.S. Dollars.

"Where did you get the money?" She asks.

"Scavenging. Why don't we just enjoy the day?"

"Okay, but it would be nice to know more at some point."

We walk through the town, and Ada enjoys looking at the shops.

There are few. We pass a school and children play, and then we go by the simple village church.

She asks, "Are you religious?"

"Not exactly. It seems to me that religion is doing something to achieve spirituality, like performing acts to be accepted by God. It raises the question of how perfect one's performance has to be? I believe that we can work our butts off and never reach God. He knows this, cares, and gives a solution by reaching out to us. We can know him, and all it takes is faith. My faith isn't always strong, but that's my bottom line when it comes to religion."

She smiles. "Simply said, but I got it."

"And what's your belief?"

"I'm like you. We can talk directly with God without going through intermediaries."

That was a revelation. Here is someone in harmony with me, at least on the spiritual plane. Besides cultural divergences, the religion question often became a barrier with the women I met in California.

We walk to the edge of the village, and then, on another street, we circle back to the beach. At the coffee bar, we take a table, and I order two *café con leches* and a plate of Panamanian cookies. It's too early for lunch.

Just as the drinks and cookies are served, I see Enrique Colon arrive and look for a table. He spots me, waves, and approaches us.

With a smile, he says, "Bartholomew, it's so nice to see you. How are you?"

"Just fine. Would you like to join us?"

"Yes, thank you, if it is not an imposition."

"May I introduce you to my friend Ada, ah . . ." It's awkward that I don't know her last name. And, to Ada, I say, "This is Senior Enrique Colon."

He bows slightly and says, "It is a pleasure to meet you."

Enrique takes a chair at our table and orders a coffee, the waiter showing him the highest respect.

"I didn't expect to see you again," Enrique says.

"We have a day off, so we decided to come over here."

"It's a glorious day to sail," he exclaims.

"Ada is a fabulous sailor. I didn't have to do a thing."

"You are lucky," he says.

153

Ada remarks, "I didn't realize that Bartholomew knew anyone on this island. So how did you meet?"

Enrique smiles and says, "It is easy to meet people in a small village. Bartholomew and I became acquainted and had interesting discussions."

His answer was warm and gracious, and he honestly answered her question without giving too much information. From this, I imagine his discretion as a lawyer.

He asks us, "How is your work going?"

I answer. "It's progressing but not without challenges. We have enjoyed being on Isla San José, but in a few days, we will be finished and then return to the United States."

"Isla San José is magnificent. It's one of the few unpopulated islands in our archipelago. Recently a new owner purchased it, and I hope he doesn't destroy it."

"It's a paradise," Ada states. "May I ask what you do here?"

"I am mostly retired, enjoying this time in my life."

He and Ada continue a lively discussion when she asks him questions about the islands and what it is like to live here. Enrique describes the Pearl Islands, life in his village, Panamanian culture, and his sadness at seeing how some islands are being overdeveloped. They laugh, and I see how he is at ease with people, speaking with a soft, gracious voice. Yet, simultaneously, I notice how he peers at Ada and me with experienced, discerning eyes, as though he sees us beyond a superficial level.

At one point, Ada excuses herself to go to the restroom, and Enrique bends over to me and says, "She is lovely."

I smile. "I agree."

"And intelligent. Do you have feelings for her?"

That was straightforward. I take a breath. "That's a good question. Honestly, yes."

"She seems to be someone to spend the day with and a lifetime."

That statement hits me. The refined, cautious Latin man gets straight to the point, which is unsettling. "I need to think about that," I state.

"You better not think too long before someone else is quicker."

"Thank you, Enrique. I need encouragement."

"You need more than that."

"What do you mean?"

"Too often, when opportunities present themselves, most people let them disappear without acting. This happens for many reasons, and one of them is fear. Does that describe you?"

His questions are penetrating. I grin, swallow, and say, "You know how to go for the kill. I have no fear for many things, but I'm hesitant to ask someone to walk with me for a lifetime down an unknown path."

"Does anyone know what the next hour will bring, let alone the next year? We have two choices. Either live in fear and let events control your life, Or navigate unfamiliar waters with faith and courage, making choices while going along."

I nod. "I also wonder how our relationship will work out."

He speaks with a soft but sure voice, like a lawyer advising his client. "Bartholomew, I have found that in business and in life, it comes down to one thing. After gathering the facts, one must act or walk away at some point. No relationship can be healthy if the two parties tiptoe around each other."

"So you are saying to jump in the deep end."

"I'm not saying to impulsively decide, although it is a simple equation. You must ask if you have enough information. Do you know enough of this lovely young woman to commit? And I mean a lifetime commitment?"

"I've seen how she acts in stressful situations and is concerned for others."

He nods, waits a moment, and says, "You don't need to know everything about a person. Everyone is a deep mysterious well, and discovery takes time. There comes the point where you say I know enough, and it seems right, and you make a choice, and it's then that you sign an invisible contract. Remember, I am a lawyer and know about these things."

"But, what after that?" I ask, with a realization that I'm fearful and lack confidence.

"It is simple," he states. "You become partners, lovers, walking that unknown path, knowing you will work together and look out for each other. So what I say is not only words of encouragement but a truth formulated by life experience. But it is not always easy. For a relationship to endure, it takes willpower. In fact, love is a choice, ongoing each day. Sure, there is romance and feelings, which are important, But choice is central."

"Enrique. How do I know," I say in desperation, understanding that I've been running from choices, hunkering down at a corner desk in Hollywood.

He says, "The eyes tell a lot about a relationship. I see how you look at each other and how there is an unexplainable bond. Do you sign the contract or not?"

He gave me a lot to think about. I'm unsure how to respond, but what he said was right. Is it too soon to make the commitment he was alluding to? Maybe the invisible contract was already signed without realizing it. Hesitating, all I can say is, "Thank you, Enrique."

Ada comes back, sits down, and says, "I could live here."

Enrique smiles. "It is not for everyone. Only those who want to live differently."

"What do you mean?"

He looks her in the eyes. "Do you want to go with the culture or find a unique direction?"

That was a strange question, and I think he lost something when translating from Spanish to English, but maybe not.

Ada tilts her head as though realizing he speaks figuratively. She smiles and says, "It seems most important to find a life path that gives purpose, which then gives satisfaction."

"And what is that for you?"

Ada hesitates. "I have a following on the internet, mostly younger women searching for identity. So I try to be a positive influence. But I wish I could do more. So many people need a helping hand."

He smiles. "You sound very much like Bartholomew in my discussions with him. Is there a way for you to work together?"

I'm nervous about where he will take it from here. Do I really need a matchmaker?

She glances at me. "Bartholomew is good at helping people. So yes, I could see myself collaborating with him."

He says, "When I met my Maria, that encounter seemed more than human, but divine. She was from an aristocratic family on the mainland, and I came from this primitive island. No one would have ever thought those two divergent people could form a life together. Yet, from the beginning, it was a special relationship. Every day we enjoyed each other's company. We were so much in love. Now she is gone, and my heart has an empty place. Yet, I do not regret a single day with her. When we first met, we would have missed something precious if I had walked away from her or her from me. Throughout our years, we worked together, and life had struggles, but our souls were always one."

"I'm sorry to hear about your wife," Ada says.

"Thank you." Enrique turns to Ada and then to me. "I am not a prophet or one to force the future, but I have many experiences with people. Life is fleeting. Sometimes there is too much fear. When you see that other person who lights a spark, and the spark works both ways, then why not recognize this and take the risk?" He looks at his watch and says, "I must go, for I have a meeting this afternoon in Panama City. It was a pleasure to talk with you, and I hope you don't think I am too forthcoming. I wish you everything and hope we can meet again someday. I'd like to know about your journey."

Enrique gets up, shakes our hands, and then speaks with the server. The server slightly bows his head in respect, and Enrique disappears down the street.

Ada looks at me, takes a breath, and says, "Wow, that's quite a cultured and intelligent man. It's baffling that you met him."

"He is respected in this village."

Her eyes shift to her coffee cup, one finger touching the cup's handle. Then, finally, she whispers, "He was straightforward, wasn't he?"

I smile. "I should say so, but it was done uniquely."

"That cuts through days of back-and-forth discussions and dancing around delicate questions."

"There's not much room for maneuvering after what he said." Looking at her, I realize I must be like Enrique and get to the point. "So, what's our response? I feel the spark. Do you?"

She waits a few seconds, but it feels like a lifetime. "Yes," she whispers.

I take a deep breath. "He mentioned something daunting because it deals with the unknown. Do we take the risk?"

"And you?" She asks.

"We should," I pronounce, knowing we speak in vague expressions. Still, we talk about something specific, committing to each other for a lifetime. That's not a little thing. And this is moving so fast, maybe too fast.

"I agree," she says, sticking out her hand. I shake it.

"It's a deal," I smile.

She releases my hand and puts her hand on my shoulder, leans across to me, and touches her soft lips against mine. After that, time ceases to exist, for our lips stay together for what may be a second or eternity. Eventually, we pull apart, but I desire more.

"I'm in a cloud," I say.

"I think a crazy decision was made," she responds.

I laugh. "We hardly know each other."

"But we do know each other. In stressful situations, we have watched each other. Those days on the island have been like years."

I grin. "Let's have lunch, get in the boat, and sail together in the same direction."

"Forever?" She asks.

"Yes, forever."

We order from a handwritten menu and are served fresh grilled fish, fried potatoes, vegetables, and a tomato salad. We talk and laugh while enjoying the meal. It's good to be away from the pressures in the camp. Yet, it feels like tectonic plates shifted under us.

After lunch, we shop, buying a couple of large bags of fresh cookies for the survivalists. I also buy them five baseball caps with Panama written across the front. Then we leisurely sail the Lux back to Isla San José. There isn't much talking along the way, mainly glances back and forth combined with warm smiles. Finally, we put the Luz in its hiding place in the Mangroves, and I carry my backpack and the things we purchased to my beach camp, where we stop to rest in the two camping chairs.

"Is this where you live?" Ada asks.

"Some of the time. This is a great spot to enjoy the sunsets, but the same could be said of any viewing point on the west side of this island."

"Where did you get the chairs?"

"They resulted from negotiations with June. I wanted to leave the show early, and she persuaded me to stay. The chairs were part of the deal."

She laughs. "I bet that was an interesting discussion. Are you glad you stayed?"

"It has made all the difference. If I had left early, I would now be sitting at a corner desk, logging receipts and controlling expenses. The additional time here has been a life-changer. I met interesting people, and today made an amazing choice."

"Do you regret it?"

"I need to get my mind around it, but no regrets. This was an amazing day, probably the best of my life. How about you?" I ask.

"No one could believe it. Your friend, Enrique Colon, was unlike anyone I have ever met. He spoke vaguely but directly at the same time. His challenge to us came unexpectedly out of the clear blue sky, but it was done diplomatically. I bit the hook."

"Happy?"

"It's living a dream, and if you are wondering, I meant what I said, getting in the same boat and going in the same direction, whatever that is."

"We will figure it out."

"Who is he exactly, Enrique Colon?"

"An unusual man of wisdom, a prophet, someone with experience. He is a lawyer, semi-retired."

"A lawyer?"

"He has an office in Panama City that his son runs. It's in a modern high-rise office building. That city is incredible."

"Have you been there?"

"Yes, about a week ago."

Ada's eyes open. "What have you been up to? I saw you the day you arrived with nothing. You seemed so timid and lost. Now, you have that boat, clothing, money, and friends. And you have been off the island. The rest of us have existed in our little world around the camp."

I smile. "We came here to survive, and that's what I have done."

"There's one thing I can't figure out. Your campsite here is in a wonderful place, but it seems too simple. You bring jerky to us. Where was that made? I know you have additional clothing. Where is it?"

"There is another place." With Ada, I must share everything, but not all at once. "I will take you there sometime."

"I would like that."

We walk to the trail going over the bluff, and at one point, Coco joins us, wagging his tail, glad to be back with the pack.

Descending to the other side, we cross the stream at the end of the lagoon. Ada says, "Now I know you are not a ghost disappearing into the spooky depths of the forest, and I know how to find you."

I laugh. "You are welcome anytime. Only, please don't tell the others. I'm not ready for visitors."

"It's between us." She stops and looks at me. "Thank you for today. It was special, wasn't it?"

"It gives much to think about. But, let me confirm that I want to share the future with you even though little is clear now."

"I'm not worried. I'm with some resourceful guy who walks onto a tropical island with nothing and does magical things. I look forward to anything life throws at us."

I laugh. "Don't get your hopes too high."

"Whatever happens, I want to do things with you. My first task is to get to know you better. I know little about you besides working as a bookkeeper for this film company. Where are you from? What have you been doing? What is your family like?"

"And I need to learn the same things from you. Isn't it strange to commit to someone with such little knowledge?"

She says, "We know enough, and that's all that matters."

Ada takes a step toward me, raises her lips to mine, and we kiss, staying in a long embrace. We finally step apart, and I say, "Let's go to the camp."

"Regretfully."

Coco bounds ahead of us into the campsite, where June talks to the survivalists. Frank films their interaction.

"Are we safe?" Pandora asks.

"I don't know," June answers.

June sees us and says, "I'm glad you are here. Something terrible happened today." She hardly notices Ada's new hat and sandals.

"What was it?" I ask.

"We had to evacuate Bob and Carlos."

"Why?"

"They had the same symptoms as Diego, only not quite as bad."

"What do you mean?"

"After breakfast, they both had stomach cramps. I didn't hesitate and called the office in Hollywood, which sent the medical plane over here. Roger, Harry, and Pandora went with us in the speedboat to help carry Bob and Carlos on stretchers, but they managed to walk from the boat to the airplane. They were not as bad off as Carlos, so it seems."

"That's terrible to hear," Ada exclaims. "How is Carlos doing?"

"Not well, and the hospital doesn't yet know the problem."

"Could it be a stomach virus?" I ask.

"They don't know," June answers. "It seems more like food poisoning."

"So, now we are without a medic," I state. "What is Hollywood suggesting.

Frank captures our discussion on camera.

June states, "Our producers are screwballs. We only have a week to go, and they want us to finish the challenge with our existing resources, not wanting to spend more money."

Frank puts the camera to his side. He says, "That's no problem. We can create something exceptional in the days to come." Frank voice is cool and calm, sounding like a reasonable person, no longer the psycho.

I ask, "Shouldn't we call it quits and go home? What if more people get sick?"

Frank says in a reassuring voice, "Don't worry. The film company will take care of everything. I'll arrange a bonus if everyone stays to the end."

"How much?" Pandora asks.

"Double what's in your contract."

He emphasized the word 'contract,' and I'm sure that is to keep the participants in line."

Pandora asks the survivalists, "So, what do you think."

"I don't want to starve," Roger says. "Give us food."

"That's no problem," Frank affirms. "We have plenty of food over in the production team camp, enough for you with the absence of three crew members."

"But it might be bad," Pandora says.

"Don't worry about one can of ravioli. There's rice, potatoes, vegetables, cans of tuna, and many other things. All you need to do is fulfill the contract."

There goes the contract word again.

"Okay, I can act out the last days. I need the money," Roger says, "but only an hour of acting each day."

Except for Ada and me, the others nod in agreement.

Frank glows with enthusiasm. "That's wonderful, although we still need footage of suffering and maybe we could introduce fear of the puma. June is still the coordinator, but I can help script the scenes. So we can create the best Naked Fear show yet."

Frank sounds like a coach getting his team ready for the big game. And he appears to be submissive to June, which is new.

Frank turns to me and says, "Bookie, can we put our differences aside? I may have gotten a bit out of hand and will try to do better. We could use your help around here to complete the production."

"Sure. Let's be the best of buddies."

"Good, then we can continue filming tomorrow morning. See you then." Frank turns and leaves the campsite.

I tell June, "He didn't seem concerned about his sick colleagues."

She says, "Frank is a strange guy. He sees the world from the perspective of the lens, believing that controlling the camera puts him in a powerful position. There is something to that, for he determines how viewers see the world. Do you think viewers of the show will care about Bob, Carlos, and Diego? Their suffering is nothing more than entertainment captured through the eyes of Frank."

"But he's getting something from this that is beyond entertainment. Rather than empathy, it seems he has perverse enjoyment."

June says, "It seems that way." She turns to the group. "Let's just survive the coming days and keep him in line. If anyone feels uncomfortable, please let me know."

I say, "I need to go, but I have something for you." Reaching into my backpack, I take out five hats with 'Panama' written on the front and hand four to the participants and one to June. "Enjoy," I say. Ada wears the Panama hat we bought earlier in the day.

"Where did the hats come from?" Pandora asks. "Ada, you were with him all day. So, where did Bookie get them? And you have a Panama hat and sandals."

"We had a nice day wandering, and I can say that Bartholomew is resourceful from what I've seen."

I smile as Ada gives me a slight wink.

Coco and I head to the beach and walk past the lagoon. The sun lowers in the sky, and I want to get to my beach hut to watch the sunset and reflect on the day, which was crazy, none like any other. Enrique Colon certainly set us up, and I am grateful for his intervention. I needed a push, and Ada probably did too. In fact, we both needed a big push. We made a significant commitment, but not out of nowhere. There was a spark, as Enrique called it. I've had feelings for Ada from the first moment I saw her in that jungle clearing. Observing her character over the past weeks confirmed that she is a caring and thoughtful person, lovely and solid. Yes, I have things to think about.

Fundamentally, it's absolutely crazy to think we decided to marry after only knowing each other for such a short period of time. Who else would do this? Surely something must go wrong.

Other than thoughts of Ada, the news of Bob and Carlos is disturbing, and I hope a stomach virus is not sweeping through the camp.

DAY 23

When the first light of the morning hits my campsite, I rise from my bed, get up, and stretch. I'm tired and my brain feels fried. Yesterday was long, unique, and marvelous in every way, except when hearing about Bob and Carlos getting sick.

I skip breakfast, make coffee, and then go to the beach. Coco runs ahead of me and corners a giant crab in some rocks, and he jumps around, attempting to sniff it while avoiding the crab's outstretched claws. The dog needs to go through a serious learning curve.

Sitting in a camping chair, I drink coffee and enjoy the morning, and this gives me time to think about what happens in five days when we leave the island. My future is as ambiguous as ever, except that I locked myself into a couple of agreements. The first was with June, to resign from the Naked Fear Production Company. The second, which is more significant, was made with Ada. Both are the right decisions, but they open a universe of uncertainty. It's one thing to agree on a future act, but another to fully comprehend the consequences.

I plan to visit the survivors' camp in the afternoon, as I want to check how things are going. Is there any news about Carlos, Bob, and Diego? Of course, there is a more important reason for going over there. Was yesterday a fanciful dream, or is Ada fully committed to our decision? All I know is that my desire is to be with her.

Once finishing the coffee, I walk to the lagoon, where I wash with soap and shave. Then I put on a clean t-shirt and shorts.

After lunch, Coco and I walk over the bluff to the survivors' camp, and as we arrive, I hear gagging noises. Roger, Harry, Pandora, and Wilma are vomiting in the bushes. They are naked, and Frank films them. Ada lies on the ground in front of her hut with her hands on her stomach. June kneels next to Ada, and she touches Ada's shoulder.

Rushing to Ada and June, I ask, "What happened?"

With a frantic voice, June says, "We started filming for the show, and then suddenly, they all got sick."

"All at the same time?"

"Yes. This is not acting. It's the real thing. So, what can we do?"

"Call Hollywood and tell them to get urgent help over here. We certainly can't fit all of them in the small medical airplane. It holds two sick people max."

June looks at me with anxious eyes. "I can't. The battery in my satellite phone needs charging. I must have left it on after my last call."

"Can we charge it?"

"That's what I'm trying to do, but something is wrong with the solar panels, or I don't know how to properly use them. Bob is the expert with those things."

The participants in the bushes continue vomiting with deep, savage, retching sounds. Frank goes from participant to participant, focusing his camera on their faces and the blasts of liquid coming from their mouths. My eyes shift to Ada, and I deeply worry about seeing her in such a condition.

"Did you say they all got sick at the same time?"

"Yes. It was almost like clockwork."

"When did it happen?"

"They had an early lunch, stew with javelina and yams, then they got ready for filming, and it happened."

"Did you eat some of the stew?"

"No. Frank and I ate tuna sandwiches."

I think for a moment. "This can't be stomach flu. Perhaps the javelina got spoiled."

June looks up at me. "Then, what about Bob, Carlos, and Diego. Diego got sick one day when he ate ravioli, and Bob and Carlos the next didn't eat javelina."

"Was it the water?"

"It can't be. The production team has bottled water, and the participants boil water from the lagoon."

"We need to do something," I exclaim.

I bend down and put my hand on Ada's back. "How are you doing?" I ask.

She moans, "My stomach hurts like crazy."

"Did you throw up?"

"Not yet.

"Did you eat as much stew as the others?"

"I wasn't all that hungry, so I ate very little. I had other things on my mind." Ada smiles slightly.

"I wasn't hungry either, as there were some important things to think about."

Ada's smile widens.

June looks at us. "What's so important?"

"Our secret," I say. When looking at the participants, I think of something I learned from my village in Guyana. "I'll be back in ten or fifteen minutes but get some water boiling. We will need a lot of water."

I rush from the camp and sprint for the bluff. Coco runs ahead of me, excited about this new game, which is anything but a game.

Fifteen minutes later, I return with large branches of leaves from *cordoncillo negro* shrubs. I had seen them growing in the dry areas on top of the bluff. In Guyana, we know them as *mantico*. The leaves are chewed to treat digestion problems like vomiting and dysentery or rubbed over cuts as an antiseptic.

Going to each person, I give them leaves to chew and then hand several leaves to June to put in the boiling water. When someone became sick from bad food in our village, they chewed these leaves and drank them as tea.

The participants sit on the dirt while chewing the leaves. Roger and Harry seem worse off than the women. I suspect they ate more stew than the others.

I go to Roger and ask how he is doing, and Frank yells at me. "Bookie, stand back. You are ruining the shoot."

"Frank, you're a birdbrain," I say. I put my hand on Roger's shoulder and ask, "How's it going?"

"My stomach got hit by a freight train."

"Keep chewing the leaves. Then, spit them out and chew some more when the taste is gone. Tea is coming."

I go to June and ask, "Do you have proper cups for drinking tea?"

"Yes, at the production team camp. I'll get them and start boiling water on our camp stove. We have plenty of drinkable water, so let's stop using water from the lagoon."

June rushes away, and I go to the participants asking each one how

166

they are doing

Frank continues to film close-up shots and then steps back for a wide-angle. He says, "This is fantastic, the most dramatic scene ever for a Naked Fear show. Our audience will love it. We need a good extraction scene now, and this show is good to go."

"Frank, why don't you help these people?"

Frank says with a calm, controlled, almost spooky voice, "Bookie, I've told you many times you don't belong here. You know nothing of television drama. You possibly do a fine job of typing expenses into a computer, but beyond that, you are way out of your league. Now, step back and let a professional do his work." He raises his camera and pans across the survivalists who sit on the dusty ground hunched over.

I go to Ada and kneel next to her. Chewing a leaf, she asks, "What is this?"

"*Cordoncillo negro* leaves, but from where I come, we call it *mantico*. It has powerful medicinal properties, especially for stomach sickness."

"What do you mean, from where you come from?"

"I grew up in the jungles of Guyana, which make this island look like a manicured park."

"Guyana?" She groans.

"Yes. Please don't tell that to the others."

"Where's that?"

"On the northern side of South America, next to Colombia."

Ada smiles. "It looks like we have much to learn about each other."

"We have a lifetime together to do that."

"If I live," she says.

"You will. Chew the *mantico*. Tea is coming."

She bends over, hands on her stomach. "Thank you, Bartholomew."

I hesitate and, with a soft voice, say, "I love you, Ada."

She grins. "This is a strange time to get romantic. But it means the world to hear that. I'm amazed by you."

June arrives with water bottles and hands them out, and we spend the afternoon providing tea and *mantico* leaves. When stomachs are settled, we give them clothes and move them to the production team camp. The three women take the cots of Bob, Carlos, and Diego. Roger and Harry lie down on thick mats on the floor.

June and I stay busy while Frank retreats to the production tent.

He fiddles with equipment and downloads footage from the camera to the computer. When walking by the tent, I see him sitting in a chair, looking at a computer monitor. He has a smile of satisfaction, and I hear him chuckle.

In the evening, the survivalists' condition improves. There is no more vomiting, and the pain is less. Even so, June and I continue to serve tea. Eventually, they sleep, and June and I prepare a meal for ourselves. We take food from the supplies tent, cans of potatoes and sausages in tomato sauce, and heat them. I wonder if this will make us sick.

I open a can of cooked beef and give it to Coco, who is thrilled to receive gourmet food.

Frank does his own thing but moves his cot from the tent with the sick people to the equipment tent.

Around one o'clock in the morning, I find a mat and blanket and put them in the supplies tent to spend the night. June has her own tent, being the only female production team member. I lie on the mat, cover myself with the blanket, and put my head on my backpack. Then, I remembered Frank and his rifle threats. I don't trust him. So, I remove the pistol from my pack and put it near my leg to easily reach it, wondering if I'm being paranoid?

Out of caution, I get up, find a blanket amongst the supplies, put it on the ground just inside the tent's opening, and call Coco. "Sleep here," I say, patting my hand on the blanket. Coco immediately lies down, happy for the five-star treatment, and I'm glad to have a guard dog, knowing Coco doesn't like Frank.

Going back to the mat on the floor, I quickly fall asleep.

DAY 24

I sleep well beyond sunrise and stretch after rising from the mat on the floor. Sleeping there was okay but not as good as the bed at my hut. I wonder how the sick survivors are doing.

Coco is not on his blanket. He is always hungry in the morning, so I take a can of boiled meat from the food supplies and walk outside. It's a warm day and one that most people in the northern states of the U.S. would envy, where March can still be bitterly cold.

On one side of the production team campground, Carlos and Diego had fastened the corners of a long, wide tarp to four palm trees to give shade. Under the tarp is a table, chairs, camping stoves, and utensils where June is making coffee, and Coco sits close by, waiting for handouts.

Before going there, I peek inside the tent with the sick participants. They are all sleeping. My eyes are drawn to Ada, who peacefully sleeps on her side, an angelic look on her face. I hope the medicinal tea helped. My heart hurts for her.

Closing the tent curtain, I go to June, and she asks, "Coffee?"

"Yes, please. I need it."

She hands me a mug of fresh black coffee and asks, "How did you sleep?"

"I was out like a rock. How about you?"

"Troubled. In the middle of the night, I went to check on everyone. Roger and Harry felt feverish. I think the women are doing better."

That was bad news and good news. "Should we evacuate the two guys?"

"Let's see how they are doing this morning and then decide. I need to get the satellite phone working to contact Hollywood to see what they want. The phone needs to be charged. Do you know anything about solar panels?"

"Not much. I think that Roger has a technical background. Maybe he can help when he is able." I look toward Frank's tent. "Is Frank up yet?"

"At least an hour ago. As you know, he went to bed early."

"Where is he?"

"He took his camera to get videos of the island. He hoped to film birds and animals as dramatic inserts in the final cut."

"What do you think of him?" I ask.

June rolls her eyes. "I think less and less of him. It seems his reality is nothing more than filming scenes. He has lost all empathy."

I comment, "We saw that yesterday. He was most concerned about filming agony rather than trying to help anyone. Assisting others is outside his frame of reference. In fact, he seemed to show delight in their suffering."

"What do you think made them sick?"

"I would have said stomach flu because it appeared to have spread from Diego to Bob, Carlos, and the others. If that's the case, we are lucky not to have caught it. But I think it's something different, most likely from food or water. This sickness is a mystery. I'm sure the hospital in Panama City will discover the cause after doing tests on your team members."

"In the meantime, let's help these people."

Pandora emerges from the hospital tent and holding a hand to her head, she stumbles toward the bushes. She joins us a few minutes later and groans, "Morning."

"How do you feel?" June asks.

"Dizzy."

June puts her hand on Pandora's forehead and says, "I don't think you have a fever."

"Maybe not, but my guts have gone through a microwave, and someone beat my head all night with a sledgehammer."

"Sit down," I say. "Can you drink some tea?"

"Tea? Do you mean that bitter medicine drink you forced on us?" She slowly lowers herself onto a chair.

"Either that or real tea," I say.

"Black tea would be great."

June pours boiling water over a tea bag in a mug and hands it to Pandora, who then waits for it to cool. "Thank you," she says, looking back at the hospital tent. "How is Roger doing?"

"I checked him this morning," June says. "He felt hot. I wish we had the medical kit because it contains a thermometer."

"What do you think happened to it?" I ask.

"I have no idea. Carlos was responsible for it. He probably put it somewhere, and now it can't be found."

"It's a pity."

Pandora asks, "What was that stuff you gave us?"

"In Central and South America, it's called *mantico*, named after the Spanish explorer who discovered the tree. He used it as an antiseptic. It has many other names but is commonly used to treat digestion problems.

Pandora sips the tea, takes a breath, and says, "Bookie, I completely misjudged you. I apologize for being malicious by calling you nothing more than a useless wanderer. It was unacceptable. Obviously, you know more."

I nod.

"But how do you know these things?"

Avoiding the question, I deflect and say, "Beliefs can be based on false assumptions."

She smiles. "So, you won't tell me. What I've seen is that you out survived all of us. And you kept us fed when we were unable to do so. You are a welcome mystery, and I suspect your magical potion may have saved our lives. Thank you for all you have done."

"Now, you need to rest," I say.

Pandora shakes her head. "I can't. I want to see how Roger is doing."

"I'll go with you," June says.

They walk to the hospital tent, and I finish my coffee. I want them all to get well, but my primary concern is Ada. That sickness was nasty, and it will take time to recover.

After several minutes, June comes out of the tent and says, "Ada and Wilma are getting up. Harry and Roger are still sleeping, and it feels like Roger still has a fever. Pandora wants to stay with him."

"He needs to keep drinking the mantico tea," I state. "It will wash the poison from his body."

June sits down and remarks, "What Pandora said was correct. When they started to fall apart, you raised them up. That wasn't in the script. The bookkeeper was supposed to tap out after a few days, but I don't care if that didn't happen. So why did you stay?"

"I don't know. First, I made a promise to you to stick around. Then, I didn't like to see what was happening to the survivors. It's one thing to watch this on a television show, but the reality is different. It involves real people and real suffering. So irrespective of the show's success, I wanted to do what was right for them."

"We only have four days before extraction. Do you think we will make it?"

"Does it really matter? If we leave today, back at the Naked Fear studios they can make this show look any way they want, whether twenty-eight days, thirty days, or whatever. Television viewers can never verify how many days we were on this island. It looks like you now have enough footage to make a show."

"Then, why don't we pack up and go home? I'm ready to get on with my new life."

"Me too, but I still don't know what that is."

"Are you sure about that?" June asks.

"What do you mean?"

"I see how you and Ada look at each other."

"Is it that obvious?"

She laughs. "Maybe the others don't see it, but for me it is clear as day. Isn't Ada somehow a part of your future?"

"It's a possibility," I say.

"You are discrete, that's for sure." She grins.

"And what about you? Have you given further thought to where you go from here?"

"You challenged me. I will look for an organization that restores people rather than putting them in degrading, punishing conditions. It probably involves a drop in salary, but the reward will be greater."

"Whatever you do, you will be good at it, for I've seen how you operate."

"Thank you, Bartholomew."

Ada and Wilma emerge from the tent, squinting their eyes in the morning sunlight. I'm delighted to see Ada, even though she looks like she has been through a hurricane.

"Uggh," Ada says. "What happened?"

Wilma shakes her head. "Was it food poisoning? Maybe that pig meat sat in the pot too long."

Their questions are right on the money. What caused this? If it is a stomach bug, will June and I catch it? Somehow it seems different than a virus, and it certainly doesn't have the characteristics of amebiasis with constant diarrhea.

June and I help Ada and Wilma walk to the shady area, where they sit in chairs. I'm glad to see them up but concerned about their health. Whatever they caught, the symptoms may last longer than twenty-four hours. Ada's face looks gray in the morning light. June prepares tea for them.

"Get some rest today," I say.

"Do we have a choice?" Ada smiles.

"Probably not. Is there anything we can do for you?"

"Pray."

Grinning, I say, "I can do that."

There is noise on the edge of the camp, and Coco raises his ears. Frank emerges from a jungle path. He whistles a simple tune, happy birthday to you, but way off key.

Walking to us, he smiles and says, "Good morning."

I nod, and no one answers.

Frank says, "We are doing good. I need one more shoot, along with extraction day. After that, this show will be exceptional."

"What do you mean, one more shoot?" June asks.

"We need to see the survivalists back at their camp recovering from this illness. The drama from that sickness is fabulous, with all of them becoming ill simultaneously. We have never had anything like this. The television viewers will be captivated, wondering if anyone will complete the challenge. I need a scene with ultimate drama, maybe to have one survivor get angry and tap out. Then the remaining few will victoriously walk to the extraction point."

"Is that all you think about?" I ask. "We have some very sick people here. Don't you care?"

"Bookie, I keep saying you have no reason to be in this business. The entire purpose of this show is to exhibit maximum suffering and then to answer whether they will survive. There will be hardship and sickness along the way. It's normal and expected. Then, only the resilient make it, and the viewers vicariously experience the victory as our naked winners bounce away in the back of a truck or boat at the end of the show. Let's be grateful for the sickness that swept through this camp. Otherwise, without it, the show would be a flop."

Ada shakes her head. "So, do you want people to endanger their health for television viewers, even long-term?"

"It's the risk you sign up for when you come on this show."

"It's not worth it," Ada says.

Frank looks in the direction of the hospital tent. "Are the others ready for a shoot today?"

"You won't get it," I say.

Frank smiles. "Bookie, you're too pessimistic. Believe me, I will get one more dramatic scene. They must appear to be emaciated and broken. It will be fantastic."

June says, "As the show coordinator, I decide what happens."

Frank sneers. "June, you've lost it and need to step aside. We will get that shoot, and these sick puppies have no negotiation in this. Sick or not, we need the scene. Don't worry. I will tell them what to say and how to act." He walks away to the tent containing the technical equipment.

"That guy lives on a strange planet," I state, sensing that Frank is unhinged.

* * *

June and I deal with the participants for the rest of the morning. Ada and Wilma return to their cots and sleep, whereas Pandora seems in the best shape. She sits by Roger putting a cool cloth on his forehead and occasionally wiping off his sweaty body. Harry sleeps, but he doesn't seem to have a fever.

Around noon, Harry is up, and we give broth and crackers to the sick participants, except for Roger. It's almost like he is in a coma. June tries to charge her phone, but the solar panels are still not working. The best thing would be to fly Roger to a hospital on the mainland.

After lunch, I come to a decision. It is essential to speak with our bosses in Hollywood because they need to take urgent action, and there are two choices to contact them. The first is to run the speedboat to Isle Pedro Gonzalez and make a call from there. Or, even quicker, take the speedboat to the guesthouse and ask them to use a phone. Of course, going to the guesthouse is not a pleasant thought, but probably the best alternative.

After discussing the options with June, I go down to the speedboat and realize the key is missing. Who was the last one to use the boat?

With the motorboat not running, I consider sailing the Luz to Isle Pedro Gonzalez. However, the round trip is five or six hours, depending on the wind. We might even put Roger in the Luz and take him to Isle Pedro Gonzalez, where we could arrange a medical extraction. Still, the risk of taking him on the boat might be too high.

Walking to the guesthouse is a quicker option, so I decide on the guesthouse.

After explaining my plan to June and commanding Coco to stay with her, I head off through the jungle. It takes fifty minutes to get to the hill to the south, where I use my binoculars to observe the buildings. Then, I crouch down behind a bush and see the two caretakers sitting in chairs in front of the main guesthouse.

These men make me nervous, as I remember the last time I was here. How should I approach them?

They drink beer from bottles, and the taller one laughs, his white teeth showing under a dark mustache. The smaller man raises his beer bottle to salute the larger man and then puts the bottle to his lips. There is a white wrapping around his right hand, where Coco's fangs did their business. Dog saliva is nasty. Did it leave an infection?

Then, I'm surprised to feel something press against my side and a hot panting breath on my face as Coco licks my cheek. His tail wags in joy to see me, but my heart drops. The dog shouldn't be here. I was an idiot to have left him loose at the camp. Indeed, he picked up my scent and tracked me here.

I attempt to put my arm around Coco to calm him down, but he skittles around, lifts his nose in the air, sniffs something, and immediately runs toward the guesthouse. My stomach tightens, and I could kick myself for being so stupid. With all that was happening back at the camp, I wasn't thinking straight. My mind was on Ada, worried about her and the others.

Coco approaches the terrace and barks. Then, he immediately charges at the shorter man and viciously bites his lower leg. For some reason, that man is Coco's mortal enemy. Both men are surprised, and the smaller man yells out a stream of words in Spanish that are difficult to discern. Then, he reaches down and attempts to lift his semiautomatic pistol, but he fumbles it because of the wrapping on his injured hand. He grabs the gun, lifts it, and awkwardly fires it in the air. Coco dodges around the building, having enough sense to run. The man stumbles forward, follows Coco, and fires the gun off balance, emptying the clip. Miraculously, Coco isn't hit with a bullet. Instead, the dog runs in my direction as the man reaches into his pocket, pulls out another long clip, and exchanges it with the empty one.

Why does Coco have such a deep hatred for that man?

I'm not sure if the man saw me, but as Coco disappeared into the bushes, the man aims toward me and sprays the trees with bullets. Crouching, I hurry down the opposite side of the hill and sprint into the jungle. I suppose I could have fired back at him with the pistol in my backpack, but it would be difficult to hit anything at that long distance. And in any case, it is not my objective to get into a gun battle with them.

I sprint a hundred feet and then jog on a small path winding through the undergrowth. Coco joins me and in less than an hour we are back at the production crew camp.

"How did it go?" June asks.

Out of breath, I describe what happened and tell her we must be careful. We don't know why these men are so hostile, but it leaves an awful taste in my mouth. We need to get off this island, but there is a problem. "What about Roger?" I ask.

June smiles. "His fever broke, and he drank some tea. Hopefully, he is recovering."

"I'm happy to hear that."

"Let's prepare them a meal," she says.

In the late afternoon, June and I serve broth and crackers to the participants. Pandora is recovering better than the rest, and Roger is still wiped out but awake and conversing.

We all go to bed when night falls, but I have difficulty sleeping. The thought of those bullets buzzing over my head is disturbing. Why are these men so unfriendly, and why do they trigger a reaction with Coco?

The other concern is Frank's insistence on doing another shoot. He seems happy the survivors are sick, and that worries me. I'm glad

Coco is curled up on his blanket at the entrance of my tent.

DAY 25

I am the first one up in the morning, and June appears from her tent soon after. She goes to the camp stove, boils water, and makes tea and coffee. The survivors exit slowly from their tent, and Roger is the last to emerge. He is uneasy on his feet and keeps a hand on Pandora's shoulder for support.

When Ada sees me, she smiles, the pale gray gone from her face, and it's a relief to see she is doing better.

Everyone except Frank sits in chairs around the camp table, and June serves coffee. Frank is over at the survivors' camp and seems to be working on something. Breakfast consists of crackers with cheese squeezed from tubes, and the campers eat little.

I turn to Roger and ask, "How are you doing?"

With a slight grin, he says, "The world spins like a merry-go-round. All I need is music."

I smile. "You went through a rough patch."

"What was it, some kind of twenty-four-hour flu?" He asks.

"We're not sure. It seems something like food poisoning." However, that is not a plausible answer because Bob, Carlos, and Diego ate different food.

"I'll never ever eat javelina again," Roger exclaims. "The taste of javelina barf is still in my mouth."

I wait a minute, then ask him, "Do you know anything about solar panels?"

He frowns. "Why do you ask that?"

"I believe you once worked as an electrician for a phone company or something like that. The satellite phone needs to be charged, and the solar panels are not working. We need to call the Naked Fear film company in Hollywood to get us off this island."

"Why not take the boat?" He asks.

"The key is missing."

"Then, hotwire it."

I feel like an idiot. Despite all my survivor abilities, sometimes I omit some basics. I say, "With all that was going on, I hadn't thought of it. You're the expert. Can you help?"

"If a couple of you can help me get over to the boat, I'll do it, but first, more coffee. My head is ringing like a church bell."

Roger has lost weight, but one would still take him as a linebacker.

As Roger drinks his coffee, Frank comes into the camp. He laughs, "Well, it looks like the happy bunch is up and around. Are we ready for another shoot?"

"What are you talking about?" I ask.

"I need one last small shoot showing the recovery of the survivalists from that terrible illness. That's it. It will be less than two minutes in the final cut. So, you can do that."

"I'm not doing anything," Pandora states.

Frank glares at her. "Fine, we can just say you died from the sickness or had to be taken to the hospital. But that won't work. I spoke with Hollywood, and their lawyers are lining up, ready to take you to court, and you better respect the contract. This episode of Naked Fear was headed for disaster, but now we are back on track. I saved it. Just give me a short scene of you emerging from your shelters. You need to act like you are recovering from sickness, and I will tell you what to say."

"Okay, two minutes, and that's all you get," Pandora says with fiery eyes.

Around the table, the other survivalists nod their heads, except for Ada. I suspect they are so beat down they would agree to anything.

Frank smiles like he's running a victory lap. And then says, "Of course, there is the final extraction scene. That should only take ten or fifteen minutes of filming."

Roger shakes his head. "Let's talk about that."

"One step at a time," Frank states.

June says, "Frank, we have enough footage to make three shows. So let's call it quits. We need to get off this island." She glances at me, and I know she is thinking about the men at the guesthouse.

"It would be better to complete the twenty-eight days," he says.

"No, we need to get off the island today."

"Fine," Frank says. "I'll see you all at your campsite in an hour." He jabs his finger in the air in the directions of the participants' huts, and then storms away and disappears into the tent with the technical equipment.

Roger says, "Let's go to the boat."

Harry and I stand on either side of Roger, and he supports himself by holding onto our shoulders, and we slowly walk to the boat. Roger goes to the control panel, and with my hunting knife, he pops open the fiberglass covering. He carefully considers the wiring, detaches three wires, and uses my knife to cut off the insulation. Roger touches one wire to another, and nothing happens. He tries again with no success.

"I think the battery is dead," he says.

Roger moves to the back of the boat, removes a cover, and looks at the battery. "Can someone find a wire or metal long enough to stretch across the battery pins?"

"Will a machete work?" I ask.

"Perfect," he says as he drops onto a seat in the boat.

I jog up to the camp, find a machete, and bring it back to Roger. He lays the machete across the battery and touches the two pins. There is no spark.

"It's dead," he says. "We can try and charge it with the solar panels."

"That's what I mentioned earlier," I say. "They are not working. Can you check them out?"

"I guess," he says, "but I'm not doing well." Then he leans over the side of the boat and vomits.

I look at Harry and say, "Let's get him back to the tent."

This time we carry him. I'm glad Harry is here because Roger is a heavy man.

We get Roger back to his mat on the floor, and he curls up, shuts his eyes, and goes to sleep. Pandora enters the tent carrying a wet cloth and wipes Roger's sweaty forehead.

Harry and I leave the tent, and Frank emerges from his tent and yells, "Everyone to the survivors' camp. Lights, camera, action."

"Roger isn't doing well," I tell Frank.

"What?"

"He had a relapse."

"How bad is it?"

"He's sleeping and feels warm."

Frank grins. "This could be a first."

"What do you mean?"

"Imagine if someone was on the point of death and even succumbed. That has never happened in one of our shows. The viewers will love it, and the show's ratings will skyrocket. The publicity will be enormous on the internet with a zillion social media sites debating it."

To clarify his thinking, I ask, "Are you talking about the death of someone?"

He smiles. "You said it and I didn't. I used the word imagine, but this could be fantastic. What eventually happens to Roger is beside the point. We could leave it a mystery to the viewers, as though the show is hiding something."

"Isn't the storyline up to June?"

"June is hopeless. I'm sure Hollywood will go with my scenario. But I must work on this." Frank disappears into his tent.

Harry says, "This guy is crazy."

I nod.

We go back to the camp table and sit down.

June brings us mugs of coffee and asks, "How did it go."

I explain about the dead battery and Roger's condition. "Without the solar panels, we are stuck," I say. Then, I have an idea, to sail the Luz to Isla Pedro Gonzalez and make a call. "Can you give me the phone number of the Naked Fear office in Hollywood?"

She says, "I just remembered something. Today is Sunday, and the office is closed."

"Do you have the personal number of the producer?"

"I do, at least for his work phone, but he plays golf on weekends and always turns off his phone."

"Maybe there is someone else?"

"I have personal numbers for some people in the office."

My only option is to sail the Luz and make a call, but first, I want to check out the solar panels. The two large panels are next to the technical tent, so I examine them. On one of the panels, several wires are frayed and disconnected. It's the same on the second one.

Frank charges out from his tent and asks, "What are you doing?"

"We need the solar panels to charge the satellite phone and the battery on the boat."

"Are you an electrician?"

"No."

"Then, I wouldn't mess with this. You could cause damage worth thousands of dollars."

"Are you suggesting saving the solar panels is better than having someone die out here?"

Frank glares at me. "Roger is a tough guy. He won't die." Then, he walks over to Harry and Wilma and says, "Go get Pandora and go to the survivors' camp. I need to film a scene."

I turn to the solar panels, wondering how Frank is able to charge the camera's battery unless he has backups. After analyzing several frayed wires, some seem to have been cut. What caused this? Is it possible an animal chewed on the wires? Using my hunting knife, I peel off the plastic at the ends of the wires and then connect red to red, blue to blue, and yellow to yellow. And then, I do this for the second panel. Catching June's attention, I ask her to put the satellite phone in the charger in the equipment tent where Frank is working on his scenes."

She comes out with a smile on her face and says, "It's charging."

"How long will it take," I ask.

"An hour or two. That phone needs a lot of power."

"Okay, let's wait." This means I don't have to sail the Luz, as I'd rather stay here to give help if needed.

June and I return to the camp's kitchen, and she makes more coffee.

Five of us sit around the table, June, Harry, Wilma, Ada, and me. Ada asks, "Do you think we can leave this island today? I've had enough of the place."

"Me too," Wilma says.

June replies, "Once the phone works, I'll call Hollywood, and we can get the wheels turning. We planned the extraction for you to walk through the jungle to a beach on the island's southeast side, where the speedboat would meet you, and then we take you to the airport. Ideally, we should have about ten minutes of footage to complete the filming, and I hate to admit it, but Frank is right on this one. But, at this point, I really don't care. With the state of health of all of you, I'd rather leave this place as soon as possible. And there may be other dangers."

"What dangers," Ada asks.

June looks at me as if waiting to see if I tell them about the men in the guesthouse.

I nod and say, "I had an incident, but I am not sure it concerns us." Then, I describe going to the guesthouse and getting shot at.

"That's weird," Wilma says.

"Maybe they are protecting the guesthouse from thieves or vandals," Ada states.

"It could be that," I say, suspecting it is something more.

June says, "Let's not worry about them, but we should do our best to pack up and leave. Your passports and clothing are in plastic bags in the supply tent. You can go and get your things. Once you leave, I will need to stay here to supervise a team of people to pack up the tents and equipment."

"I wish you could leave with us," I say.

"Me too, but I want to fulfill my agreement with the film company."

We spend the rest of the morning talking, and at one point, Ada and I walk over to the beach. Coco follows us. We sit under the shade of a palm tree and talk.

"How are you feeling?" I ask.

"Much better," she replies.

"I was worried about you and the others. When we took Diego to the airport, he was in terrible shape, and I hoped you would not also get sick."

"That sickness was anything but pleasant, and my brain still feels like someone went through it with a grinder." Finally, she looks at me and asks, "Do you have any thoughts on where we go from here?"

I smile. "I'm trying to get my head around that one. Living here on this island is different than the world back there. I feel we need to spend time with each other to get to know each other rather than rushing into our professional lives." I pause. "Isn't it strange to make the commitment we did with such little knowledge of each other?"

"Do you have doubts?" She asks, her head tilted with a furrowed brow.

"I'm just asking if this is what you want."

She smiles. "Of course. We both know this is right. Seeing how mysterious you are, it may take a lifetime to know you. Still, I'm looking forward to the adventure."

I laugh. "I'm not that complicated, but definitely, we will have an adventure." This makes me think of my parents, medical missionaries, who stuck with each other through all the joys and challenges.

We stare out at the turquoise sea. Ada asks, "So, you are sure about this?"

"One hundred percent. Quit asking."

We laugh, and I lean across and kiss her.

She pulls away from me and says, "I have a headache."

"This time, that excuse may work, but please don't use it in the future."

She grins. "Believe me, I won't."

We talk and describe our upbringing, and I tell her about growing up in Guyana. She grew up on a ranch in Texas close to the Gulf of Mexico. That's where she learned survival skills, and with the sea so close, she learned to sail. After going to university, she decided to do other things than ranching. She left that to her older brother, who works with her parents. Ada developed a social media business by chance, but she wants to do something more. She has been fortunate to have good parents who taught her the value of work, personal responsibility, and the meaning of human life. Those are based on the foundation of an almighty, loving God and His eternal order. Ada and I sing from the same song sheet, which is good.

We return to the campsite, and I ask how the phone charging is going.

"Very slow," June remarks. "It's barely at five percent."

"Maybe only one of the solar panels is working," I say.

"At least it's charging," she replies.

We eat lunch, and everyone takes a nap. The sick survivors need it. By mid-afternoon, everyone is up, including Roger, and they agree to make a two-minute shoot with Frank. However, Wilma and Pandora complain about walking around nude in front of Frank and vow to never do it again. This leads to an argument between Frank and Pandora about making the final extraction scene.

The phone is fully charged by late afternoon, and June calls Hollywood. After trying to get through to several people, she eventually talks with someone on the production team. June stands off to one side of the clearing, and it is not easy to hear her conversation.

Finally, she returned to us and says, "The Production Manager wants us to spend another night, as he needs to discuss this with the other decision-makers. It's Sunday, so no one is available today. The question is whether we wait for them. Should we leave the island now or wait for tomorrow? I could bypass them and call a company in Panama City, and we might get a boat over here by this evening. Please tell me what you want to do?"

"We need to shoot the extraction scene," Frank says. "There should be no discussion."

Pandora sneers at Frank and says, "You can take your extraction scene and shove it." Then, she turns to Roger and asks, "How do you feel?

"Better," he says. "I'm not sure I can survive a boat ride to the mainland. So staying here for a bit longer would do me good."

Pandora turns back to us and declares, "He needs rest."

June says, "I suggest we spend the night and then leave tomorrow."

Frank interjects, "There's no other choice. First, we need the extraction scene, and then we can arrange transportation."

Because of Roger's condition and not wanting to go on a boat, we all agree to spend one more night on the island. After that, I could care less about Frank's extraction scene, and I believe the others feel the same.

We make dinner, and the sick survivors eat small portions. Tomorrow, we leave this place.

DAY 26

I am up early before dawn, go to the beach, strip down, and swim while Coco wildly digs in the sand. It's odd to think we will leave this island today, just as strange as arrival day when I awkwardly stood in front of two beautiful women. The purpose was to survive, and I feel satisfied achieving that objective. There was both skill and luck in this. The luck was finding the sailboat providing things that made life easier. The Luz gave me mobility, and the money on the boat enabled the purchase of clothing and provisions. Even without that, I am confident I would have survived this event.

Even more important than surviving, there is the reality that one of those beautiful women will become my life partner, my wife. That's a strange thought, but true. I've seen how Ada managed throughout this event, showing strength and compassion, even during times of hostility. How people go through stressful events tells a lot about their true character.

What was astonishing was to see changes in the others. Pandora went from tyrant to leader to caregiver. While beginning as antagonists to each other, she and Roger now show affection. June made a critical life decision to leave the film company. She is a lovely, beautiful woman with leadership capabilities, and I hope the best for her.

Harry and Wilma were strong through this challenge, and except for Harry's fight with Roger, he became a stalwart. Wilma is a survivor, quiet and thoughtful.

The only negative was Frank. He emerged as a despot. In the beginning, He delighted in filming suffering nude female survivalists. As the challenge went on, he came out as someone with a bizarre personality, showing little empathy for others. He perceives reality through a camera lens, and he continues to puzzle me, especially after seeing how he reacted to the sick participants. It's almost as though he found joy in their misery.

It's troubling that Bob, Carlos, and Diego left in a sick state. I hope we have news of them once getting to the mainland.

Today's task is to get out of here.

I look at Coco with his nose buried deep in the damp sand as he sniffs for something. What's going to happen to the dog? I can't leave him here. In fact, I've grown attached to him. He provided welcome company during a time that might have been lonely. Is it fair to bring him into my uncertain life? At least I can find him a good home, although it would be hard to see him go. One becomes attached to animals.

I get dressed, head toward our camp, and hear a boat's motor. Coming from the north, I see a speedboat and recognize it as the one from the guesthouse. My stomach tightens. Knowing the men in that boat dislike Coco, I walk with the dog into the jungle.

In a small clearing, I take Coco's homemade leash from my backpack, and tie him to the base of a strong branch. Then, opening my last bag of jerky, I put all of it in front of Coco, and he gladly gets to work, gulping down the meat.

Then, I take the pistol from my backpack, place it behind my back, hidden by my t-shirt, and sprint to the camp.

The two men from the guesthouse approach the camp just as I get there. They left their boat next to our boat in the small harbor. Each man carries a weapon, the smaller man holding a semiautomatic pistol, and the taller one with the black mustache and green hat carrying a rifle. The smaller man has a wrapping around his right hand and walks with a slight limp. It's good that I left Coco tied up.

June and Ada are at the camp stove heating water, and Roger, Harry, Pandora, and Wilma emerge from their tent. Frank comes from his tent, holding his camera to his side.

"Good morning," I say to the men.

"Buenos Dias," the one with the automatic pistol answers.

"Do you speak English?" I ask.

"We speak," he answers.

"Can we help you?"

Both men take a moment to look at us more closely. Eventually, the one with the pistol says, "Have you seen a man with a dog around here?"

All those in my group look at me.

"What do you mean?" I ask.

"There is a man from Colombia on this island. We found his camp, and he should not be here."

"What does he look like?" I ask.

"He is brown-skinned, mestizo."

I feel relief. They are not looking for me. I say, "We haven't seen a man like this, although a dog sometimes wanders into our camp from time to time. May we know why you are interested in him?"

"The Colombian is dangerous. You should immediately leave this island."

Frank speaks out. "We can't do that. There's work to be done. A contract was signed with the owner of this island that we can film here."

Both men stare at Frank, and the one with the pistol says, "I told you to leave."

Frank scowls back at him. "Sorry, pal, but we are going to stay."

I look at June, and she raises her eyes.

The man with the rifle points it at Frank, and the other says, "Leave now."

Frank raises his camera and begins to film the two men. Does he believe that will give him magical protection from a bullet? He moves forward and then circles the two men to capture the entire scene with everyone in it.

"Don't film us," the man with the pistol commands.

Frank continues moving to the side.

The second man steps toward Frank, and with the barrel of his rifle, he knocks the camera from Frank's hand. Then he fires several bullets into the camera, with loud bangs, metal pinging, and glass shattering.

Frank stands frozen as though unable to believe what just happened. Then, in anger, he charges toward the two men, and the taller one with the rifle slams the rifle butt into the side of Frank's head. Frank flops to the ground like a rag doll. He stays still, mouth full of sandy dirt. I'm glad the man used the rifle butt, for if he had shot Frank, we might all be in grave danger.

"He is *muy loco*. Get off the island today," the smaller man commands, waving his pistol back and forth.

The two men walk away from us, and as they get to the solar panels, they look back at us and then riddle the solar panels with bullets. The one with the automatic pistol steps into the equipment tent and empties his gun, sounds of breakage filling the air. He yells out, "Leave now," as he loads his pistol with another clip.

Our group is shocked as we watch the men go to their boat. Before leaving, the taller man with the rifle puts several bullets into our boat's motor.

We stand looking at each other as they speed away to the north. I quickly consider if I did the right thing. There is a pistol stuck in my pants behind my back. If I had been on my own, I might have tried to use it, but not today. It would have put our group in danger.

June goes to Frank, who is still out cold on the ground. Roger, Harry, and I carry him inside the equipment tent, put him on his cot, and June fetches water. My heart sinks when I see the satellite phone with a bullet hole in the screen. The laptops and electronic gear were blown to pieces. That likely means the entire shoot over the last twenty-six days is destroyed. Frank and the show's producers will go berserk.

Now, there's a question for which I don't have an answer. How can we get off the island with the phone and boat out of commission? Those two men with the guns weren't thinking straight.

While June attends to Frank, I go outside the tent and walk over to Frank's camera. It will never be used again. Frank's film bag lies near the camera as it fell off his shoulder when the man hit him with the rifle. I open it and pour the contents onto the ground, and I'm surprised to see the key to the speedboat and a pair of pencil-nosed wire cutters.

More disturbing is a plastic bag with shiny green leaves. The leaves are finely serrated, and the bag contains a few greenish-yellow flowers. They are very familiar to me. They come from the manchineel tree. The Caribs of the Caribbean make poison from the tree's sap for the tips of their arrows. It has a fruit that looks like an apple, and in Central America, it is known as the *manzanilla de la muerte,* or little apple of death. It is one of the most toxic plants in the world.

My heart sinks, and pieces of the puzzle come together. Those leaves explain the illness that went through this camp, and everyone is lucky to be alive. I suspect that Frank knew about the properties of this tree, and he experimented with them. Diego was the first, and he received the most potent dose. We had difficulty getting him to the airplane, and I hope he is still alive. Manchineel is bad news and nothing to play around with. Bob and Carlos were second, and while quite sick, they were not as bad off as Diego. On the third day, it was the survivalists, and Frank's goal was to produce horrifying scenes for the show. Ada didn't eat as much as the others, so she was less sick. June and I were lucky not to have tasted the stew.

This confirms my theory that Frank is perverse, an evil person who has no feelings of right and wrong. His goal was to create something that television viewers would enjoy even by endangering the lives of others. It's appalling to know he did this.

The question now is, what to do with Frank? First, I need to show the evidence to June, and I'm afraid that if Roger and Harry learn about this, they will break Frank in pieces. Or Pandora would do it on her own.

June comes out of Frank's tent, and I ask, "How is he doing?"

"He's out cold. Wasn't he a fool to take on those men with guns? I was terrified."

"We have another issue to deal with. Can you come with me?"

She nods, and we walk away from the destroyed camera. And I tell her about what I found in Frank's bag.

"Are you sure about those poisonous leaves?" She asks.

"Absolutely. The natives in this part of the world treat that tree with utmost caution."

"What shall we do with Frank?"

"He needs to be turned over to the police in Panama. And I suspect he has broken U.S. laws, as he perpetuated dangerous acts against U.S. citizens, but I'm no lawyer. Someone needs to investigate this. Until the legal system is informed, Frank needs supervision. He might use a knife or other weapon. I suggest that Harry takes responsibility for him."

"Agreed," she says.

"We have another pressing problem."

"I know. It's how we get off this island," she states.

"Without a phone and the speedboat, I have an idea."

"What's that?"

"I can call the office in Hollywood or find some help from another island or the mainland."

"How will you do that?"

"Trust me. It will take anywhere from six to seven hours until I return. I'll ask Ada to go with me."

"Do whatever you can. We are in a terrible situation."

"We'll get out of it," I proclaim while not feeling confident.

We walk to the camp, and after reviewing my plan with Ada, she agrees to go with me. I was sure she would. Then, I go into the forest to Coco, release him, and bring him back to the camp, where June will watch him. Then, Ada and I head for the bluff. She walks more slowly than the other day, but seems to have strength enough to make this trip. We plan to sail the Luz to Isla Pedro Gonzalez to make phone calls and find help to get off this island.

* * *

Ada and I cross over the bluff, and where the trail branches off to my camp, I notice the footprints of two men.

"Let's go this way," I say, pointing to the small path on the right.

"What's there?" Ada asks.

"I need to check something out and want you to see it."

We follow the footprints leading into my camp. The hut is still intact, but some things are destroyed. My clothing is spread across the floor. One coffee mug is smashed. It's distressing when one's possessions have been ransacked, even if of little value.

"Is this where you lived?" Ada asks.

"Yes. It seems the two men from the guesthouse were here."

Ada looks around. "This is a five-star hotel compared to where we were living. Did you find this hut here?"

"I built it."

"And where did all these things come from?"

"Nearby islands."

"Bartholomew, you continue to astonish me."

"Don't get too astonished. The presence of those two men changes everything. I can never use this camp again. It's not a safe place anymore."

"It's another reason to leave this island."

"Certainly. Let's get the Luz."

We leave my camp, take the trail to the beach, and pass by my beach camp. Walking over the rocky breakwater, we follow the path to the thicket of mangroves.

When we get to the hiding place of the boat, my heart sinks. The Luz is gone.

"It's not here," I stammer, knowing we are stuck with no way off the island and no way to call for help.

"What happened?"

"It must be the two men. They found the boat and took it."

"It means we are their captives until they decide what to do with us," Ada states.

"It seems that way."

"What shall we do?"

There seems to be only one solution. "I need to find the Luz or someway off this island, but I don't want you to go with me."

"Will it be dangerous?"

"I'll do my best to avoid risks. Can you go back to the camp and tell everyone to be careful? We don't know what those men will do with us. I have theories, but it is only speculation at this point. Be cautious, and everyone there should hide in the jungle if the men show up. You know the paths well enough to disappear."

"I wish I could go with you," Ada whispers.

"You can't. Go help the others."

"How long will this take?" She asks.

"If the Luz is tied up over at the guesthouse, I will need to wait until the middle of the night before taking it. Then, I'll go to Isla Pedro Gonzalez and call for help. If all goes well, I should be back before noon tomorrow. Everyone must stay on guard."

"Okay." Ada hesitates and then gives me a tight hug. "Please be careful," she states.

She turns and walks toward the direction of the camp.

I hate to see her go, but I have no choice. What I told her about returning to the camp tomorrow is speculation. While it is a hopeful plan to get the Luz, there is no telling what I will find at the guesthouse.

I head northeast, weaving my way through jungle trails.

* * *

Reaching the small hill to the south of the guesthouse, I crouch down and peer over the edge, remembering the last time I was here. The sound of a semiautomatic pistol is frightening when aimed in your direction, and when bullets smash through trees above your head.

The guesthouse is quiet, with no one visible. Three boats are tied up at the dock, the guesthouse speedboat with the two large outboard motors, the *Sueño del Mar* catamaran, and the Luz.

Taking my binoculars from my backpack, I scan the buildings, imagining the best way to approach the dock in the middle of the night and sail away quietly. It is almost noon, and the air is still, and I wonder if there will be enough wind to propel the sailboat. Of course, taking the speedboat would be better, but will the key be in the ignition?

I reach into my backpack and sip from a bottle of water. This will be a long wait.

After an hour of sitting on the hill, I observe four men appear from the guesthouse, walk to the dock, and then go into the catamaran. A few minutes later, they emerge carrying large cardboard boxes. One of the men places a box on the deck, opens it, and pulls out a brown plastic bag about the size of a small loaf of bread. He opens a pocket knife, sticks the blade in the bag, and pulls it out. He wipes his finger across the knife and then puts his finger in his mouth. He laughs. The others join in the laughter, taking his knife and repeating what he did. The plastic bags contain cocaine, and they are sampling the goods.

They move the boxes to the black SUV and drive to the warehouse at the back of the property. After disappearing into the warehouse, they emerge carrying more boxes. Then, two men get into the SUV and drive on the road going toward the airport. They are the two that came to our camp. It's unclear why they move these boxes around and do they only contain cocaine?

The other two men go to lounge chairs on the terrace in front of the guesthouse, open bottles of beer, and relax in the shade. Each has a semiautomatic pistol.

It is impossible to get to the Luz during the day, and if those men sleep on the catamaran, I need to be especially cautious.

There is a faraway sound of a motor. Across the top of the trees, an aircraft approaches the island. It swings out over the water, descends, and then I lose sight of it because of the trees near the runway. The two men in the lounge chairs get up and walk to the warehouse.

The plane leaves, and ten minutes later, the SUV reappears and stops in front of the warehouse. The two guesthouse workers get out of the car, and another man gets out from the back seat. With my binoculars, I zoom in on the third man. He has blond hair. Somewhere I've seen him before. Then, I remember. This is Jim Olsen, the multibillionaire who recently bought this island. It confirms one of my theories that he is working with drug runners and explains where he got his fortune.

As he gets out of the car, something odd happens. An argument breaks out, and the two men point their semiautomatic pistols at Jim Olsen. As a result, Jim Olsen is roughly pushed into the warehouse.

From their body language, I suspect a long discussion will occur, which might give me a window of opportunity. There could be enough time for me to get to the dock, check the speedboat for a key, or sail away on the Luz. Of course, if it's the Luz, the motorboat will need to be disabled, so I'll cut the fuel line. But, taking the sailboat is a stupid alternative because it is slow, and the catamaran would quickly catch it.

I decide to at least check out the speedboat. After putting the binoculars in my backpack with the .38 pistol, I sprint down the hill to the dock. Then I move swiftly, attempting to not make running noises on the dock's wooden slats.

I quickly look into the speedboat and am disheartened seeing that the keys are not in the ignition.

At the foot of the dock, I notice movement, and a voice yells, *"Quédate donde estás,"* which means stay where you are, and there is the sound of a shot.

Crouching low on the dock, I raise both hands in the air.

* * *

The man with the automatic pistol leads me into the warehouse where Jim Olsen stands with the other three men.

The shorter of the two guesthouse workers asks, *"¿Qué es ésto?"* What is this? He seems to be the leader.

"Ask him," The man with the semiautomatic weapon responds with a Spanish accent.

The leader stares at me and says, "You were at the movie camp. I told you to leave the island. So why are you here?"

"You left us no choice," I say. "We found a bullet hole in our phone, so how can we call anyone? You shot holes in our boat's motor and took the blue sailboat."

"That sailboat belongs to our Colombian rival. We thought we had taken care of him, but we found his camp near a bluff south of the island. He and his dog are here somewhere."

"We have never seen this Colombian man, and the camp is mine. I found the boat and painted it."

He hesitates and says, "We will find out more about this. Now, stay here with him." He points at Jim Olsen. Then, looking back at me, he commands, "Put your backpack on the table and go into the room.

One of the men opens the door to a small storage room and waves his gun at us. We walk to the room, and I leave my backpack outside the room on a table. The door shuts, and there is the sound of a latch.

A little light comes into the room through a crack high in the wall.

"Who are you?" Jim Olsen asks.

"My name is Bartholomew, and I'm with the film crew on the south of the island. A couple of those men came to our camp early this morning and shot up our equipment, including a satellite phone. And they disabled our boat. Then, illogically, they ordered us to leave the island. It's a long swim. So, I came here looking for a solution." I paused. "Why are you being held like this."

"They demand a ransom."

"What for?" It was a stupid question.

"Before you arrived, they threatened my life, asking for millions."

"Why are you here?" I ask.

"I bought the island two months ago, sight unseen, with the idea of keeping it as a natural reserve. This is my first trip here, and I now realize it was foolish to come here without security. Only a few tourists used the guesthouse when the island was on the market. Caretakers were looking after it, only it seems the caretakers are not what I had assumed."

"Do you know what they do?"

"Obviously, they kidnap people."

"More than that. They are drug runners, and I'm guessing they have used this island for the past two years as a transfer point for drugs coming from Colombia. That's when the island was on sale, so the previous owner was not interested in this place. So they moved in as caretakers, which gave them control of the island, enabling them to bring the drugs up the coast and load them onto boats or planes headed north. The small private airport is an ideal place to serve their purpose."

"I'm shocked. How do you know this?"

"I've been here almost four weeks with the film crew and put the pieces together."

"Then, these are more than kidnappers," he says.

"They are evil people, and from what I've seen, they would kill you as easily as look at you."

"I'm sorry you got into this. When I bought the island, I was told that a television show would be filming here. I didn't like that idea, but the contract had already been signed by the island's previous owners." He hesitates. "What happens now?"

"Honestly, my guess is that our lives are in grave danger. It's unlikely they will let me live. They probably would have let our crew off the island if I had stayed in our camp. Now, I've seen you. They can't leave witnesses, which means our entire film crew will be wiped out unless something is done. And, even if they get ransom money from you, they can't let you live. Once we are all taken care of, they will disappear from this island and find another place."

"What can we do?"

I think for a moment. "We only have one solution. Would you agree to try and escape?"

"The odds are against us."

"I know. There are four of them, and they all have high-powered weapons. In my backpack on the table out there, I have a gun. If I can get to it, it's better than nothing."

"Let's try," he says.

Jim Olsen goes to the door and bangs on it with his hand. In a minute, the latch sounds, and the door slowly opens.

The smaller of the two caretakers, Coco's enemy, stands back from the door and points a rifle at us. Perhaps it is easier for him to handle a rifle with a wrapped hand than a bulky semiautomatic pistol. "What do you want?" He asks.

Jim says, "We have to pee."

The man hesitates and says, "Come," waving his weapon toward the large door of the warehouse.

At that moment, I see a white flash, and Coco bounds full speed into the open area. This time he is a welcome sight. Obviously, Coco left our camp, picked up my scent, and followed me here, exactly as before. He heads straight to the man with the gun and sinks his fangs into the man's leg, growling, shaking his body back and forth, and not letting go. The man screams in pain and drops his rifle when reaching for Coco. I take a step forward and connect my fist to the man's head with one well-placed punch, and he tumbles down and bounces off the floor. Coco growls and continues to bite the leg.

"Stop," I command Coco while rapidly grabbing my backpack and the man's rifle. From his pocket, I pull out a full clip of bullets. Then, with a quick glance at Jim Olsen, I say, "Let's run. Turn left for the jungle."

Jim sprints past me, and Coco joins him. It's not easy to keep up with them. Remembering his age from my internet search, Jim is twenty-two years older than me, but he seems to be in great shape. He runs half marathons. It's clumsy to run with a backpack and a rifle, but my Marine training is returning.

As we arrive at the road going north toward the airport, there is the cracking sound of gunfire. I glance back, and two men run in our direction. A third man, Coco's mortal enemy, emerges from the warehouse, limping, and he aims a semiautomatic pistol and fires. Additional guns must have been in the warehouse. Fortunately, his aim is off.

There is a large open area before we can reach the jungle, and we will be sitting ducks out there, so I yell, "Go to the bungalows."

* * *

A window shatters just behind my head when we reach the first bungalow. Their aim is perilously closer. We sprint around the side of the building. Jim seems ready to run to the next cottage, but there is open space between them, and we would be exposed.

"Wait here," I cry out while quickly reaching into my backpack and taking out the .38 pistol. "Do you know how to use this?" I ask.

"Yes," he says.

I give him the weapon, and he swiftly moves to the opposite end of the building's wall and cautiously peers around it. Coco's enemy sees me and fires his automatic pistol, bullets hitting the building. Splinters of wood skim my shoulder.

Coco stays next to me, somehow knowing not to attack the man.

Quickly pivoting my rifle around the building's corner, I return fire, and Coco's enemy goes down. The other two men scatter. There is another one somewhere.

Suddenly, I see movement as a man moves around the corner of the next bungalow. He swings his automatic pistol in our direction, and Jim crouches and fires my .38 pistol, and the bullet hits the man in the chest, and he stumbles and falls. Jim rushes to the man and picks up the automatic pistol.

There are two men left. I peek around the corner again and see a man attempting to hide behind a large palm tree. With a quick aim, I fire and hit the man's leg. He stumbles backward, gains balance, and limps between trees. It's the taller one of the original guesthouse workers. The remaining man grabs the injured man by the arm, and they disappear around the side of the guesthouse.

Turning to Jim, I ask, "Are you okay?"

"Yes, and you?"

"Good for now. There are two remaining men, and one is wounded. Hopefully, they will give up the fight.

Jim and I cautiously go to the beach in front of the bungalow, and we see the two men headed for the speedboat. One of them releases the tie ropes and helps the wounded man get into the boat. He puts the key in the ignition and starts the powerful motors. It takes a moment for the boat to gain speed, and then it takes off like a rocket.

I aim the rifle and fire off several rounds, and the boat driver realizes he is being shot at. Maybe a bullet hit him or the boat, but he yanks the wheel to the right attempting to zigzag to avoid incoming bullets. However, he turns too tight without reducing speed, and the boat suddenly flips, violently hitting the water with a loud crashing bang. It takes time for the water around the speedboat to settle, and a minute later, one of the men floats to the surface, face down. There is no sign of the second man.

Jim goes to a chair by the bungalow and sits down, and I join him, taking a second chair.

Jim shakes his head and asks, "What just happened? That was insane."

"Are you okay?"

"My legs are shaking."

"Take deep breaths and try and relax."

"Everything happened so fast," he whispers.

"You did well," I state.

"And you," he asks. "How are you?"

"I was in the Marines and saw horrible things. One might get used to it, but that's not the case. It's a shock the way things suddenly happened here. These men would have killed us, so we did the right thing."

Jim stares at the overturned boat in the water. "What do we do now?"

I don't have an answer. There are two dead men on land and two out in the water. In the warehouse are boxes of cocaine. How do we explain this? But then, I have an idea.

"I know someone who might help. He's a lawyer and despises these kinds of men. Is there a phone in the guesthouse?"

"That's what I was told."

"Let's go see."

Holding our weapons, we walk cautiously to the guesthouse and go inside. There is a large room with shiny wooden floors, a vaulted ceiling, and elegant furniture where high-net-worth people would relax. On one side of the room are a reception desk and an office. We go to the office, and Jim lifts the phone, which works.

I take out Enrique Colon's business card from the back pocket of my shorts and call his personal number. After three rings, he answers, saying, "Enrique Colon."

"Senior Colon, this is Bartholomew."

"Ah, Bartholomew. It is so nice to hear from you."

"I'm calling to ask advice, even for help. I need a lawyer."

After silence, Enrique says, "That is my business, and I would be pleased to represent you. What can I do?"

I give him a brief overview of what happened, and he tells me to not touch anything. He will immediately go to his airplane and fly to the island. He thinks he can be here in less than an hour.

After hanging up, I explain the phone call to Jim Olsen. He agrees, knowing his lawyers in Florida are far away.

Then he says, "Thank you for saving my life."

I smile. "And I have to say the same thing to you. You managed that pistol quite well."

"I have a gun permit in Florida and had training. I needed to know how to protect myself, which paid off. But honestly, you took the initiative to get out of that warehouse. You were a godsend. Can you tell me more about yourself?"

I give him a quick summary of my experience, starting with the Marines, university, working for the film company, and looking for my next step in life. I left out the part about Guyana, as that gets too complicated.

He asks, "So, what do you want to do?

What do you mean?

What do you want to do with your life?"

"My preference is to find something that helps people, which sounds nebulous."

Jim nods. "That's a good goal. You certainly helped me."

I ask, "Now that this has happened, what are your plans for the island?"

"Nothing changes. It will remain a wildlife sanctuary with no more permanent construction." He looks out at the dock. "When I purchased the island, a boat charter company came with it, including that catamaran and other sailboats. I was thinking of selling the charter company, for I certainly don't have the time to manage it."

"Are you sure you want to sell the catamaran?"

"Do you like it?"

"I enjoy sailing. Do you see that small blue-trimmed sailboat? It's mine." I laugh.

He pauses, then says, "Quite a contrast." Again, he takes his time. "Why don't you take the catamaran?"

"What do you mean?"

"I'd like you to have it."

"There's no way. That boat cost millions, and I couldn't afford it."

"It might sound arrogant, but that's not much for me."

"Pocket change?"

"I guess you could call it that, but I try to manage wisely. I want you to have the catamaran if you can use it. You saved my life."

"Not really. It was that thing that saved both our lives." I point to Coco. "Maybe he should get the boat."

Jim smiles. "I see your point. So let's pretend the boat is yours, knowing he's the true owner."

We laugh, maybe because of the aftershock, because we need some levity to help us through this situation. My legs still tremor. I'm overwhelmed and not sure what to do with it. Could I even afford to operate it? "Let's go take a look at it," I say.

We walk to the dock, go to the catamaran, and climb aboard. It is a magnificent boat, and I know it will require ongoing maintenance. We descend into the sizeable left hull, where a long walkway leads to bedrooms and a small bathroom. I open the door to one of the bedrooms and stand in shock.

"Please come here," I say to Jim. "We have another problem to think about."

Stacked from floor to ceiling are bundles of one-hundred-dollar bills.

Jim says, "It looks like they were running drugs north and transporting money south."

"Their bosses will want it back," I state. The cartel behind this has the resources to track us down, and everyone in our camp would also be in danger.

"Maybe your lawyer friend will have an idea," Jim says.

* * *

Enrique Colon taxis his airplane across the runway and parks it next to the SUV where Jim and I wait. He gets out of the aircraft wearing a lightweight beige suit and blue shirt without a tie. I make introductions and describe what happened at the guesthouse, going into detail. I don't want him to be shocked to see the bodies.

Then, I drive the SUV to the guesthouse, and Enrique doesn't seem bothered by the bodies when getting out of the car. Instead, his comment is, "Good riddance."

I'm still shaken when looking at the men on the ground, and I'm sure Jim feels the same.

Enrique wastes no time getting to work. He says, "Do you both agree that I will represent you legally?"

In unison, Jim and I say, "Yes."

"Good. I've had time to think about this when flying over here.

Here is the story of what happened, if you agree? Mr. Olsen arrived on his island today and found these men like this, and he called me asking for legal representation. After I arrived on the island, I did a careful examination of these buildings and discovered boxes of drugs in the warehouse. In determining the illegal business of these men, it's obvious they were in a gunfight with a rival gang. Did you say there were two men in a boat that capsized?"

"That's correct," I say.

"Those two tried to flee the rival gang, and something malfunctioned on the boat. It flipped over at high speed, and they drowned. It's as simple as that. If we give a different story, it will become dangerous for you. Your names might be published in the news, and drug cartels would be interested, and we don't want that. So it's best to blame it on a rival gang, which makes logical sense. A good friend of mine is the Chief of Police in Panama City. If I call, it may take time for him to get here. Do you agree to this explanation?"

Jim and I look at each other, and we nod.

"Then let me do the talking when my friend arrives here."

While Enrique embellishes the facts, he knows best how things work in this part of the world. We acted in self-defense, and while the outcome is horrible, Enrique is correct. Jim and I could be in danger. Our film team and the survivalists would also be in trouble, and I want to protect them. Enrique's advice must be accepted.

Enrique asks, "Do you have a phone in the guesthouse? Unfortunately, my cell phone doesn't get a signal."

Jim leads Enrique to the office in the guesthouse, and a few minutes later, they come out on the terrace where I am waiting.

"My friend is on his way," he says.

"There's one other thing," I say. "There is quite a lot of money in the catamaran. What shall we do with it?"

"How much?" Enrique asks.

"It has to be many millions," Jim says.

"That's interesting," Enrique answers. First, if the cartel wonders what happened to the money, it will be reported that a rival group took it. That's the official story. Regarding moving the money, the specialty of my office in Panama City is creating structures for managing funds. We form trusts and foundations. You could let the Panama Government have the money or consider directing it for a good cause.

Bartholomew, isn't that what you wanted to do?"

This is moving too fast. First, Jim gave me a high-end catamaran, and now Enrique is offering a foundation. I turn to Jim. "What do you think?"

Jim replies, "It's a good idea, but I shouldn't have any legal connection with it. So, you will have to deal with it on your own."

"Can you help in some way?" I ask.

"How's that?"

"The money needs to be invested, and I will need advice."

"Certainly. I can help with that."

"We must do something about the catamaran," Enrique says.

"What do you mean?" I ask.

"Surely, the cartel knows its name. I deal in Panama boat registrations and can arrange paperwork so no one can trace it. You need to think of a new name for the boat, and I have acquaintances at several boatyards in Panama where they can paint on a new name."

"Thank you for thinking of this," I say.

Enrique smiles. "It looks like we have solutions for all the problems." He pauses. "Bartholomew, you should not be here when my friend arrives. You don't fit in the story. Did you say your film crew was on the island's south side?"

"Yes."

"Then, please go."

"Okay, but there's another thing. Our film crew must leave the island tomorrow. Can you help with that?"

"I can do that," he says. "Be ready tomorrow morning."

"Oh, and there is one more thing where I could use your help, but I don't want to complicate things. I will tell you later." I wonder what to do about Frank, but right now I don't want to add more complexity.

Enrique smiles. "It sounds intriguing. Of course, I can help. I am your lawyer."

I thank Enrique and Jim and head to the Luz. Coco runs ahead of me and jumps into the boat as though he is at home. After untying the boat from the dock, I raise the sail and navigate to deeper water. Looking back at the guesthouse, Jim and Enrique wave, and I wave back. Floating next to the dock is the *Sueño del Mar*. It is a magnificent boat, and it's crazy to think it is mine. Jim made a quick decision to give it to me. Maybe it resulted from the aftershock of what happened, a form of Post-Traumatic Stress Syndrome. Or perhaps that's how some wealthy entrepreneurs operate, having quick minds that swiftly decide and act. Whatever the reason, I must figure out what to do with this catamaran.

What happened in the past few hours is unimaginable and will take time to absorb and process. It was a horrific experience, and I need to get back to the camp to check on everyone and reassure them that everything is okay.

* * *

After sailing south around the island with Coco next to me, I anchor the Luz in the small harbor near the camp. In a few minutes, the sun will set. Then, I wade to the shore as Coco swims ahead of me. When reaching the sand, he energetically shakes the water from his fur and then charges up the beach. I see why. Ada runs toward me, and when she reaches me, she almost knocks me over, hugging me tightly.

Slightly panting, she says, "Bartholomew, I was worried. You were gone a long time. I'm so glad you are back."

"It took time to make arrangements," I say.

"What happened at the guesthouse, and did you find a way to get us off the island?"

"Do you remember Enrique Colon, the man we met at the coffee bar by the beach in Isla Pedro Gonzalez?

"Of course, how could I forget him? He was the one who challenged us most extraordinarily." She smiles.

"He is arranging for us to get off the island tomorrow."

June, Pandora, Roger, and Wilma walk briskly down the beach. I assume Harry is with Frank. They approach us, and June says, "We were worried about you."

"Thank you, but I'm doing fine."

"Ada told us you were going to the guesthouse. Did you run into those two evil men?" June asks.

"They decided to leave the island."

"So, what did you do?"

"It took a while, but I arranged for us to leave here tomorrow morning."

"That's good news," Ada says.

When I asked Enrique to help us, I wasn't sure he would bring an airplane or a boat.

Roger points at the Luz and asks, "Where did you get the boat?"

"It was tied to the dock at the guesthouse."

Roger laughs. "I don't suppose we could all sail to Panama City in that."

"It would be tight," I grin. "How is Frank doing?"

"He's in his tent lying down, and he may have a concussion."

"Did you ask him about poisoning everyone?"

"Yes," June answers. "He confessed to that and cutting the wires on the solar panels. His strange reasoning is that the show was bound to be a flop, and we needed the illness's drama to make it the best show ever. And he swears his actions were noble, for the right reasons, and he would do it again. And he detests you. So the question now is what to do with him?"

"Tomorrow, we can decide. I know someone who may help." Certainly, Enrique and his police chief friend will have ideas. Legal action must be taken with three poisoned patients in a Panama City hospital and the sick people here. Frank committed a criminal offense, even though he doesn't see it that way. And, with his twisted method of reasoning, maybe he never will.

* * *

We go back to the beach by the camp and sit and watch the orange colors in the sky to the west, no one speaking, everyone lost in their own thoughts. Harry joins us. Frank is asleep.

This is our last night on the island, and I have mixed emotions. This has been an exceptional experience for all of us, a disperse set of personalities who started as antagonists and have now become friends.

Scenes from the day flash through my mind. It will take time to get over the trauma from what happened at the guest house.

Ada sits close beside me on the sand, leans against me, and it is fantastic to feel her presence. I never want to lose that.

DAY 27

By mid-morning, everyone is ready and waiting for our transport to leave the island. June needs to stay for one more day. It was prearranged that once the participants and cameramen left the island, a cleanup crew would clear the camp of tents and equipment. June will supervise their work.

We wait at the production team camp, and Ada asks, "How are we getting off the island?"

"I'm not sure," I reply.

Just as I say that the *Sueño del Mar* appears from around the island's southern tip. The sails are down, and the boat is powered by its motor. It turns and then navigates into the small harbor. Jim Olsen is in the front, and he waves.

"Is that how we are extracting?" Roger asks.

"It appears so," I reply.

Roger laughs. "You mean, no bumpy ride in the back of a jeep? This is a first-class extraction. That boat is a beauty."

June goes to Frank's tent and calls for him, and Frank comes out on wobbly legs. Harry moves beside him, and then we all walk to the harbor.

Two mid-sized, brown-skinned men expertly navigate the boat with its rudder and stern to the shore, then anchor it. They have the movements of experienced seamen.

Wearing shorts and a t-shirt, Jim hops into the water and wades ashore. He smiles, shakes my hand, gives me a solid man-hug, and says, "Bartholomew, how are you doing?"

"Just fine, and you?"

"It's a good day."

I introduce him to the group and see Jim's eyes fixed on June for a long moment. Then, he turns to the rest of us and says, "Are you ready for a boat trip?"

"For sure," Pandora replies.

"Well, get on board Bartholomew's boat," Jim commands.

"What do you mean, his boat?" Pandora asks.

"He is the owner," Jim answers.

The survivalists look at each other, spellbound.

Pandora turns to me and says, "Bookie, there's something weird about you. First, we saw how you came to this island with nothing. And then you were like a guardian angel looking out for us, even though we didn't deserve it. And now this. Do you have an answer?"

"I do. Get on my boat."

The survivalists wade through the water, Roger and Harry assisting Frank. Finally, the two men on the boat lower steps into the water, and everyone climbs onto the catamaran.

I stand with Jim and June. Jim looks at her and says, "Could you excuse us for a moment?"

She nods and walks away.

Jim states, "What happened yesterday was horrific and indescribable, and again, thank you for saving my life."

"You did your share of saving," I say. "And let's not forget the mutt here." Coco is next to us, wagging his tail.

"Just so you know, the Chief of Police had no problem with Enrique Colon's story. First, they found the bodies of the two men in the sea and brought the speedboat back to shore. Then, Enrique told me he would find reliable staff to guard and run the guesthouse.

"That's good news."

Jim points to the catamaran where the survivalists are waiting. He says, "Enrique also found those men to sail the boat and flew them over here."

"I was wondering how difficult it would be to sail that boat. Enrique seems to think of everything."

"There's one more thing. In knowing your background and seeing the way you operate. I'd like to offer you a job."

"A job?"

"I started several humanitarian organizations, donated to others, and realized I need someone to oversee this activity. This job doesn't mean managing the day-to-day activities but keeping track of what's happening. I try to do that, but too many other responsibilities fill my time. Running my investment company is more than a full-time job. You already have experience in cost control, so would you consider this job? It would fit with running your soon-to-be foundation, and I could introduce you to the investing side of the business. What do you think?"

I don't know what to think. This is a shock, overwhelming, and unexpected. "Do you really believe I could do it?"

"Of course. Consider it high-end bookkeeping."

I smile. "Around here, they call me Bookie."

"There you go."

"May I ask where it would be based?"

"At my company headquarters in Florida."

As Jim is a fast thinker, I need to be the same. "I'd love to take this on, but do you see that blondish young woman in the t-shirt with 'Panama' written on the front?" I point to Ada.

"You mean, 'I Love Panama'? Yes. She looks lovely."

"We have plans and will need time off."

"A honeymoon?"

"Yes. At least three months."

"Take whatever you need. It's a deal." He sticks out his hand.

We shake hands, and I realize this so-called 'deal' happened so fast that I didn't have time to ask about salary and working conditions. What have I done?

June joins us, and I state, "It looks like it's time to extract."

"The best show ever," she laughs. Then, she hugs me and says, "Bartholomew, thank you for everything."

"And thank you," I say. "I hope we can keep in touch."

I head to the water and turn around. Jim is talking with June, and I ask him, "Are you coming?"

He says, "I think I'll stick around here."

June smiles.

"How will you get back to the guesthouse?" I ask.

"Loan me your little sailboat." He points toward the Luz, dwarfed by the *Sueño del Mar*.

June looks at Jim and asks, "What do you mean about that little sailboat belonging to Bartholomew?"

"Both boats are his," Jim replies.

June shakes her head and says, "Bartholomew, someday I want to hear the whole story."

I wade through the water, Coco swimming beside me. Then, I lug Coco up the steps and onto the catamaran. Quickly the two crewmen raise the anchor and motor away from the island. As the sails rise, I see Jim and June talking with each other and laughing. They seem lost in their own world and are oblivious that we are leaving.

This is day twenty-seven of our challenge, and all participants are tapping out one day early. It doesn't matter because this episode of the Naked Fear television show doesn't exist. A couple of drug runners destroyed all the footage.

What matters is that we all changed. The experience had some rough patches, but we grew in positive ways.

The sail catches the wind, and the boat speeds through the water. I lead Ada up to the wheelhouse.

Ada asks, "Is it true what Jim Olsen said about you owning this boat?"

"Yes."

She shakes her head. "This is crazy. How did you get it?"

I wait a moment. "Ada, I never want to have secrets between us, but would you mind if I kept just this one? All I can say is that it's best for both of us if yesterday is forgotten."

"Bartholomew, you are a mystery. I can live with that."

Nodding to the crew member piloting the boat, I ask him to move aside.

Then, I take Ada's hands and put them on the wheel while I stand behind her, putting my arms around her waist.

"Sail her," I say.

"Where?"

"Panama City, and after that, we can decide."

EPILOGUE

One Year Later

Ada and I swim together beyond the breakers in front of my old beach camp at Isla San José. She is as lovely as the day I first saw her. Coco chases seagulls along the water's edge. He seems happy to be back on the island.

It's the first time we have been here after a whirlwind year. The Luz had been docked at the guesthouse, where high-net-worth visitors sail her around the island. This week, the little sailboat is for us. We sailed it here to my beach camp, loaded with a tent, camping equipment, and enough food to last seven days. We need this quiet time with just the two of us, plus the dog.

My temporary driftwood shelter still stands, and June was wrong. Pacific storms didn't blow it over.

I think back to all that happened.

On day twenty-seven of our Naked Fear challenge, we sailed to Panama City, and Harry and Wilma flew back to their hometowns to resume their lives. Once they left, the two Panamanian sailors took the *Sueño del Mar* to a boatyard where they painted a new name. The boat is now Panamanian-registered and owned by a company connected to my newly formed foundation. The foundation is helping to fund jungle hospitals on several continents, including the hospital run by my parents. They are thrilled to have additional money to cover the cost of medicine and equipment.

After discussions with Roger and Pandora, they said they wanted to continue their adventure, so they agreed to sail the catamaran for a year. First, they took the catamaran to the Caribbean for a couple of weeks, where the two crewmen began training them to operate the craft. Then, Roger, Pandora, and the two crewmen sailed across the Atlantic to the Mediterranean. From Spain, the crewmen flew back to Panama. Between Roger and Pandora, I have yet to figure out which is captain and co-captain. It's surprising how well they collaborate with each other.

From Panama, I flew to California, handed in my resignation to the Naked Fear film company, packed up my few possessions in my tiny apartment, and then, with Coco in my car, I drove to Florida. My bosses at Naked Fear were furious about what happened on the island, but nothing was said about clothing, props and store-bought food. Frank got the blame for destroying the show.

In Florida, I was given a large office in Jim Olsen's modern building, where I now work for him. It's somewhat different from my corner desk at the film production company offices in Hollywood. Jim has taken me under his wing. I'm now doing more things than overseeing humanitarian organizations, which turned out to be a bigger job than he first described a year ago.

The salary and working conditions are generous.

When Ada and I said goodbye in Panama, she flew back to Texas. We didn't see each other for six weeks, except for a weekend trip where I went to Texas to meet her family. But we talked every day over the internet. Then we were married in a small rural Baptist church, and after that, there was a Texas-sized celebration on her family ranch. My parents and sister were there, along with Jim Olsen, June, Harry, Wilma, Bob, Carlos, and Diego. Roger and Pandora couldn't make it because they were somewhere in the Mediterranean Sea with the catamaran. Enrique Colon flew his airplane across Central America and Mexico. He loved the trip and was a big hit with the ladies at the wedding reception.

Frank didn't make it, as he wasn't invited. He had other things to think about, as he resided in an inhospitable institution in Panama, where he remains. Prisons in Central American countries are not pleasant places.

Frank is incarcerated in Panama because he poisoned two of their citizens. Criminal charges were also filed in the United States because he poisoned U.S. citizens. All that is now stuck between slow-moving government bureaucracies, which may take years to work out, even before he goes to trial. Out of goodwill, I recommended an excellent Panamanian lawyer, but unfortunately, Frank wanted nothing to do with me.

After our wedding and two days of non-stop partying at the ranch, Ada and I went on our honeymoon. The party merrily continued for several days without us.

When Ada and I had lunch at the coffee bar on Isla Pedro Gonzalez, she expressed her desire to see everything from Spain to Israel. So, therefore, for our honeymoon, we flew to Barcelona and met up with Roger and Pandora. Then, we sailed our catamaran with them from Spain to Italy, the Greek Islands, Turkey, and Cyprus and finally docked in Haifa. Being with Roger and Pandora was fun, as they had one side of the catamaran, and we had ours.

Seeing Israel was exceptional, with so much history, past, present, and future, the land of Abraham and the place where Jesus walked.

After three months of travel, Ada and I went to Florida, where she manages our foundation and still mentors younger women on her social media site.

Jim spends a lot of time with me, explaining venture capital and investing. Like two soldiers who went through a battle together, we formed a special bond because of that horrid time at the guesthouse. Occasionally, when he and I are alone, we talk about it, which is therapeutic for us. It leads to topics about ethics, spirituality, and the hereafter.

Several months after we left Panama, Enrique Colon called me. He said there was little to worry about what took place at the guesthouse. Shortly after that event, there was an all-out war between two rival cartels, and many were killed, including drug lords. Cartel members were imprisoned, new drug lords emerged, and priorities changed. Now, anything that may have happened on an insignificant island in the Pearl Island archipelago is forgotten by them, even though millions in drugs and cash were lost. For those depraved criminals, it's just the cost of doing business.

On day twenty-seven of the challenge, we sailed the catamaran away from our camp on our so-called extraction day. I remember how June and Jim stayed behind on the beach, talking as though nothing else existed. When Ada and I returned to Florida, Jim and June were married. The engagement period was short, but they figured why waste time. I figure it was that spark between two people that Enrique spoke about. I'm happy they found each other, and that June is still part of our life.

Roger and Pandora eventually sailed the catamaran from Europe to Florida and when they arrived, they had a civil wedding, with Ada and I as the witnesses. Then, we endured another two-day party at Jim Olsen's massive property, with June as the organizer. It was a fantastic event. Harry and Wilma came, and she no longer had purple hair. It is now fluorescent green.

Roger and Pandora then sailed the catamaran back to the Pearl Islands. We decided to continue with the charter company, with them running it. The plan is to grow the business by adding more charter boats, but that will take time. Pandora still calls me Bookie, but it is no longer condescending. It's done out of love and respect.

* * *

Ada and I are back at my beach camp on our island, and we have set up the tent nearby the large pile of driftwood. We visited my old hut, and it would take quite some work for us to camp there. The jungle fights back when you let it, and it always wins. While the hut still stands, it is overgrown with vines. Some items, like mugs and the teapot, are still usable. But rodents chewed holes in my clothing, and ants claimed my bed. Surprisingly, my archery bow is still in good shape. I will take it back to Florida as a souvenir.

Over at the survivors' camp, there is no sign it was ever there, not even the wooden huts or the stone fire pit. The cleanup crew did its job. The world changed, and the survivors made it through that event. Frank is the only casualty, and I'm not sure it could have been avoided. It's a sad fact, but sometimes individuals are responsible for their suffering because of how they view life and their choices.

The Naked Fear film company continues to produce episodes with only two survivors and a trimmed-down film crew. And each show is carefully scripted, with the participants selected because of their acting skills. The sites they choose have few actual physical dangers. Makeup artists do wonders in transforming survivors' faces into emaciated facades of distress and misery. Our episode was never seen on television, and our producers learned lessons after losing money. Nevertheless, television viewers continue to revel in the show. It's a wonder how starving naked people bring such enjoyment to TV viewers who sit on comfortable couches while eating potato chips and drinking beer.

Sitting in the beach chair, I observe the magnificent colors as the sun sets in the west. Ada swims toward me, and it is a joy to have this Texas gal who delights in nature. As I think back, our Naked Fear challenge was remarkable, knowing I came to this island with nothing and found a treasure. She means everything to me, and I love her with my entire being.

This makes me realize that the One who creates these magnificent sunsets has been good to me. As my parents say, "Trust in Him." A year ago, I was caught in a rut working at a desk in Hollywood with little personal vision, and this island experience opened a new world. I'm genuinely thankful, enjoying another one of His glorious sunset paintings.

We will be alone for a week, relishing every second.

As night comes, Ada and I enjoy a meal of fresh fish and a salad, and Coco gets a can of high-end dog food. Surprisingly, June's two camp chairs are still usable. Tomorrow I will look for oranges, lemons, avocados, and bananas behind the derelict house. But this night is for us. We go to the tent, and I close the tent flap, and we lie in each other's arms. Coco stays outside.

In seven days, we will sail the Luz back to the guesthouse, where Roger and Pandora will meet us with the catamaran along with Jim and June. Then we will all spend another week exploring the Pearl Islands, including a visit to Enrique Colon. It's a strange feeling to know I have a Panamanian lawyer who is also a friend.

When Enrique asked me for a new name for the catamaran, I had to think fast, and one thing came to mind. So now, there is a small blue-trimmed sailboat called the *Luz* and a large catamaran called the *Luz II*. They make quite a sight when floating next to each other.

It turned out that the Naked Fear producers were right. Our episode was the best show ever. Only it was never shown on television.

ABOUT THE AUTHOR

I am a full-time writer who grew up in the United States and now splits my time between Spain and Switzerland. You can find out more about my books by going to www.casstell.com.

A request: I hope you enjoyed *NAKED ISLAND*. If you would consider leaving a review on Amazon or Goodreads, I would be grateful. Reviews help independent authors, even if just a line or two.

Here are more of my books to enjoy:

The SAVANT: What would you do if you could predict future events? This compelling story follows the journey of a boy with a unique form of 'savant syndrome.

If you like coffee, you will love **The COFFEE LOVER**.

Dance With POETIC SEA: A man suffering from burnout is brutally attacked. Was it a random act or deliberate? To escape danger, he makes a radical decision to flee New York by enrolling in a quirky poetry workshop in Spain. There, he is out of place when he meets a group of literary types who exist in an artsy realm of prose and fantasy. Searching for insight, he is forced to confront his broken past.

CASS TELL

Dance with
POETIC
Sea

a novel

The MUNICH SHIFT - Wings Series 1: Wings is on a mission to protect the Gathering from annihilation, as depraved powers do everything to stop him. Get these adrenaline-driven, Christian contemporary fantasy novellas, two-hour reads.

The COOKBOOK: Do you still have your grandmother's old Betty Crocker cookbook? What if it contained shocking secrets that dramatically changed your life?

PALE TIDES: Expecting to find love and acceptance, he faces nothing but legalistic rules. Can he survive?

Printed in Great Britain
by Amazon

32458804R00126